THE
DARKER SIDE
OF JUSTICE

THE
DARKER SIDE
OF JUSTICE

CONVICTING JAIME DAY

GERALD PRICE

TATE PUBLISHING
AND ENTERPRISES, LLC

Published by Tate Publishing & Enterprises, LLC
127 E. Trade Center Terrace | Mustang, Oklahoma 73064 USA
1.888.361.9473 | www.tatepublishing.com

Tate Publishing is committed to excellence in the publishing industry. The company reflects the philosophy established by the founders, based on Psalm 68:11,
"The Lord gave the word and great was the company of those who published it."

Book design copyright © 2014 by Tate Publishing, LLC. All rights reserved.
Cover design by Rtor Maghuyop
Interior design by jmensidor@tatepublishing.com

Published in the United States of America

ISBN: 978-1-63185-405-7
1. Christian / General
2. Crime
14.03.07

ACKNOWLEDGMENTS

Thanks to my wife Sherri who is my best critic and editor.

Special recognition to Lisa Hebert Photography.

CONTENTS

PREFACE

The judicial system, which is a part of the form of government, within which we all as Americans conduct our lives, was established by the founding fathers and others who have come before us to provide justice for all Americans. It is apparent that their intent was to include "due process under the law" and "justice for all" in any proceedings relevant to the laws of a state or of the nation itself, where any individual finds themselves under indictment for failure to obey such laws. The following is a story of the failure of this system. This story exemplifies the transformation modern-day politics has imposed on this system. It is troubling to see that in America, the prosecutors and participants of our court system have become so politically charged that they have ceased to be in pursuit of truth and justice. Somehow, that directive, which is mandated by our constitution, has been replaced by what it is now a score card to maintain a record of wins versus losses in the process of developing a career. Unseen to the public eye, there is a methodology working in our system that stops at nothing to win a conviction without regard to a defendant's innocence or guilt. It is a shocking revelation to realize that the prosecutors of our judicial system would much rather send an innocent person to prison than admit to a mistake and be publically embarrassed. Most importantly and in the larger view, this is a story of God's deliverance and provision. It chronicles the events that occur when an innocent woman from a Christian family is wrongfully accused of a horrible crime, God's promise of deliverance, and ultimately, the process and fulfillment of that promise. My hope is that this story will eventually become public and will somehow prevent the type of injustices that we have experienced in our own lives from occurring in the lives of others in the future.

> *The righteous cry and the Lord heareth, and delivereth them out of all their troubles. Psalms 34:17* KJV

THE EARLY DAYS

I grew up in Vicksburg, Mississippi, through the sixties and seventies. Ours was a poor family, and poverty was just the way of life. My mom was a single parent working on an assembly line in a Westinghouse light factory. She had been raised in a sharecropper's home and had learned early in life there were no free lunches. I have listened to her tell of working in a five- and ten-cent store at fifteen years of age to earn money to pay for her own school lunch and buy school clothes because there simply wasn't enough money in the family to provide these things. My youngest brother, Robert, and I found ourselves at an early age, living in a very dysfunctional environment. As a small boy, I remember our entire family living in a rented country shack on what was then called old Highway 61 North on the north side of Vicksburg. My grandparents, Jake and Erma Price; my two aunts, Elsie and Sherline; my uncle Sherman; my mom; and my two brothers, Robert and Darrell, along with myself, were all under one roof. There was no running water in the house, and I remember taking our baths in the winter in a #3 wash tub on the kitchen floor. By the time I was in the first grade in school, Mom had gotten an apartment in town. My youngest brother and I went to live with her while my oldest brother Darrell remained with my grandparents. Then when I was about the age of ten, we relocated back to the country. Three families, including ours, lived on eleven acres owned by Mr. Stanford McBroom. The McBroom Estate as we called it was about seven miles outside the city limits of Vicksburg. It was country living with chickens, hogs, horses, and a truck farm-style garden that provided vegetables for everyone living on the place for the entire year. While these were good, hardworking country folk, there was still an element of fast living accompanied by alcohol, violence, and a largely sinful environment that was continuously part of their lifestyle. By the time I reached the age of fourteen, I was smoking pot and did pretty much anything else I felt like trying on. At eighteen, I had a felony on my record and was a full-fledged IV drug addict. During that time, I was sentenced to three years in the Mississippi State Penitentiary at Parchman. That sentence was suspended, and I, instead, was sentenced to one year in a rehabilitation program in Meridian, Mississippi. I served five months in this program before being released on good behavior.

It was an era of rock and roll music, bell-bottom jeans, and promiscuous drug use. The memories of the Vietnam War were fresh in the minds of that generation. Jimmy Carter was the president of the United States. I had left home at sixteen and had been on a path of self-destruction for all of my life. I simply got weary of the heartache and disappointment of the life of sin I was leading. I think I always knew there was a call of God on my life. I just didn't understand or acknowledge it in the early years of growing up. I do remember rolling up on my knees in the privacy of my sleeping quarters on a towboat and praying to God, "Lord, please don't let me die in the condition I'm in." At twenty-two years of age, in the year 1979, I turned to God after a life of sin and hardship.

I became a born-again Christian and was filled with the spirit of God at a small church on Halls Ferry Road in Vicksburg. Like most others, I can still remember the exact moment and place where I stood the day I was filled with God's Holy Ghost. The pastor of that church was a man whose name was Grady Ladner. He was, at that time, in the hospital stricken with pancreatic cancer. I met him only once, in the hospital before his passing. Even so, he left an indelible impression upon me as he lay on that hospital bed, facing certain death. When someone tried to encourage him and asserted that he would soon recover and be back in the pulpit, I will never forget the faraway look he got in his eyes as he gazed upward and declared, "It will be all right. I know in whom I have placed my trust." I remember feeling the weight of his words and thinking to myself, now this is no game, this is really where the rubber meets the road in life. I never forgot the feeling that day as I realized, here was a man who was about to cross over into eternity and was hopeful and fully prepared to meet God. This provided a sharp contrast to the mentality I was so accustomed to, one of perpetual fear of meeting God without preparation. In the end, Pastor Ladner passed away, having succumbed to the cancer, less than a week after my own first real experience with God.

Within a few days, I learned through a family member of a powerful spirit-filled church in Wisner, Louisiana. Wisner is a small farming town about seventy miles southwest of Vicksburg. I visited that church within a couple of weeks of my new birth experience and was astonished to find a church of around four hundred in a community of fifteen hundred. There was such an overwhelming presence of God. Worship was boisterous, powerful, and fervent. I returned to Vicksburg that week, rehearsing the many questions that swirled through my mind relevant to what I would do with my life. I had spent the previous three years working on riverboats and was at that time a first mate for a company called Central Towing located in Alton, Illinois. I had in those recent months been training for the wheelhouse with plans of becoming a riverboat pilot. The first day after receiving the baptism of the Holy Ghost, I called Jack Delaney who was the then port captain to submit to him my resignation. I had no idea as to how I would make a living. I only knew that my mind was made up to follow God and having lived the "river life" for the last three years, I was convinced that the two worlds just couldn't coexist for me.

Two weeks later, my uncle, Russell Hartley, who was attending the Wisner church at the time, showed up unexpectedly and suggested that I might consider relocating to Wisner and basing out of that church. I took it as a word from God and did not hesitate to quit the local job I had taken and move myself to Louisiana. I arrived in Clayton, Louisiana, with the only possessions that I owned in this world, my clothes, and my 1974 Chevy Monte Carlo. Russell was married to my mom's sister Sherline, and they had three children at the time, Keesha, Melaney, and Jesse. They all lived in a conventional single wide mobile home on the banks of the Tensas River at Clayton. There was no room in the home for me, so I moved into Russell's storage shed, which we converted into a bedroom. Russell or someone before him had added a screen porch to the front of this portable building. It had a toilet and shower in what amounted to a closet off to one side, and there was a stove and refrigerator setting on the concrete floor of the screened area. We moved all of his storage to one end of the building, added a partition and a window fan, and suddenly, I was looking at my new home.

I remember the first day I arrived, there was church that night and as everyone got dressed to go, I took a walk down on the bank of the river to pray. As I prayed, I asked the Lord for guidance. I remember specifically asking Him to show me that I was doing the right thing to move to this new life for myself. We went on to church that night, and almost immediately, there was a sweeping presence of God and a prophecy of tongues and interpretation given. The interpretation of the message was. "My will has been done. I have brought you unto this place. Abide here and I will use you in greater ways than you have ever known." At that moment, I was overwhelmed with the presence of God, and I knew most certainly I had heard from Him. Most of all, I remember being so amazed that the God of glory took time to talk directly to a man such as myself and how He was apparently so acutely aware of the details of men's lives.

There were constant times of fasting and prayer at Wisner, and it was obvious that I was among a body of believers who loved and sought after God in a phenomenal way. Here, I began a journey following the ministry of Pastor Sonny Nugent. After the first year at Wisner, I married my wonderful wife, Sherri Salter. That was one of the best decisions of my life. She has been an anchor for my life and my best friend for thirty-three years. I consider myself extremely blessed to have been able to associate my life with Pastor Nugent and his wife Joann Nugent. He has always been a unique visionary with a burden for souls and a love for the work of God. He always demonstrated an exceptional love for humanity. He is a pastor's pastor and a leader among Christian leaders. Furthermore, he is a modern-day prophet of God. Accordingly, he possesses a phenomenal ability to walk in the spirit and listen for the voice of God. Those of us who know him would testify that he has led as a pastor for decades, listening to and obeying the voice of the Spirit. No other human being has impacted my life more than this man. If ever there was a woman who set the standard for all others in the role and ministry of a pastor's wife, it was Joann Nugent. She is a godly woman of prayer and great spiritual strength. I have never seen or heard of her exhibiting anything but goodness and the love of God. Only eternity will measure the impact that these two pioneers of the church have had on the lives of countless souls throughout their more than forty years of leadership.

WINDS OF CHANGE

It was in 1983 that Bro. Nugent informed the congregation at Wisner that God was leading and had begun to call for him to leave Wisner and accept a call to assume the pastorate at Livingway Pentecostal Church in Lake Charles, Louisiana. He obeyed that call, moving himself and his family into the school building at the church, and began his ministry at Lake Charles of reaching the lost. One year later, my family followed. We loaded everything we owned into a U-haul truck and moved to southwest Louisiana. It was Sherri and I with our three children, Shane, Jaime, and Jason. I had a beautiful red chow who we called Ching that rode shotgun with me in the U-Haul while Sherri drove our family car with the kids.

Sherri was involved with music ministry as a singer, and we were always involved with outreach in one form or another. Bible study in the homes of people in our community was a part of our weekly function. Additionally, we have worked with bus ministry for most of the years that we have been in Lake Charles. Practically, every Saturday of every week, for most of the more than twenty-eight years we have attended Livingway, we spent at least a couple of hours on outreach, going from door to door, meeting new people and inviting them to the house of God. Most of my Sunday mornings were spent driving the church bus. We currently participate in weekly Christian fellowship meetings at a church facility in Sulphur, Louisiana. The facility's official name is The Outpost. Our meetings at The Outpost work in conjunction with our current bus ministry. The purpose of these meetings is to provide a platform, which becomes a "first step" for new people to become familiar with the church environment. We spent all of our years at Lake Charles laboring with the church for the kingdom with our lives built around the church. We raised all of our children there, and they all attended school at Lake Charles Christian Academy, which was the church's private Christian school. I thank God for the anchor the church has been for our lives.

Livingway experienced great revival throughout the years with Pastor Nugent at the helm. We experienced constant and consistent growth and continuous outpourings of the Holy Ghost. We were a church completely driven by the mission of reaching the lost. There were roughly eighty to ninety people attending when we first arrived in 1984. That number grew to probably around six hundred in the late nineties after we moved into the newer sanctuary.

In the spring of 2003, we were at regular Monday night prayer meeting when Bro. Nugent informed me that evening of my daughter Jaime's pregnancy. We had just begun praying when he walked up to me and placed his arm around my shoulder. He gently hugged me with one arm and said, "I love you." He then said to me, "Your daughter is pregnant." If you know Pastor Nugent, then you know that he is a master at delivering bad news with love and grace. My wife and daughter, being unable to bring themselves to be the ones who brought this troubling news to me, had asked him to tell me. Jaime was not married at the time, and we were temporarily devastated. The fact that our family was considered to be in leadership roles in the church added to the difficulty at least in our minds. However, once everything sank in, we set forward on a path to make proper adjustments and prepare ourselves for a new grandchild.

Sometime in the fall of the same year, Jaime and Murry Day approached me at my home to ask my blessing upon his proposal of marriage to my daughter. We all agreed that they would be married, and on December 12, 2003, Jaime and Murry became man and wife. They were married at our church facility known at the time as the Wedding Chapel. This building had originally served as the main sanctuary before the construction of our current sanctuary. I will never forget and have sometimes laughed when I remember Jaime's wedding. I was to lead her down the aisle and give her away. As I stood in the back of the church with her, I said, "It's not too late to change your mind. You can walk out right now, and I will go up front and take the heat for it." I have laughingly told that story to others on a number of occasions since that day, but in light of this story, that may have been the best advice I ever gave my daughter.

On January 1, 2004, Jason Kolten Day was born into this world and became the joy of our lives. I personally, upon the first moment of his birth, instantly fell in love with this child. I have always believed that something special occurred in my spirit concerning Kolten the moment I saw him. I realize that most grandparents love their grandchildren, but I believe something extremely acute happened to my heart on that day, concerning this child. I now believe it came from God and was to prepare me against the trouble that would come in just a few short years. It was on September 16, 2005, that the second of these two grandchildren, Dalton Kyler Day, was born to add to the joy that we had. His birth will always be most remembered by the arrival of Hurricane Rita to Calcasieu Parish. Our first days with Kyler will always be marked by our flight from Rita with him only a week old. We drove fourteen hours to reach Vicksburg, Mississippi, from Lake Charles. This was due to the extreme overflow of people on their exodus of Calcasieu Parish. Vicksburg is normally a four- or five-hour drive.

GABE

At the time of Jaime and Murry's marriage, Murry had a son, who was born out of a previous relationship between himself and a girlfriend of his. Her name is Nita Hanks. The child's name is Gabriel Hanks. Gabe, as he is commonly called, was two years old at the time of Jaime's wedding. Through negotiations, an agreement was eventually made with Nita regarding Gabe and visitation for Murry. In its beginning, the arrangement was that Gabe spent alternate weeks with Jaime and Murry. When he wasn't at Jaime's, he was with Nita. That agreement was short-lived, and eventually, Nita reduced her interactions with Gabe to an arrangement that allowed for her to visit on alternate weekends and have nightly calls by phone. Their interactions gradually declined to the point that in December 2008, Nita relinquished all parental rights and Murry became the sole custodian of Gabe, pursuant to the orders of the family court judge.

During those initial years with Gabe, he would often return from visits at Nita's with bizarre injuries to himself. The explanations for these injuries were usually difficult to accept. On one occasion, he had a serious injury to an arm, which was explained to be a result of a fall from bed. On another occasion, he had a huge bruise and knot on his forehead. We were told another child had hit him with a baseball bat. Upon each of these occasions, Jaime and Murry took Gabe to the hospital for treatment. Jaime additionally reported the instances to the Department of Children and Family Services (DCFS). The other thing we began to notice was Gabe's extreme and emotional reaction to any mention of his mom and the difference in his overall demeanor upon his return from stays at her home. This increased more as time went on, in so much that eventually he became extremely emotional and combatant when he thought he would be even speaking to her. It should be noted that Nita had an extreme drug history and had been under indictment for her involvement and participation in drug-related crimes.

The visits with Nita and Gabe eventually came to be conducted at a local facility known as the Whistle Stop. This is a place where troubled family visits are facilitated for a fee. By this time, the relationship between Gabe and his birth mother had deteriorated to the point that he refused to speak to her on the phone, and finally, at a Whistle Stop visit, he refused to get out of the car to go inside. He was hysterical to the point that the attendant finally informed Jaime that they would not force him to participate in the visit. He was screaming and crying uncontrollably. We initially suspected that he didn't want to be around her because of some neglect or abuse he was receiving from Nita. That may have represented a portion of the reason for his actions, but we would later realize that this method of operation would be common for Gabe any time he thought he was not getting his way.

I should say that in the beginning, all of us in the family were very supportive of the fact that Gabe had become a part of our family. Initially, he came across as bright beyond his years, neat, and polite. He did well at first in school, and we saw ourselves as rescuing him from a very bad situation. We enrolled him at Lake Charles Christian Academy, which was our church's private school. Our family paid for all cost and tuitions for Gabe's education. It all started well, but eventually, things began to evolve in the wrong direction. By the time he was eight, Gabe had begun to exhibit strange behavior, both at home and at school. At first, the problems seemed light enough; as a family, we thought it would just be things that could be corrected through parental influence. But things soon got much worse.

He developed habits of stealing, disobeying rules, or defacing things at home or school and then totally denying that he had committed these actions when everyone involved knew he had. It really didn't matter if you were an eyewitness, he could still look at you very convincingly and tell you that you were wrong. As time went on, there was a continuous escalation of the behavioral problems. They ultimately became so severe that it came to the point he was inflicting injury on himself. He refused to eat, and he would defecate and urinate on himself and at various locations throughout the house. Sometimes, he would defecate and toss the feces under a piece of furniture or behind the TV. He would deliberately defecate in his clothes at school so he would be sent home. Jaime was called to the school because Gabe was banging his head on his desk or hiding under the desk, refusing to participate in the class activities.

In the presence of visiting neighbors, he would walk into the room, drop his pants, and relieve himself on the floor, and when confronted and asked why, he would state that he did it so they would go home. He seemed to feel that visitors somehow were a threat to him. He would deliberately destroy property wherever he was at. He would find ways to harm himself at home until finally all furniture in his room had to be removed, except his mattress for his protection. Gabe's health declined to the point where there was significant weight loss, and you would constantly see him with bruises or contusions where he had banged his head or whatever he could do to harm himself. On three occasions, he harmed himself seriously enough that he had to be taken to the emergency room. Some examples of his self-injurious behavior are flipping backward off a bed into the floor, injuring his back. This wasn't a boy playing too rough, but rather, he did this in a deliberate attempt to inflict injury on himself. The nurse, who treated him at the clinic, had recommended we take the bed from his room and leave only the mattress. On another occasion, he attempted to stab himself with a screwdriver in the face. The screwdriver passed through his upper lip. My daughter called my wife, frantically seeking help. He was taken to the emergency room for treatment. Gabe's explanation for this injury was that he wanted to kill himself so "he could be reborn by entering into my daughter and she would really be his mom." He explained that he had heard somewhere you could kill yourself instantly by stabbing yourself through your nasal system into your brain.

As his self-injurious behavior escalated with him, continuously finding new and different ways to harm himself, he finally came to the point that he refused all food. Attempts to force-feed him were met with tantrums. For some unknown reason, he would only eat Ramen noodles or instant grits. Neighbors on either side of Jaime who frequently visited in Jaime's home became eyewitnesses of Gabe's self-injurious behavior. Regardless of what the family purchased, cooked, or provided in any other manner, the Ramen noodles and grits were the only foods Gabe would eat. Attempting to get him to eat initiated many outbursts and temper tantrums at family events, in his home, in our home, in restaurants, and many other public places. I personally have been present on multiple occasions when he would go into a tirade when presented with food. Christmas and Thanksgiving at our home, in 2009, was, to say the least, eventful. We would hope to simply have a good family time and that would be interrupted by Gabe's tirades. Gabe just refused to eat, and when pressed, he would get angry and if you pressed him to much he would cry and throw tantrums.

The family shares a story of Gabe on a visit with Murry's mom, Dana. Early in the day, Dana had been showing Gabe some old pictures and things. This included an old Valentine's card and some handwritings she had apparently kept for a long time. She explained to Gabe that these were precious keepsakes. Later in the day, Dana was entertaining a guest in another room. She had ordered Gabe to leave the room so that she and her guest could talk. Gabe refused and made multiple attempts to stay in the room with them. Finally angry, he returned to the room where the Valentine's cards were kept. He set the cards on fire and then attempted to set the curtains on fire with a burning card. Dana, somehow detecting what was happening from the other room, rushed in and stopped the ordeal. He was obviously attacking her for not allowing him to have his way. It was obviously an attempt to destroy what he believed to be precious to her in retaliation for what he perceived as her selfishness.

On another occasion, Gabe was spending the night at my home. He had gone to bed, and I was up watching television in the den. I became conscious of a tapping sound. I turned just in time to see Gabe, lying on the floor, half in and half out of the room where he was to be sleeping. Just as I turned, he jerked himself out of my sight. It reminded me of something I have often seen while hunting, a squirrel peeping around a tree to see me, then jerking himself behind the tree. Curious, I went down to his room to see what he was up to. Upon investigation, I discovered that he had taken a white paint marker normally used on my job, which had been inadvertently left in the bedroom, and with this, he had defaced several items in the room. This included the bedspread, headboard, the entire face of the clock in the room, and the area of the floor in the hall just outside the bedroom. When I questioned him, he, with big-eyed innocence, declared he had not made any of the markings. I then realized the tapping I was hearing was deliberate and it was Gabe "calling me out." He was seeking confrontation. The thing that struck me was the sincerity he could display all the while obviously lying. I found it eerie. Here I was with a child who had maliciously created as much controversy through the destruction of my property as he possibly could and then went looking for me to challenge me and invite confrontation. I think the most fascinating thing is that when you were one on one with Gabe, you had the sense that he was intelligent far beyond his years, almost as if he were an adult in a small boy's body.

I dismissed the conversation and told him it was all right and to just go to bed. I waited a couple of days and decided to approach him on the subject again. I asked him, "Are you ready to talk to me about what you were doing in the bedroom the other night with the paint marker?" He said to me in a brooding and, I thought, odd tone, "I don't remember that, I only remember good things." I ended the conversation at that point, having this strange sense that I was dealing with a child who had serious issues. Upon the next opportunity, I discussed the matter with Jaime and Murry. I suggested to them that there was a serious problem residing in Gabe, which needed professional help. I am persuaded that the central issue was he was seeking attention. I believe he is driven by a need to feel elevated above all others or simply by a need to be recognized, but his need seemed to drive him to a point of unreason.

Upon each of Gabe's visits to the emergency room, the hospital staff would conduct an evaluation and place him on the psychological ward for a five-day stay. Gabe loved these stays because the hospital staff catered to him completely. If he ordered two large pizzas, someone got them for him. Anything he wanted, he got. He treated it as room service. During these visits, he would transform into the young boy who first came to our family. He later admitted that he had deliberately self-inflicted so that he would be taken to Memorial on these occasions. We would learn that he simply loved to go to the hospital because of all of the special treatment.

In September 2009, Gabe was being treated by a child psychologist, Dr. Charles Murphy, at Memorial Hospital. Dr. Murphy started him on Risperdal or Risperidone, which is its clinical name. This is a drug normally used in treatment of schizophrenia in boys thirteen years of age or older. At nine years of age, Gabe was being prescribed the maximum dose of three milligrams. In December, the drug Depakote (valproic acid) was added to his daily intake. Both of these drugs have similar side effects listed in their warning labels, but valproic acid states clearly that it can cause depression and thoughts of suicide. I have always believed that these drugs were major contributors to Gabe's behavioral issues.

By this time, his behavior had deteriorated at school so badly that he was placed in a program called "homebound," which provided state-certified teachers to come to his home for classes. This is a program that can only be initiated by the school and only when there is a student who exhibits behavior that makes him unmanageable in a normal school environment. This is significant because the teachers from one of his elementary schools would later provide conflicting testimony in court, saying that Gabe was an exemplary child at school and would deny any serious problems with him. Their testimony proved to be very significant in these court proceedings.

Also, he was being seen by counselors from a program called Helping Hands. They also came to the home each week to visit and advise Jaime. By this time, he had been enrolled in three separate elementary schools, including the private Christian school we started him in. As we drew near to the latter half of 2009, his condition grew intensely worse. At each of the schools Gabe attended, lying was one of the most frequent indictments against him. He appeared so convincing when he would lie to you that you would think, "I must be mistaken," when you knew for a fact that he was lying. The lies were usually in the form of a denial of some sort of destructive behavior of which Gabe was accused. Another phenomenon regarding Gabe is that he was and remains extremely intelligent. When he wishes to, he makes remarkably high grades in school. As I said earlier, I always got that same sensation that I was communicating with a grown man in a small boy's body when I would visit with him one on one.

A WARNING FROM GOD

January 16, 2008, marked a new error in the history of Livingway Pentecostal Church. We were blessed with the addition of Pastor Massey and his wife Madonna along with their children, Easton and Chapel. Brother Nugent assumed the office of Bishop. What I think is most notable is that that there was no significant change in the direction of the church or its ministry. Pastor and Sister Massey are compassionate, dedicated, and loving leaders. Brother Massey is a spiritual man who shares the same vision and love for the work of God that we have known from brother Nugent for the last twenty-five years.

Over the course of its history, Livingway has experienced constant revival and steady church growth. Our attendance has grown from its average attendance of approximately one hundred in the early eighties to eight hundred to a thousand attending over the course of any given week. Our services are always spiritually packed. There is a constant presence and operation of God in the house each service. Once in the middle of a weekly worship service, probably less than three months before all of our trouble started, we received a prophetic message, warning us of great impending trouble like we had never known. This message was very specific. It came as an interpretation of tongues. I remember feeling warned as though God were dealing with me personally when I heard the interpretation: "You are dealing in foolish things, and there is more trouble than you have ever known waiting just down the road." The problem for me was that at that precise period, only I knew the true state of my carnality. But you see God always knows right where we are, and He is every bit as alive and powerful as we find him in the New Testament book of Acts. Little did we know what we would face in the next few months, but God was attempting to warn us.

December 2009 begins the crux of our story. For perspective, I feel I should describe the overall condition of the family or, more to the point, the overall description of Jaime and Murry's marriage and home. Murry was always problematic as a husband. Having worked in the industrial sector for almost thirty years, I had acquired a certain amount of influence, which enabled me to assist Murry in obtaining employment in the industry. Murry could never keep a job for more that five or six months. He would always start well, but eventually, his lifestyle and work ethic would catch up with him. I can name numerous good-paying jobs he squandered away. He was very unreliable and would constantly cycle in and out of the drug world. The position that my daughter was in was that she wanted to somehow save her marriage, hold the family together, and be a mom to all three of the boys. I can only describe Murry as if he were a perpetual adolescent. His "friends" and his "right" to have his party life were far more important than raising a family. He could always play the role of a father at a birthday party or some similar event, but there was simply no substance to him.

In late December of 2009, I was working as a project manager for Remedial Construction Services. We had a construction project in Coushatta, Louisiana, on a subcontract basis for BE&K. I hired Murry to work on this job as he had lost his most recent employment with the Pilot's Association in Cameron. This job would require that he stay in Coushatta and come home on weekends when possible. This fitted Murry's lifestyle perfectly. He was able to dive into a new season of party life without the problematic burden of a family to be responsible towards. Jaime was left at home to try to hold things together on her own. All of this was happening as Gabe's problems were escalating to their highest point.

A couple of months earlier, someone had observed Gabe in public and had made a report with the Department of Children and Family Services (DCFS). There was an investigation conducted by the sheriff's office. Their findings were there was no abuse occurring at the time. However, this set off an alarm ringing loudly in my mind. I was both angry and concerned when I called Murry and stated to him with much emphasis that he had to involve himself with Gabe and stop leaving the entire burden on Jaime. I followed up on this call by driving to Coushatta and taking Murry to dinner, discussing the situation with him. When addressing me, Murry was always at least respectful, but still unresponsive to my suggestions. When Jaime placed pressure on him to help, it would usually end with him cussing her out. He told me he was tired of hearing Jaime complain to him about her need for assistance with Gabe. He said to me, "That's all she ever wants to talk about." I suppose it never occurred to him that maybe he should just try being a father. That in itself would have eradicated most of Jaime's complaints.

By this time, I was very concerned that we needed to get Gabe into a professional help program. One thing I fully understood was that this problem had become much larger than any of us could possibly handle. In desperation, on Gabe's final stay at Memorial, I advised Jaime that she should refuse to pick him up from the hospital when his five days had expired. My reasoning was that no repercussion could be worse than what she was dealing with or what it could come to. We had already learned that there are no long-term help programs for children with mental conditions such as Gabe's. We applied with every agency available and were in the process of getting assistance through Helping Hands and the coroner's office when everything finally fell apart.

Murry's sister, Katie, and his mom, Dana Day, for a reason only they could explain, apparently, had some vendetta against Jaime.

Their relationship was always strained at best. Katie, at Dana's advisement, and that according to Dana, called the sheriff's office and made a report of a child "locked and tied" in a back room of Jaime's house. She also reported that he was being starved. I am certain had she any idea what the outfall of her actions would be, she would not have made this ridiculous report. Katie knew full well that nothing akin to what she reported was the truth. She was fully aware of Gabe's bizarre and self-inflicting behavior.

A deputy from the Calcasieu Parish Sheriff's office was dispatched to Jaime's home. Upon his recommendation, Gabe was taken to Memorial Hospital for an observation. At this point, he had reached his lowest level. His weight was at thirty-eight pounds. This was a point that would be overemphasized throughout the investigation by the sheriff's office. Thirty-eight pounds in reality was approximately ten pounds beneath his normal weight. He was always small, and at nine years of age, forty-five pounds was his normal average. At the time of his arrival at the hospital, Gabe had physical indications on his body that were consistent with the self-inflicting history, for which he was by now so well known. However, the hospital and the sheriff's office immediately began a pursuit of proving someone was abusing Gabe and my daughter was the prime suspect. What I knew for certain was that within the first hour of Gabe's arrival at the hospital, there was an instant transformation that took place in him. The hospital staff initially attempted to get Gabe to eat something. In response, he started his usual "I want my grits" tirade. When it became obvious that he was not going to cooperate and eat something, Katie volunteered to go to the store and get him some grits. The hospital staff at that moment decided they would have to install an IV to get some nutrients into his body. When Gabe realized they wanted to stick him with a needle, he began a new fit. Detective Mike Primeaux, who was present at the time, then suggested to Gabe that if he would agree to eat, then he wouldn't have to take the IV. Gabe instantly reversed himself and, in a few moments, was sitting up in bed laughing and talking with Murry while eating a large plate of hamburger steak and rice and gravy. When Katie returned with his beloved grits, he had lost all interest in them. This transformation was nothing less that astounding. It was as much of a Jekyll and Hyde experience as you will ever see. Part of the oddity was the fact that he was laughing and talking with Murry at all, because for the last several months, he had developed the same attitude toward Murry that he had for Nita. When Murry would come home, he would go into a tirade. If Gabe heard his truck outside, he would start screaming, "Tell him to leave!" He had developed an unexplainable hatred for Murry, so this new behavior, of a big-eyed love and reverence for Murry, all in a moment was troubling and bizarre. Additionally, everything that happened that day was in sharp contrast to what was actually reported later. Katie had told someone that a doctor had thanked her in the hall for making her call and that it had it had probably saved his life. According to her, the doctor had suggested to her that he was probably only days from death. Nobody knows for sure what the exact words were the doctor used, but from his comments, the story evolved to Gabe being within two days of death and that he had to be kept under a blanket for several days, bringing his core body temperature up. There is no official hospital record of this version that I know of, nor was that rendition ever provided to Mr. Sanchez's office.

TROUBLE COMES

Gabe was kept in the hospital for observation. The next morning, my wife and Jaime were at the hospital when Gabe commented to them both, "Mom, you know what they are trying to get me to say? They want me to say that you hurt me! Ha-ha." Gabe had always openly admitted his self-inflictions. Up until this moment, the idea of accusing Jaime was something he hadn't thought of. Looking back on this event, we now wish we would have had the insight to bring in hospital staff and have Gabe repeat what he said to us and make a formal record of it. Within a couple of days, we were made aware that a criminal investigation was ongoing. A search warrant was issued, and Detectives Mike Primeaux and Elizabeth Zaunbrecher executed the search. I was present at the time, and seeing this horrific nightmare unfold, asked a question of the detective. After spending a few minutes attempting to convince them that they were barking up the wrong tree, I asked Mr. Primeaux, "Are you searching for the truth, or are you only in pursuit of an indictment?" His reply was, "Both, Mr. Price." The remainder of this story will bear out the insincerity of that statement coming from Mr. Primeaux.

Under the duress of what we saw happening in our lives, we asked a lady in our church, who had worked for years for attorneys, who she would recommend for legal counsel. She replied immediately and with no hesitation, "Mr. Walter Sanchez." She told my wife, "He is the best." Our daughter contacted him and provided him our story. My wife and I later met with him in his plush tenth floor office at 901 Lakeshore Drive. I was very impressed with the view from his glass-enclosed office overlooking the lake and city of Lake Charles. Walt listened to our story. At the end, he said to us, "You are in the right place," and we agreed that he would represent us. We paid him seventy-five hundred dollars that day and the balance of the retainer of fifteen thousand dollars a few days later to get things started. We left that day with assurances from Walt that the retainer would probably cover the cost of defending Jaime. No one could have foreseen how wrong we were.

Within days, Detective Mike Primeaux called me to request that we send our grandchildren over to the CASA office to be interviewed. I originally agreed to bring the boys for that meeting, but then recanted and called him to advise him of my new decision. I remember me telling him that I had solicited an attorney and would wait on his recommendation. He then asked me, "Mr. Price, do you mind if I ask who your attorney is?" To which I replied, "Some guy named Sanchez, I think his name is Brent." The tone in his voice rose when he asked me if possibly his name was Walt, to which I replied, "Yes, that's it, Walt Sanchez." I am being a bit facetious when I say he seemed to know the name well. He then said, "That's why we live in this great country, Mr. Price, so we can exercise the right to make these decisions."

The most alarming observation that ultimately became obvious through the course of this investigation was the realization that once committed to a direction in a case, this law enforcement agency and the associated prosecutors would not be in pursuit of truth, but simply a win at any cost. What occurred over the course of the next two years was shockingly revealing as to how the system can work if in the hands of the wrong people. One must understand the position DCFS, law enforcement, and/or prosecutors are in, once they have committed in a high profile case, to a suspect if such a case has been exposed to the public by the media. It is for political reasons that they can never publicly admit they were wrong. In fact, in this case, when they found evidence to corroborate my daughter's story, there were principle players within the state's powerful machinery who attempted to conceal that evidence.

Within days, the most horrifying event of our lives occurred. I was at work on February 24, 2010, when my wife called in a panic and almost shouted on the phone, saying she had just received a phone call from DCFS Investigator Veronica Garret, saying she was on her way to our home to take our grandchildren. I remember the sinking feeling I had in the pit of my stomach when she, with obvious pain and anxiety, cried, "They're taking the boys! They're taking the boys!" I ran to my truck and drove with the emergency flashers blinking, driving as fast as I possibly could, only to arrive too late to even tell the boys good-bye. When I arrived at my home, I stopped my truck in the street at the point where there were a couple cars from DCFS and the sheriff's office parked. My grandchildren were already loaded in the car and I was being ignored. We watched in horror in our own front yard as DCFS along with the sheriff's office drove away with our two wonderful grandchildren whom we had come to love more than anything in this world. We would willingly have died for either one of them. And there we stood, Sherri, my daughter, and me, devastated, broken, and helpless. I tried to comfort Jaime as she simply leaned against the wall and loudly wailed, desperate and with a broken heart. We did not see those boys again for one full year. Words cannot describe the pain and brokenness that started in that instant and continued for all of the following weeks and months. I remember being jarred out of sleep in the middle of the night to the sound of my wife sitting up in bed beside me, wailing out loud to God, for Him to move and bring our grandchildren home. She later told me of the days traveling alone in her car after a day of trying to hold it together in front of coworkers, as she would cross the I-210 Bridge on her way home, she would just scream in travail, weeping, seeking release and an answer from God. I fully understood.

But the trouble had just begun. On March 8, 2010, Jaime was arrested on an indictment of thirty-two counts of cruelty to a juvenile, five of which were listed as second degree cruelty. Her bail was set at five million dollars and our daughter, who while not perfect, but had certainly committed no crime, was arrested and placed in the parish jail. My only indictment against her was that she had not listened to me when I advised her not to pick Gabe up at Memorial Hospital on his last stays there. I recall that in response to my advice, she said "Dad, I know you don't understand this, but I have been his only real parent. I feel a strong responsibility for him, and if anything would ever happen to him, I would always blame myself." How very ironic.

The following Monday, as is always our practice, I got ready and made my way to the church for prayer meeting. I didn't want to discuss this thing. I wasn't feeling like speaking with anyone, so I just slipped in quietly and sat in the back. In a few minutes, as we began to pray, the Bishop made his way around and slipped up behind me. At first, he just laid his hands on me and began to pray. He then leaned into my ear and said to me, "You are not in this thing alone. We are in it with you." I leaned against him and wept and moaned, "Oh, Brother Nugent!" I was feeling so broken and so guilty for past failures. You see, at that moment, I wanted to be able to cry out to God, saying, "This is not fair!" I wanted to declare, "I have been faithful and I have always tried to do what was right!" I wanted to be able to declare my righteousness to God and say, "Oh, I deserve better than this!" But I knew that to say so would be a horrible lie. I knew the failures of my flesh and worse things I was capable of. I knew how easily I identified with the writer in the New Testament who said, "Oh, wretched man that I am. Who shall deliver me from the body of this death?" I knew that if the truth were known, at least where I was concerned, I was probably getting what I deserved and I had no righteousness of my own to declare to God. I could only be hopeful that I would be able at some point to identify with Paul in his letter to the Hebrews, where in the thirty-fourth verse of the eleventh chapter, he said that there were some who "out of weakness were made strong."

My wife and I visited with Sheriff Tony Mancuso at his office within less than a day of her arrest in an attempt to have their agency more thoroughly investigate the case. We felt that if he would just order a follow-up to the information we were able to share with him, we could clear this thing up. Our hopes were dashed in that very hour. Based on pictures of Gabe taken at the hospital and his condition, Mr. Mancuso basically shouted us down and excused us out of his office. He said to me, "Somebody is going to jail over this!" I attempted to provide information to him relevant to past hospital stays and the doctors under whose care Gabe had been. I could not get him to even listen to us. In fact, he stated to me with anger and in a loud voice, "This child has not seen a doctor in more than a year! More than a year! That is inexcusable!" I was so taken aback by that statement that I didn't immediately respond, except to try to convince him he needed to fully investigate. It was obvious his detectives had misinformed him, given the fact that Gabe had been in and out of hospitals and under multiple medical and psychological professionals for the previous several months. I shook Mr. Mancuso's hand as I prepared to leave. At that moment, I said to him, "If there is a God in Heaven and if there is any justice in this world, your entire case will fall apart." His reply was "Good luck." Within a few days, Mr. Mancuso appeared on KPLC Channel 7 news and basically convicted Jaime before trial. He stated, speaking I suppose of our visit to his office, "The family claims she is innocent, but the evidence is clear." His appearance in the media had, I suppose, its desired effect, which is to solidify public opinion in the favor of law enforcement and the prosecution in the case.

Local media immediately went to work after Jaime's arrest. What they reported was completely off, wild, and irresponsible. They describe horrible events that never took place. They reported a nine-year-old boy rescued by a deputy in a back room. The report said he was tied to a doorknob with a dog leash and starved. What made that report preposterous was the obvious fact that if a nine-year-old boy were tied to a doorknob, he would simply untie himself. They described a urine- and blood-soaked mattress in his room. By this time, my family was literally in shock. We could not possibly recognize what was being reported, except we certainly recognized our daughter's picture on the front page of the *American Press*. The events occurring in our family were happening so rapidly, we were simply punch drunk. None of this was true. Officer Jason Schnake who was the deputy who first arrived at Jaime's home later testified in family court to that effect. His testimony stated that all of the media reports were false. In his testimony, he stated that all of the sensationalism reported in the media was simply that. His story was that he had simply arrived at Jaime's home, found a boy sleeping on a mattress in his bedroom, and based on Gabe's condition and the nature of the complaint, recommended that Gabe be taken in for observation. Jaime and Murry simply complied with his recommendation as he followed them to the hospital. Obviously, if he had in fact found a boy tied and starving in the back room of a home, he would have made an arrest without further investigation. The arrest came several days later, after Mr. Primeaux and Mrs. Zaunbrecher completed their investigation.

The local TV station, KPLC and the *American Press* of Lake Charles carried this story laced with sensationalism and apparently with their own rendition. Within the week, it had been carried on every news station in the gulf south. The *American Press* retracted their version of the report the next day after receiving a call from Mr. Sanchez. It should be noted that they printed a large front-page cover story the first day, but the correction was a small block similar to a classified ad inside the paper. Anyone can go to the Calcasieu Parish sheriff's office's Web site, where there is a link for commendations. In it, our story appears. Deputy Schnake is identified and given a special commendation for going above and beyond the call of duty in "rescuing" Gabe. The story as it appeared in the media is cited on this web page. The deputy testified that when he was notified of the intention to give him special recognition, he objected, telling his superiors the story was not true. He testified he was told to just keep quiet and accept the commendation.

In a few days, KPLC news showed up at our church, looking for an interview. Bishop Nugent met them under the breezeway at the main entrance. What he did not realize was he was on camera as he spoke. He was on the news the next day. He had simply refused the interview, saying, "We will do our talking in court." Somehow, the news media had discovered the affiliation between my family and Livingway and were there to get our side of the story. We simply had no trust for their report to not be biased in favor of law enforcement and felt that no good could come out of getting in the media right now.

I should mention that within days of my daughter's arrest, the children were interviewed extensively by the sheriff's office and CASA workers at the Lake Charles CASA facility. These interviews were recorded. The content of these videos were kept secret for many months. During all of the months that followed, the state alleged in family court that very incriminating testimony from the children was on the videos. We in the family would often discuss these claims and always come to the same conclusion that what they were saying was impossible because we knew the truth about Gabe and the children certainly did too. It was not until more that a year into the court proceedings that our attorney and my daughter were allowed to view the videos. After seeing the films for themselves, both Walt and Jaime came away, saying that there was simply nothing on them, just two little boys wanting to go home. This should shock all of our minds to think that the people who we as citizens are expected to trust and rely upon to defend our rights and civil liberties would lie to the entire public and the judge presiding over the case in an effort to deceive all and to delay, in hopes of coming up with some actual evidence. All of this was at the cost of two small children's happiness, the destruction of an innocent woman's future and reputation, and the pain and emotional and financial devastation of her entire family.

We continued a horrible and nightmarish march through the courts, fighting to win this case for more than three years. We intensified our focus on our God and the enduring hope that He would deliver us out of the trouble that had come to us. We expended all of our energy and resources. Our prayer life intensified as we sought the Lord daily for His will. I discovered that there was an intimacy with God that from my view could only be attained through an individual's pain. I realized something that I could not have fully comprehended before, and that is that trouble can be your friend. It will propel you to places in prayer that nothing else will. It will cause you to make decisions about yourself and who you want to be. I recall a comment from Bishop Nugent to me. We were both leaving one of our weekly services and were standing on one of the landings on the west side of the building. He said to me, "You need to pray for the will of God. That will get you somewhere. You need to pray until you have prayed all of the hate, all of the anger, all of the resentment, and all of the bitterness out of this case. When you do that, there is no case." I remember feeling a little puzzled by that statement, not really understanding what he meant. I asked myself the question, "I understand the need to pray all of the hate and resentment away, but how does that diminish the case?" For the next two years, my family would have the tremendous challenge before us to accomplish and understand this in prayer.

At the time of her arrest, Jaime was pregnant with our third grandson. I was so very concerned about her being in a jail cell on a hard floor with poor jailhouse fare for food while pregnant. It was another nightmarish concern, when in my mind, I would envision her in the jail and what she must be feeling and thinking. We made as many visits as allowed to the jail, never missing even one visit. We paid for phone calls and provided money to a jail account to provide her with any personal needs she might have.

She described a miraculous event that occurred while she was incarcerated. She said that anytime she was transported anywhere within the confines of the facility, the other inmates would jeer, curse, and spit upon her. As one would imagine, she was terrified. I recall on our first visit to the jail, we were waiting at the glass window for her to arrive for the visit. All visits were conducted through the glass partition. When she came through the door into the room opposite of ours, I was shocked at the terror in her face and the way she physically shook, all the while trying to compose herself.

Upon one of our scheduled visits as she was being returned to her cell after the visit, she later described to us the following. I have provided the quote as it was listed in a Facebook post from Jaime to an evangelist friend of ours, Reverend Jerry Holland.

I bowed my head with tears going down my face and just talked to God. I told him that I couldn't take it much more, would he just please protect me and keep me safe. I looked up towards the door and I have never in my life seen anything like what I am going to try and describe. Standing in front of the door facing it was this majestic angel. He was as wide and as tall as the ten foot door he was facing. He had a long white robe and these enormous wings that went up to the ceiling and flowed out behind him on the floor. He was there just briefly. The guard opened the door and I stood up and the same people were in the hallway, but the walk back to my room, I did not hear a sound. I could see that their mouths were moving and by the look on their face it was not nice, but I couldn't hear a single sound at all. God covered me.

I can only say, if we believe our Bibles, then obviously, we believe in angels.

Jaime remained in jail for thirty days until a bond hearing at which her bond was lowered to two hundred twenty thousand dollars. Our home and everything we could come up with was not enough to get her released. We were in the middle of the hearing when a close friend from the church approached me and without saying how, he advised that he may have a solution for the twenty thousand dollars we were short. A short while later, another friend called to inform me that he would provide the twenty thousand dollars needed. I am humbled even as I write this to think that he or anyone would extend themselves that much for our family. When I later spoke with him, I was emotional. Choking back tears, I thanked him for standing with us and providing such a tremendous blessing. His simply said to me, "There was never any doubt." I will never be able to aptly convey how thankful we are for the people of God in times of trouble.

KATHAN

Then on September 1, 2010, Kathan Stanton Day was born. He is named after me as my middle name is Stanton. Three days later, we were preparing to be discharged from the hospital when the hospital attendant in reading our chart read where DCFS had made a mandate to hold the child pending a court ruling. To say I was shocked and irate is an understatement. We had spoken with our attorney and he had advised us that DCFS had in fact petitioned the judge to allow them to take Kathan, but he assured us that he had good information that the judge had denied their request. He was partially wrong. Judge Bradberry had in fact denied their request initially, but on the third attempt, they had convinced him. In the end, Veronica Garrett and Mildred Holmes showed up and took Kathan away. They claimed to have received a complaint of abuse. This we all knew was a preposterous allegation, one that had apparently been fabricated as part of a larger scheme to enhance the case against Jaime. DCFS was moving about, barking orders and notifying everyone that they had a court order to take Kathan. There was a young sheriff's deputy who was there to oversee the process. He appeared to disagree in part with DCFS and what they were doing. I remember while Mildred Holmes was attempting to make everyone believe she was absolutely in charge, the young deputy refused to allow her to take the baby until he had spoken personally with the judge. He seemed adamant about his position. I took it as an indicator of previous experiences he may have had with DCFS. I met Veronica Garrett in the hall and she commented to me, "You are having a bad day, aren't you, Mr. Price?" to which I replied, "I have a bad day every time I see you coming, ma'am." This seemed to bother Mrs. Garrett, so I was surprised to discover that she was not as callous as I had originally thought. At least some of these people are just doing their job, which calls for them to follow marching orders, no matter how diabolical those orders may be.

We reached Walter on the phone and he came to the hospital and sat on the bedside with my daughter and wept openly with her. Walter had, in the early days of our case, made a statement to us, saying that he never allowed himself to become emotionally involved with a case. Later, he confessed to me, "I need to apologize to your family. I told you that I never allow myself to become emotionally involved with a case. I have failed to keep that commitment, I and my entire staff."

The following week, we attended a custody hearing held for the purpose of determining who would have custody of Kathan. On this particular day, Judge Bradberry was out for the week and Judge Ron Ware was sitting in for him. As we saw early on, DCFS was staunchly opposed to my wife and I having custody of any of the children. Their position was an apparent indicator of their close working with the district attorney's office. It seemed to me to be an attempt to preserve an anticipated or perceived testimony against Jaime for the state from our grandchildren. They apparently believed that our grandchildren's testimony was crucial to them winning the case. I assume that consequently, they felt they had to convince the court that no children should be left in the care of our family. This would include Kathan by default. I ultimately came to believe that they were coercing the children into saying what they needed them to say in their effort to win this case.

When we entered the courtroom, Judge Ware had apparently already reviewed the case in chambers. From his comments, I knew he had also reviewed the home study done on our home. With no reason apparent, DCFS had failed our home. One comment made by Judge Ware resonated with me. He first of all said, "I intend to place this child with the Prices. Why shouldn't I? He then said, "I will not be influenced by outside sources, I intend to rule based on what is presented before me in this court and I see no reason not to place this child with the grandparents." It was Steve Berniard representing the state who stood and objected strenuously to Judge Ware's ruling to which Judge Ware tersely replied, "Noted." I was curious in that moment as to what outside sources he was referring to. We were so very grateful on that day for a strong and honest-hearted judge and for his decision to give us back one of our children. I think it was the design and hand of God that Judge Ware was on the bench that day. When I consider that it was Judge Bradberry who had finally succumbed to the pressure from some unknown element to allow DCFS to take Kathan in the first place, then I find no reason to believe he would have returned him to us at the hearing.

After court, we drove to DCFS's office to get Kathan and then made our way home. There was a sense of huge relief and victory on that day. Even though we still had many miles to go on this journey, we had at least experienced a day of victory. We had our God to thank. We thank Him for answered prayers. For our grandson being returned to us and for providing us with who is probably the best criminal attorney in the state.

A new problem arose immediately. Ms. Gwen Thompson from CASA called and questioned my wife concerning Kathan's location. Sherri informed her that she had left him with a lady in our church who would be providing day care while she was at work. Mrs. Thompson declared that for my wife to place Kathan in childcare would not be acceptable. She stated to her, "That is not what the judge ordered." At this point, we were so gun-shy that we were afraid if we didn't please them, they would come and take the baby again. Consequently, Sherri made the decision to stay home with Kathan. At the time, she was the office manager at a medical facility known as Business Health Partners or BHP. She asked her employers if they would consider allowing her to work from home for a while. They declined, and in a few days, she was completely released, and we then found ourselves financially devastated, having taken on extreme debt in the defense of our daughter and now having lost forty percent of our income. We feel DCFS and CASA are directly responsible for the loss of her job. Under the extreme pressure of the trouble that we were in, Sherri's health started a sharp decline. She became extremely sick. Finally, on a visit to her doctor, she was ordered to report to the emergency room. She spent five days in the hospital, and it was discovered that she had renal failure and would be on kidney dialysis for the foreseeable rest of her life. We contribute all of her health issues to the stress related to this case.

GOD'S PROMISE

It was somewhere during the early part of 2010 that we were in a mid-week worship service and received a prophetic message from God. Earlier that night, we were at home getting dressed for church. As was the norm during those days, our emotions were raw and we had spent a lot of time in a state of brokenness. We had done everything we could in prayer and encouraging ourselves in the word of God in an effort to summons the faith we needed to continue. We had taken turns on previous days and weeks falling apart emotionally. I would either come in from work to find that she needed me to help her up or it would be my turn to fall apart and she would have to pick me up. By this time, I had changed employers and was working for Veolia Environmental Services. I was the project manager on a fairly large expansion at PPG Industries at the time. I recall the strain of trying to focus on that project and its success while dealing every day with the fact that my grandchildren had been wrongfully taken from us and our daughter was incarcerated and under a five million dollar bond. Sometimes, I would just sit and weep, staring into my computer screen. It was Thursday evening, and as I stood in our bedroom, I looked across the room at her and said, "You know what we need? We need a word from God, we need assurance that He is on board." There is nothing to be compared to a timely word from the throne of God.

We finished dressing and made our way to the church, which was only a couple of miles away. We have always sought to have our residence as close as possible to the church. It was about the middle of the service during worship that night that the prophetic message went forth in tongues. There was an immediate interpretation. As usual, the entire service was recorded, so I later transcribed the prophecy and printed a version for home. I kept this promise in my Bible. I would take it out each morning at prayer time and lay it out before the Lord. Sometimes, I would lay it across my head as I prayed. We would pray over it together as a couple or a family. We were determined to lay hold on to the promise of God and to place our faith in that promise until it came to fruition. I have written it as shown below.

> *Be still saith the Lord, for behold I am in control. I know how you go in, I know how you go out. I know the sorrow that you bear. I know all about you saith the Lord. Be not afraid but draw nigh unto me. For I have a plan, and in the end I win. In the end I win saith the Lord. I'll lead you to victory if you will trust in me.*

On one of my visits to Walt Sanchez's office, I took the printed copy of this prophecy with me. We met in Walt's office with its wonderful view of the lake from the tenth floor. Becky Jacobs and Tom Shea, his associates, were both present. I took out the prophecy and explained to them what it was. I explained from Paul's letter to the Corinthians how that tongues and interpretation of tongues was one of nine supernatural gifts that should operate in a body of believers to edify the body of Christ. These gifts are specifically found in 1 Corinthians 12:1-11 and were exercised commonly within the New Testament church found in the book of Acts. I assured them that while I didn't know how they would win, I could assure them that in the end, they would win because of God's promise. As you might expect, they didn't have a response, but just sat quietly and listened to me. Here I sat in the plush office of one of the most prominent attorneys in the state of Louisiana giving him a Bible study on the operation of the gifts of the spirit. Walt was actually very receptive of our faith. He welcomed our prayers in the face of the seriousness of the case. He also carried an anointed prayer cloth from my wife with him at all times.

CONSPIRACY

Ms. Brandi Green is the DCFS worker who initially handled our case for the agency for a period of at least six months. Jennifer Prejean, who was a seemingly nice lady, was our case worker for the first few weeks, but she was replaced by Ms. Green who, according to her, was thought to have the experience needed to handle a high profile case like ours. As she became familiar with the case and was able to observe and to know our family and to develop interaction with Gabe, she began to report to her supervisors that they had it wrong. She reported Jaime as being a good mom. Mrs. Green was apparently doing everything in her power to do her job honestly and truthfully. The problem she was having was that the analysis she was developing through observation and interviews with all of us was inconsistent with what her supervisors needed and required her to report. It was appalling for us to learn that the most important rule of the game for an agency worker was, you did not necessarily report what was true, but rather what your supervisor felt needed to be reported in the course of winning a case. The agency actually met, developed strategy, and advised the case workers as to what the expected report should reflect. The loss of her job was the price Brandi ultimately paid for telling the truth.

Initially, we were told by the child services officials that normally in a case like ours, the children would be placed in the home of a relative, so we were confident that our grandsons would be returned to us. That would not be the case. Two separate home studies were ordered by the court and conducted on our home. In each case, we were told that our home did not pass. We lived in a good home, and at the time, we each had good jobs. We obviously loved the children very much and they loved us. No reason was apparent why we should not be approved.

After a while, we began to sense that something else was at work. It seemed every attempt to place the children in our home was met with extreme resistance from child services and the DA's office. Additionally, it was clear that everybody on their side was in concert on this issue. At first, we did not understand this. Finally, we were informed that because we believed our daughter was telling the truth that we would not be considered for placement of the children. When I consider this, I find it stunning. The fundamental concept of the American judicial system is that individuals are to be considered innocent until proven guilty and the burden of proof is on the prosecution. Yet in this instance, there is an apparent assumption of guilt. The children are consequently removed from the family with absolutely no consideration as to the possibility of the innocence of the accused. We as grandparents believe that as a minimum, we should have the children while the State attempts to prove their case. But with the assumption of guilt, the state is allowed the latitude to make conditions that bring tremendous hardship to the family and that in the face of the absolute certainty that they have it wrong.

Steve Fontenot is an extremely competent private investigator who conducted a telephone interview with Brandi Green. Mr. Fontenot often provides his services to Walt in criminal cases similar to ours. The following excerpt was taken from his interviews with Brandi Green.

[Excerpt from Brandi Green's Interview with Steve Fontenot]

BG: Exactly. I want to say about, before they you know that I was, they sent me home with, on suspension with pay until this day they cannot explain to me why. We all know why. Because they wanted to keep me away from the office.

SF: And why do you think that is?

BG: Because they knew that I was starting to question some things and I gonna tell you honestly. My fight has never been for Jaime's Innocence or whether she was guilty. My fight has been for the grandparents and I'm sorry, but they intentionally and purposefully denied that home study. Now that home study was not done by me. The home study was done by Jennifer Prejean. Ya'll put her on the stand, she's gonna flop. I always felt like they pulled me away from the office so they, in the event ya'll called.

SF: Jennifer who?

BG: Prejean. She had the case before I did. From what Jennifer told me before I got the case, they purposefully made her find things to deny the home study. Like I think it was.

SF: Who made her do that

BG: Lee Schmidt, John Nelson and Dawn Becton.

Given the fact that we did not simply believe our daughter, but were in fact eyewitnesses of what happened with Gabe in her home, we were appalled. DCFS would have us believe that they were concerned the children would not be safe in our home. It was much easier for me to believe that they simply wanted to have influence over everything the boys thought or said until trial. It just seemed that there was no way to gain any advantage in this case and the weight of it all just seemed to press more heavily each and every day. I would often awaken in the morning and simply did not want to face another day. I remember standing in the shower morning after morning at 4:30 a.m., simply fighting mentally to go on. But we never stopped declaring our daughter's innocence, regardless of the pressure placed on us by

DCFS. By this time, it was obvious that everyone on the state's side were apparently playing off the same page of music. It was equally obvious that a strong conspiracy was under way. That something or someone had to be directing traffic for all of the State of Louisiana's participants, in their position on issues, their reporting, and all of their public comments and court testimony to be in perfect harmony.

One of the most troubling accounts that occurred was Christmas of 2010. As Christmas approached, we were involved in some ongoing court proceedings and one of the things that came up in the proceedings was whether or not we would be allowed to send Christmas gifts to the children. Judge Bradberry ruled that Christmas gifts would be allowed and that we as grandparents could place names on the gifts, letting the boys know that we had not forgotten them at Christmas. We were excited and went out and did our Christmas shopping for the boys, then went to great pains to put as much message of love and recognition to the boys from us as was allowed. As instructed, we then submitted the gifts to the DCFS case worker, Ms. Brandi Green, who in turn delivered them to her regional office. Without telling us, DCFS removed all identifying names or markings from the gifts in an obvious effort to prevent the children from knowing who the gifts were from. Later in a discussion with Brandi, she told us that she attempted to comply with the court ruling but was overruled by her superiors, naming Mrs. Dawn Becton, Mildred Holmes, and Lee Schmitt. The children simply thought that Santa brought the gifts.

[Excerpt from Brandi Green's phone interview with Steve Fontenot]

BG: Jaime said, Ms Brandi, you know Gwen Thompson said you pulled the, our names and stuff off of the gifts. I said Jaime, I was getting ready to bring the gifts to Kyler and Kolten the way that they were. Lee Schmidt, John Nelson and Dawn

Becton along with my supervisor told me that I had to pull the names off.

SF: And who was your supervisor?

BG: Mildred Holmes. I had to black the names out and I had to pull the names off. I said, Ms. Mildred, well they said that the names could be left on. She said, all I know is Dawn and Lee and Catherine McGill are saying it can't have any names on it. I said OK, well I'm gonna do what they tell me to do. I'm not gonna be insubordinate. At that point, my job meant everything to me.

Much later in the next year, we were attending a series of court-appointed visits between the boys and ourselves. At one of these meetings, we discussed the gifts with the boys and learned the truth. I ask Kolten how he liked one of the video games we sent them at Christmas. As I asked the question, I saw the look of surprise on his face and I could feel the tension growing. We always felt the constant pressure of knowing that DCFS was listening to our conversation behind the two-way mirror. Oftentimes, during our visits with the boys, we would be interrupted by a DCFS worker barging into the room to confront us over some comment or question. There was always a Gestapo type environment that was very intimidating. We would ask a simple question like, "Where did Mrs. Potts take you on vacation?" or "What is your best friend's name at school?" and immediately, the DCFS worker would appear and say, "You cannot ask that question." I remember Kolten's surprise to learn that we had purchased and sent him the video games he so loved. After that meeting, he apparently returned to the foster parent's home and questioned them about this. Obviously, he had been led to believe that Santa had brought him the games. Gwen Thompson later admonished us that we "placed the foster mom in a bad position by telling the boys who the gifts were from." I responded to this by saying, "DCFS placed her in a bad position by not following the instruction from the court." She then responded, "Well, I can't speak for them on that matter." Anytime you cast light on these people's Gestapo tactics, they always became evasive.

It was in February of 2011, we arrived at a point in the court proceedings that the aforementioned visits were ordered. In an effort to move in the direction of establishing permanent residency for the boys, Judge Bradberry had ordered that a series of visits be set up between Sherri, me, and the boys. The setting was at a state-appointed child counselor's office who had been assigned to the children. Her name is Mrs. Ann Landry, owner of Ann Landry, MSW, LCSW, RPT-S, LCC. Her office was housed in the offices of Lake Area Psychology on Michael DeBakey Drive in Lake Charles, Louisiana. She was to monitor the meetings and make a recommendation to the court. Gwen Thompson from CASA also arranged to be present during the visits. This first meeting with the boys was indescribable. Kolten and Kyler walked into the room and immediately walked into our arms. There was this perpetual hug from which flowed overwhelming emotion and tears. Neither of us wanted to let go of the other. It was like something I have never experienced, and it was obvious that the feeling was mutual all around. Once we got past this exceptional moment, we began the first of a series of six visits with these boys that were, as I said, indescribable It was very apparent that we loved them and they loved us and that we belonged together. As I have already stated, the purpose of the meetings was to determine if we would make suitable guardians for our own grandchildren. We paid a little over two thousand dollars for these meetings to Mrs. Landry. This was an amount that we gladly paid even while strapped for money. The visits were scheduled two each week. The reason for the high frequency of the meetings was that the judge wanted us to have six visits within a period of approximately a month. This was so that all of the sessions would be complete prior to the next scheduled hearing.

You would almost have to be me or at least another grandparent wildly in love with your grandchildren to appreciate the significance of what I am about to share. From the time that Kolten and Kyler were in those toddler years up until the time they were taken, I would often play Tickle Monster with them. They would hide under a blanket or some sort of covering and I, with a deep, monster voice, would declare myself to be the "Tickle Monster looking for a little boy." After pretending to be on a search for a few moments, I would suddenly "discover" them under the covers and they would roar with laughter as I attacked with tickles. As we were nearing the end of that first visit in Ann Landry's office, we were in the hallway just outside her office preparing to say good-bye. Here we were, holding in our arms the boys for whom our hearts were broken and had yearned after for a year while DCFS held them captive. I knelt on a knee beside Kolten and hugged him, and he leaned into my ear and whispered, "Papa, you didn't forget Tickle Monster, did you?" For me, it was an unforgettable moment!

I had a picture on my phone of Kolten and Kyler. I had received the picture as an attachment on a text from someone in my family. I am not certain who sent it to me, but I think it was Jaime. I later learned that the picture originated from Brandi Green and that it had been taken in front of the Potts home. It was obviously a picture taken in a pose at close range. On one of our visits with the boys at Landry's office, I had my phone out, showing the boys' pictures, and before I even thought about it, I came across the picture of them standing together in Oakdale. Kolten immediately exclaimed, "Hey, that looks like Mrs. Roxanne's house!" to which I replied in the hearing of Gwen Thompson and Ann Landry, "It is." I immediately and intuitively knew that they probably felt that we should not have a current picture of the boys in our possession and I was absolutely correct. That brief exchange brought all sorts of foolish questions, especially from Gwen Thompson. In a later phone conversation, she questioned me about the origin of the pictures. During that conversation, she blatantly accused me of stalking the boys and sneaking around, taking pictures of them in Oakdale. She demanded to know where I had gotten the pictures. I refused to tell her, mostly because of her attitude and the fact that it was none of her business and because I wanted to protect Brandi Green if it could mean trouble for her. I told her the picture was obviously taken by someone standing directly in front of the boys as they posed, in the yard so it certainly wasn't taken by a stalker, but in any case, where I got the picture was my business. This became a sticking point with her and she even brought it up once while testifying in court, implying that I had indeed stalked the boys and exclaiming, "He refuses to this day to tell us where he got those pictures." Gwen often forgot her role as a volunteer CASA worker. She was the OCS investigator to the end.

As we neared the end of the series of meetings, we were excited at the prospect of the counselor's recommendation. We knew that our relationship was undeniable. In our minds, it was unlikely that this counselor had ever seen a relationship between children and their grandparents that was more genuine and meaningful. A few days before the reports were due to Judge Bradberry, I called Mrs. Landry to inquire as to how she felt about the visits and what we could expect of her recommendation. I was mildly concerned when she did not want to divulge the content of her report to me, but rather advised me that she would reserve that information for the report itself and for Judge Bradberry. I tried not to pay attention to it, but there was something in her tone that tipped me to the possibility that all was not well. We were soon to be disappointed in the most horrific manner. The day arrived that she provided her recommendation to the court. As the matter of course, our attorneys were provided a copy of her report. It was in sharp contrast to reality or our expectations in every way and we were shocked at its content. First of all, her initial description of our meetings was that the boys were standoffish at first and then gradually got over it and appeared more comfortable with us. This is the total opposite of the truth. As I said previously, they ran into our arms and would not let us go.

The rest is even more horrifying. During the visits, the boys would oftentimes attack me. This would begin a wrestling match, much like the many, that had been conducted in my home in days gone by. From these normal playful good times, Mrs. Landry reported extreme inappropriate touching between myself and the boys. She suggested I was seeking sexual gratification from touching my own grandchildren! In her report, she stated, "Mr. Price's face was entirely too close to the boys genitals and their genitals too close to his face." She claimed in court to see me rubbing their genitals on my chest. She advised the court that she was concerned that it was an effort to possibly achieve sexual gratification. I was shocked at first, and then I began to analyze her report. I thought, even if I were some sort of pervert, can anyone actually believe that I would attempt to molest any child, let alone my own grandchildren while sitting in a small office in the presence of a state employed counselor and a volunteer worker from CASA, One of which is an expert witness and the other a mandatory court reporter? Then I understood something. She didn't believe the content of her report at all, but was simply fulfilling a role as a witness for the state. I believe she understood the role and the result she was expected to produce. Simply put, she was a "rubber stamp."

Mrs. Landry also included in her report a distorted rendition of a trip to the bathroom. Kolten had asked while we were in Mrs. Landry's office if he could go to the bathroom. Somehow, it fell to my lot to be the one to take him. We walked together down the hall to the bathroom, and as we approached the door, Kolten said to me, "Papa, you wait out here for me," to which I replied, "Okay, I'll be right here," and leaned by the door until he came out. I remember being puzzled for just a moment, as to why he would ask me to wait outside, but then, I considered the ordeal he had been forced to be a part of for the last year so I thought, *No big deal.* When he came out, I said to him, "Okay, now you wait here for me, don't leave me," I jokingly said, thinking that I would be surprised if he was waiting in the hall for me when I came out. Sure enough, in a minute or two, I exited the bathroom to find Kolten already returned to Mrs. Landry's office where the toys were.

In her report, Mrs. Landry alleged that her receptionist had witnessed me attempting to coax Kolten into the bathroom. She stated that he had become frightened and run away. This coupled with the allegations of my seeking to molest the boys in her office made for a very interesting read in the report. A judge could hardly ignore such allegations coming from expert witnesses.

Ms. Gwen Thompson corroborated Mrs. Landry's allegations with her own concerns of sexual misconduct on my part. This, for me, was in itself a strong and clear indicator of the conspiracy they were both a part of, given the fact that I knew that nothing they alleged had one ounce of truth in it, as did they. Fortunately, we had taken pictures of my wrestling with the boys for memories' sake. As it turned out, we used them to show the actual complexion of the events and they were presented in court in our defense. The photos were humorous with the boys all over me like two monkeys as I sat in a chair with a pirate's hat on, looking quite goofy. I now realize it is simply that we have to understand that the state's witnesses do these things as a service to the state's case. It is apparent to me that Mrs. Landry and Mrs. Thompson's purpose was to create a documented suspicion that prevented Judge Bradberry from placing the boys with us. Their tactics apparently are meant to intimidate a judge who might otherwise rule against the state. He cannot ignore a recommendation made by a mandatory court reporter or an expert witness like Mrs. Thompson or Mrs. Landry. These witnesses are the folks you will find representing the state in any case for which they need expert testimony in a family court case where children are involved.

They are the state's go-to persons for an expert opinion that fits their case. What is most obvious to me is that these people would be very unlikely to be bold enough to fabricate and allege such falsehoods on their own or without inner support. I reasoned that they would have to feel protected. It is apparent to me that the participant parties have grown so accustomed to these unethical modes of operation that they simply have no conscience in regard to this. They give no consideration to the impact their words can make on innocent lives. As I heard an elderly security guard say, who befriended us in our many visits to the court, "Anything for a conviction" is the policy around here.

In the final analysis, I believe that these two women have very different reasons for the role that they are willing to play for the state. I learned in a conversation with attorney Brad Guillory, who was Kolten's court-appointed attorney, that street language among the local attorneys refer to these type expert witnesses as "whores." It is my belief that while Mrs. Landry does it simply for the contract business, Mrs. Thompson, on the other hand, being a thirty plus year retired DCFS worker does it, I would venture, for a sense of belonging to something. She is entering into the twilight years of her life, and without her involvement in the courts, she would simply not have anything to do. She once confirmed this to me in a visit in my home, explaining to me that she had become involved with CASA after retirement from DCFS so she would have something to do; she wanted to stay involved. I would recommend that she come to church with us, be born again of the spirit, and get involved. It provides a much greater reward for your services and you need not lie.

The good that came out of this hearing was that the judge apparently did not believe the account provided by Mrs. Landry and Mrs. Thompson. He ordered biweekly visits with the boys to start immediately at the Whistle Stop between the boys and ourselves. The cost of these visits started at twenty-five dollars per hour for each visit and later increased to thirty-five. This was certainly a better deal than Mrs. Landry's one hundred and thirty-five dollars an hour base rate plus a premium rate on weekends. We were allowed to bring food and clothing articles to the boys. No other gifts were allowed. We attended those meetings anytime they were scheduled. To miss one was unthinkable! They continued for two full years.

THE GOVERNOR'S OFFICE

During the early years of my early childhood, my mom was a single working parent. She would drop us off in the mornings at the Hartley home on her way to work at Westinghouse. Mom had spent many years standing in position at an assembly line assembling light fixtures. She paid Mrs. Hartley to watch us while we were out of school during the summer. It was during this time that I became friends with her son Richard Hartley. I suppose we were around eight or nine years old at the time. We spent many hours playing children's games outside in their yard on Bridge Street in Vicksburg, Mississippi. Time passed and I didn't see Richard for a few years. As a young teenager, I came in contact with him again at his new home in Ridgecrest, Louisiana, while visiting during the summer with my uncle Russell Hartley who was Richard's older brother. Ridgecrest is a small town just outside of another small town: Ferriday, Louisiana. Russell had married my mom's sister, Shirlene, around the same time that Mrs. Hartley was sitting my brother and me. Richard and I renewed our friendship while he was working at the local barbershop in Ridgecrest, shining shoes. He was probably around twelve at the time. I would walk down to the barbershop for a visit. On one occasion, he even gave me a haircut. Apparently, he had been practicing and I was a prime candidate. After that season, I did not see Richard again until his life became a part of this story. Richard went on to college and entered into public education. He worked for many years in public education both in Morehouse and Ouachita Parishes. During those years, he became well connected among Louisiana politics. After his retirement, he was appointed to the staff of Lieutenant Governor Jay Dardenne. One weekend, he dropped by to attend church with us at Livingway. This was more than forty-five years since the time we first played together as boys. Richard brought the Lieutenant Governor with him that night as a guest. It was nearing election time, which was the explanation for the visit. Politicians tend to show up at church around election time. Richard and I spoke briefly, each expressing our heartfelt gladness to see the other. He left me his card and we each promised to stay in touch.

In early July of 2011, it came into my thinking that Richard might be in a position to assist or provide some help in this crisis we were in. I was desperate and felt if I didn't ask, I may very well live to regret it. At the same time, I struggled with a question, what did God expect for me to do? Was the right choice to do nothing and simply pray and wait on God or was there a role for me to play in the physical realm? I would justify my anxious actions with scripture from the book of James, "Faith without works is dead." In retrospect, I can unambiguously declare today that God does not need our help! I called Richard and scheduled an appointment. He seemed excited to visit with me and I knew I would enjoy meeting with him and reminiscing over old times, but I was on a mission. I drove to Baton Rouge on a Friday morning and met with Richard for about an hour and a half in the State Capitol Building. They have a security guard at the door of the capitol building checking appointments. Once cleared, I was instructed as to what floor to go to and that Richard was expecting me. His office is on the same floor as the Lieutenant Governor. He was waiting for me outside his office and I was immediately impressed with my surroundings. The Lieutenant Governor's office is a large stately affair and certainly impressive to a country boy like myself. And here was the boy who used to play in the dirt with me and experimentally cut my hair at thirteen now in a suit greeting me at the governor's office. We made our way to Richard's personal office and shared a few memories. Finally, I got around to the case. I laid out all of the details of this case to him and basically just asked for help. Knowing that Richard was a spirit-filled man, I shared the spiritual aspects of the story, including God's prophetic promise of deliverance. I left that day with assurances from Richard that I would be hearing from him. I remember his promise: "I am not going to let this lie," as I was preparing to leave. I followed up this meeting with a letter to Governor Bobby Jindel. I provided him with a brief outline of the case in a three-page letter. In closing, I made the following appeal.

> *My appeal to you, sir, is that you assist us in any way possible in getting our grandchildren back in our home. OCS claims to be about reunification while in fact they are staunch in their stance against us having our grandchildren. We can provide an excellent home for them and will eagerly and gladly commit to whatever needs to be done to achieve their return. Judge Guy Bradberry is presiding over this case and our next hearing is Friday 8/20/11.*
>
> *We would be very grateful if you would launch an investigation into the wrongdoing of this case. Is it possible that in our day, we have arrived at a time when winning a case is so important that we are willing to prosecute and destroy the innocent rather that admit a mistake? My attorney is Walter Sanchez. We thank you in advance for any consideration you can provide.*

We closed the letter with our respective signatures and arranged to have it delivered via FedEx. I called Richard and advised him of the letter. He asked when and how I had sent it, to which I replied that I had sent the letter FedEx and it should arrive the next day. I was simply hoping he would monitor it so that it did not get lost in the shuffle. I have not heard from the Governor or Richard since that day.

THE PSYCHOLOGIST

DCFS and the Calcasieu Parish District Attorney's office have a certified expert witness, Dr. Lawrence Dilks. He is a psychologist commonly used as a witness in state cases such as ours in Calcasieu Parish. At our attorney's advice, we refused to allow him to examine our daughter initially. This, I think, was based on Walt's previous experiences with Mr. Dilks and would prove to be good advice. He had access to our grandchildren by virtue of his position with the state. On our part, we sought out and, through our attorney, acquired the services of Dr. Glenn Ahava from Lafayette, Louisiana. Dr. Ahavah is an expert in the field of advanced forensic psychology and, as I understand, is widely reputed to be one of the most renowned forensic psychologists in America. He examined my daughter, utilizing standardized tests that are the basis for such testing in the arena of psychology nationally. He also examined the test and results conducted by Mr. Dilks on my grandchildren. He testified in the family court proceedings that my daughter, based on the test he performed, could not possibly have committed the crimes she was accused of. He called her "Mother Teresa pregnant." He said that with thirty years of experience, she either could not have done it or she was the best actress he had ever seen.

Mr. Dilks testified that the boys had each drawn a picture of the exact same event and their pictures and stories were identical. According to him, they had each drawn a picture of Gabe hanging on a door, upside down suspended by hooks. Dr.

Ahavah testified that boys whose ages were at the time six and four would have to be coached to have drawn the exact same image. He used an illustration saying that if a masked man were to walk into the open court room and randomly shoot someone, tests have proven that each of the eyewitnesses in the room would report something different, simply because the tests have proven that it is perception rather than reality that we remember. He further testified that the test as administered by Mr. Dilks was done so in gross error, insomuch according to Dr. Ahavah, Mr. Dilks could be subject to a lawsuit for malpractice. The state, in response to Dr. Ahavah's testimony, solicited the services of a third psychologist, John Simoneaux from the Pineville, Louisiana, area, who basically leveled the ground between the two. He examined both psychologist's tests and testified that neither psychologist had been wrong, thus removing the need for the court to report Mr. Dilks to the state ethics board. First of all, I am stunned that anyone could examine this case and observe the extreme opposites in two expert opinions and provide a conclusion that both were right! I found it most troubling that the state and the court would seek and pay for an opinion to discredit Dr. Ahavah and reinforce Dilks because in effect that is exactly what they did. Besides, if neither of them had committed wrong, how do you then as the court, in ruling, make a choice? How do you discredit Ahavah and validate Dilks? How do you justify a decision to believe or disbelieve either of them? Why not have the third psychologist examine the children blindly and administer his own test, then compare the findings? It was obvious that one of them was wrong and one was not. So the question becomes is the court prejudiced in favor of the prosecution? Certainly, the court would not solicit a third opinion if it was the defense's expert's integrity that was being called into question. Our story is very revealing on this point.

Sadly, one of the lessons we were to learn from this ordeal is that eyewitness testimony is secondary in the face of expert opinion. In other words, expert testimony will carry much more weight in court than eyewitness testimony. There is a term used frequently in the courts which is "lay witnesses." This term refers to "the folks," as Bill O'Reilly would say, and it places everyday folk at a lesser level of significance than the other players in the view of the court. Accordingly, if the expert testimony opposes eyewitness testimony even if the expert is in error, or if the expert is possibly corrupt or simply providing an opinion for a fee that suits the prosecutor's need, then a defendant has a much lessened chance of convincing a court of their innocence even if they are in fact innocent and have eyewitnesses to prove it. Thus, all of the neighbors who in fact had observed Gabe's extreme behavioral issues, many of whom were frequent visitors in Jaime's home, their testimony in the end became noneffective during the course of these proceedings. Another point to be considered is that when a judge presides over a certain types of high profile cases, he has to be concerned with protecting himself from criticism. If he relies on expert testimony in his ruling, he is always protected. Consequently, many of these modern-day judges will default to ruling based on the expert's opinion even when their opinions conflict with eyewitness testimony. Their jobs could depend on it! In my view, the definition of expert testimony is simply an opinion with a set of credentials attached to it.

During the course of the testing on Jaime and the boys, we as Jaime's parents were required to spend two one-hour sessions each with Mr. Dilks for evaluation. This requirement was mandated by DCFS as part of the case plan, and we were advised by Mr. Sanchez to cooperate fully. In these sessions, Mr. Dilks attempted to build a platform from which he could create a diagnosis explaining what caused Jaime to commit the crimes of which she was accused. This was obviously based on an assumption that Jaime was actually guilty. He first suggested that I should pay for an EEG for Jaime to monitor electrical activity in her brain. He explained to me that if I would agree to this, he would be able to say she probably suffered from blackouts. He asked the question, "Wouldn't you rather be able to say that she was mentally ill than to be left with what the state is alleging as the only explanation?" I was appalled and said so. My statement to him was, "If that were the truth, then we would say so! We are all looking for the truth, aren't we?" It was shocking to me that he could suggest that we create an explanation for Jaime's alleged actions in such a flippant way. He seemed to be suggesting to me that whatever he said, regardless of the facts, would be accepted as reality in the court room. The sad reality was that he was exactly right.

The next thing he attempted was to fabricate statements from me, saying I had said to him in one of our sessions, that Jaime had been abused repeatedly growing up and that I carried much guilt concerning this. No such conversation ever occurred nor has any such events ever occurred! During my wife's next session with him, he declared this new theory to her, citing me as telling him of this abuse. She was shocked at this and told him so. She asked him, "My husband said that to you?" When she saw me later, she asked me, unbelievingly, had I made such a ridiculous claim to Dilks? "Absolutely not" was my reply." I called him the next morning and demanded how he could fabricate such a preposterous story. I remembered his making a claim of his own Christianity in court, so I ask him how he could make such a false claim and obvious fabrication and still claim to be a benevolent Christian. In reply, he said, "That is what you said, Mr. Price." To which I replied, "You know very well that I did not say any such thing." He then obligingly stated to me, "Well, maybe I misunderstood you." To which I replied, "No, Mr. Dilks, you did not misunderstand me. You know very well that I never said anything akin to what you are now suggesting." He then recanted this story and landed on the one he submitted to the court, saying my daughter had something called fictitious disorder, which is apparently synonymous to Munchausen syndrome by proxy. This is explained as a disorder where a parent harms children in secret and then claims the child or children are self-inflicting to gain the attention and sympathy of others or at least that is the best understanding I have of it. What was I to think of a system whose principal witness would stop at nothing and was willing to scandalously fabricate any scenario in order to validate their case? One of the things he said to me in our meeting was that the District Attorney's office was honor bound to prosecute the cases as they are presented to them. I asked myself that day, "What is honorable about knowingly prosecuting the innocent?"

DCFS is responsible to provide a case plan for cases like these to determine path forward for both the children and the parent or parents. DCFS's procedures by their own admission requires that reunification be their first option in the case plan. They would have you believe that the intent is for DCFS is to reunite children with family unless it becomes apparent that reunification is not a workable path forward. A part of this procedure is for the parent to undergo parenting training as part of the reunification process. The parents are tested at the beginning of a series of classes and at the end. The classes are conducted in the home of the parent. Mrs. Naomi Bellard was the instructor solicited by DCFS to provide training and testing for Jaime. Jaime was told at the initial testing that she scored higher as a parent than most parents do after training. The training is a sixteen-week course. Mrs. Bellard testified later in the November 3, 2011, family court hearing that she was comfortable that Jaime was a wonderful parent and that she had no concerns about placing her children in her care. She testified that she had scored extremely well on the standardized testing. Immediately, the state cross-examined her and asked, "What qualifies you as an expert on this subject?" in an effort to discredit her. Mr. Sanchez countered with an objection, pointing out that the state had in fact hired Mrs. Bellard to perform the training and testing on Jaime. He asked the question, "So Mrs. Bellard is an expert when they hire her, but not one if she doesn't provide them with the answer they are looking for?" These actions provide us with another peek into the "win at any cost" mentality this DA's office and DCFS possess.

In March 2011, I received a jury duty summons. As is the normal order of process, in the notice, you are advised to fax a letter if you know of any reason you would not be a proper juror. I drafted and sent a letter to the fax number provided for the Fourteenth Judicial Court. The text of that letter is shown below.

As it relates to my summons # 188955 for jury duty on March 21, 2011, I wish to express the following. I will certainly serve my civic duty as a juror, but in fairness, I feel I should express the following. I have been involved in recent months with an ongoing criminal court case and am appalled at the way that the prosecution and law enforcement in our fine parish handles cases. The dishonesty in which they operate is offensive. It is obvious that there is a policy of win at any cost or anybody's expense. It is obvious also that innocence or guilt do not play into the picture, but rather the political posture of losing or winning. There is a large portion of our community who now know this having seen it for ourselves. We hope to make changes in the next elections, but at this point, it will be difficult to believe any evidence no matter how compelling, given the fact that we have been able to see firsthand how evidence and testimony is manipulated. We believe now that a high percentage of those incarcerated are in fact innocent victims of this system. In any case as earlier stated, I will gladly serve, but this is what you would hear from me at the jury selection process.

I received a phone call the next day releasing me from jury duty.

THE JOURNAL

I mentioned earlier that the staff from Fairview Elementary had falsely testified that Gabe was an exemplary child at school. We now believe they were testifying under direction from the children's attorney at the time. The fact that the teachers perjured themselves is obvious by the virtue of the fact that Gabe was in the Homebound program at all, given the requirements to qualify for that program. Gabe's constant problematic and bizarre behavioral problems could be verified by the flow of documentation between Dr. Murphy's office and the school.

It was later established that this same attorney had in her possession and kept secret the contents of a journal kept and maintained by the foster mom in whose home Gabe was placed for the first several months after the state took custody of him. This journal contained information that was extremely contradictory to the state's case against my daughter. The attorney, Mrs. Melanie Smith Daley, apparently concealed this evidence for more than a year from the court, during which time, she argued strenuously that the only explanation for Gabe's injuries was that Jaime had inflicted them upon him.

The foster mom's journal would prove to be the most incriminating evidence against the state and its expert witnesses. Her journal's contents ultimately became the start of the downfall of the state's case. In her journal, Mrs. Semien recorded shocking behavior of self-infliction on the part of Gabe. She also records daily conversations with him in which he readily admitted self-inflicting while in my daughter's home. He declared to her, according to the journal records, that he did this out of jealousy of the other two boys. He stated to her that was why he had committed self-inflictions and that he was going to do the same to her and her family because she also had two boys and "you are not showing me enough attention." She states that on a particular event, she had removed some food he had stolen and placed in a duffel bag in his room. According to her statement, when one of the other foster children reported to her that Gabe had stolen the food, she walked into his room and took the food out of a duffel bag and returned it to the kitchen. She tells a horrific account of how he, in retaliation, screamed and growled for hours until exhausted then suddenly, he calmly looked at her and said, "I am going to do to you what I did to Jaime." When asked what he meant, he stated he was going to injure himself and tell the DCFS worker that she (the foster mom) had done it.

Later in the journal, there is an account of bizarre behavior where he claims to hear voices in his head that tell him to hurt himself. She describes finding him sitting in his room, screaming, "No, no, no, no!" He told her the voices were telling him to hurt himself. All of this behavior is mirrored in my daughter's testimony to the court. There is an entry in the journal from 7/16/10 where Gabe alludes to hearing voices that tell him to burn the house down. This mirrors the account that occurred at Dana's home.

[Excerpt from Semien's Journal]

7/15/10 – Gabe was awake before 7am, he came into the kitchen and took a box of cereal…went and put it in a dufflebag in his closet. One of my other boys came and woke me up to tell me. I got up and went in his room and took the dufflebag. I didn't say a word to him. He then got mad and started screaming and growling. I left him alone. He just got worse, he started clawing his face up and biting himself on the arms and hands.

He was screaming and said he was going to tell the worker that I am starving him. He said I don't feed him. He then got real calm for a minute and looked at me and said:" I am going to do to you like I did to Jaime."

I said to him what do you mean. He said he is going to tell the worker that I clawed him in the face and that I am not feeding him because he wants to leave here and go somewhere else. He said thats what he did at Jaime's because he wanted to leave from there and go to Memorial Hospital because he got what he wanted from there and because he got all of the attention from the doctors and nurses. He said he just wanted attention and Jaime was not giving him enough attention, she was paying to much attention to the other two boys. He told me the reason he was doing all of this today was because all of the attention was on 2 of my other kids, because their lawyer came to see them on Tuesday July 13th and their worker came to see them on Wed. July 14. He said no one was coming over to see him and talk to him about when he was bad at Mrs. Crager's house. This fit of rage lasted for hours. Gabe has said on several occasions that he hears voices in his head. That what tells him to hurt himself. (Emphasis added)

7/16/10–He says the voices tell him to cuss, steal and burn the house down with a lighter and a card. When Gabe made this statement I looked up at him and he was laughing and said that happened when I was at Nita's house.

7/17/10 – Later that evening I was fixing supper, I could hear him talking loud down the hall. I went to see, he was in his room sitting on his bed with his legs crossed and his hands under his legs. He was crying and saying "no, no leave me alone." He said he hears those voices and they are telling him to hurt himself again.

[Excerpt from Affidavit of Karla Semien]

The statements that I wrote down that were said by Gabe are accurate. He went into a rage and stayed out of control for hours, clawing his face, throwing furniture and stating that he was hearing voices in his head. He bit himself on his arm, scratched his legs and screamed for hours until he physically wore himself out.

Because Ann Landry was so concerned about his mental stability and the possibility he would hurt himself or someone else, my husband and I placed all of the children on one end of the house and made them sleep separate and apart from Gabe who was kept on the other end.

Because we were afraid for the safety of our children and ours as well, my husband and I took turns staying up around the clock from Friday afternoon until Monday morning, when he was taken to the hospital.

On the night of the 16th, after we were told that we were going to have to keep Gabe in our home until the following Monday, we took him to see our preacher and his wife, Brother Wade and his wife, Amanda. We met him at the church, Oberlin Baptist Church. We stayed there until 11:00 or 11:30 PM that night. The preacher prayed over him and gave Gabe a copy of the Bible. Affidavit of Karla Semien, Page 2, January 30, 2012

Notice in the affidavit that she makes reference to calling the Child Services officials on a weekend to report he had harmed himself and needed medical attention. She was told to not take him to the hospital but to wait until the next week. She sent pictures of his injuries, which DCFS never submitted in discovery. What could be more troubling than an agency which is fundamentally in existence to protect the well-being of children but orders a child in need of medical attention denied that attention in an apparent effort to protect their position in an ongoing court case and to conceal evidence in that case?

On July 16, 2010, when Gabe went out of control and began to injure himself, I took a photograph on my phone and sent it by text message to Brandi Green. I called her in an attempt to have Gabe placed in the hospital. I also spoke with Ann

*Landry that day, who told me that I needed to take him to
Lake Charles Memorial Hospital.*

*Mildred Holmes, the foster care supervisor, called me
back and told me that I could not take Gabe to Lake Charles
Memorial Hospital because he was in state's care and I had no
authority to sign him in. She told me that I would have to wait
until the following Monday.*

*Affidavit of Karla Semien,
Pages 1-2, January 30, 2012.*

One of the most troubling points about this information is
that we know by virtue of the dates in the journal and the foster
mom's own testimony that the State, Child Services, and all of
the state's expert witnesses, including Dr. Dilks and Ann Landry,
had copies of this journal. Mrs. Semien affirms that she provided
updated copies of the journal upon each visit to the respective
parties. It appears that there was a conspiracy between them to
conceal this evidence from the court. They successfully withheld
it from discovery for a full year, thereby denying my daughter due
process or a fair trial.

Additional from the journal:

*On July 20, 2010 I kept an appointment at the Kirkman Street
Office of OCS. This was the first visit after Gabe's breakdown.
I provided them a copy of my notes and also made a copy of all
of the photographs that I took of Gabe's injuries to himself that
night, which I had printed from the SD card in my camera.
Affidavit of Karla Semien,*

*I visited several times with Dr. Dilks about Gabe. Each
Time, I brought my journal. Dr. Dilks made a copy of my
journal on April 23, 2010. I remember him copying the
journal because, on that date, I told him that I had to leave
early because there was a scheduled visit between Gabe and his
mother, Nita, at McDonald's. He then told me that that was
not allowed; that there was a no contact order. When he made
copies of my journal for himself he also made a copy of the court*

order prohibiting contact between Gabe and Nita for me. I still have the copy of the court order that he made for me on the day he copied my journal. I remember it clearly, because when he told me there was a court order, I became really nervous because I almost put Gabe with his mother in violation of what the judge said.

On August 4, 2010, I went to visit with Ms. Ann Landry. Every time I met with Ann, her staff made copies from my journal. I remember that she made copies on that date because this was the first visit that I had with her after Gabe went to Crossroads.

Affidavit of Karla Semien,
Page 2, January 30, 2012.

GOD'S ARROW

Earlier in the year, in a passing conversation, Bishop Nugent had spoken these words to me concerning our case, "This battle will be fought in the spirit in prayer and then acted out in the courtroom." Not long after that, the Lord quickened the following psalm to me. I had often turned to the psalms in prayer for encouragement during the course of this trouble. I believed that this psalm was a word from God to our family and applied it as such in prayer.

Hear My voice O God; in my prayer preserve my life from fear of the enemy. Hide me from the secret counsel of the wicked; from the insurrection of the workers of iniquity; who whet their tongue like a sword and bend their bows to shoot their arrows, even bitter words; that they may shoot in secret at the perfect: suddenly do they shoot at him and fear not.

They encourage themselves in an evil matter; they commune of laying snares privily; they say, who shall see them? They search out iniquities; they accomplish a diligent search; both the inward thought of every one of them and the heart is deep.

But God shall shoot at them with an arrow; suddenly shall they be wounded. So they shall make their own tongue to fall upon themselves: all that see them shall flee away.

And all men shall fear, and shall declare the work of God; for they shall wisely consider of his doing. The Righteous shall be glad in the Lord and shall trust in him; and all the upright in heart shall glory.

*Psalms 64 (*KJV*)*

On November 3, 2011, the most significant hearing held to date in the family court hearings determining the future of our grandchildren was conducted. We fully understood that it had all come down to this final hearing. After all of the various court appearances, the stressful nights and days, the pain, and the cost, all would be decided it seemed in this final moment. The state, while legally responsible to provide full discovery to all officers of the court when properly requested, waited until literally twenty-four hours before the start of this hearing to submit full discovery to our attorneys. They had apparently possessed Mrs. Semien's journal and its contents for more than a year and had chosen this moment to provide it to Mr. Sanchez. Even now, it was not being provided as part of discovery in the child in need of care proceedings. This was in spite of Walt's repeated petitions for full discovery over the course of this year. On this date, it was actually being provided as part of the criminal proceedings that were to be conducted in the future and it was delivered from the District Attorney's office separate from the family court proceedings. I think one might surmise that there was a hope within the prosecutors that providing this discovery literally at the last minute would be effective in a couple of ways. First of all, it probably wasn't expected that the journal would be read by Walt's office until some later date, possibly when it was too late to have an impact on the family court proceedings, and at the same time, it would technically have been submitted within a time frame to be deemed meeting all legal requirements as it related to the criminal proceedings. This journal was buried in a banker's box of documents. Fortunately for us, Ellen Anderson was diligent. By the grace of God, she discovered and read the journal before the hearing took place. She handed it to Walt literally as he was entering the court room for this final hearing and he read it for the first time as the judge was handing down his ruling! It is overwhelming to consider how efficiently God works with absolute perfect timing! He is always in control and never late!

As Sherri and I waited outside the courtroom, there was a young attorney who I did not know, sitting across the room from us in the waiting area just outside the courtroom. In conversation, he explained that he was an attorney and was supposed to be inside the courtroom for the proceedings involving our case. He explained to me that he had arrived late, and because the judge ordered the courtroom door locked once underway, he would not be allowed inside. We talked briefly about the case. As I began to elaborate, he said to me, "Mr. Price, please don't discuss any details with me, I may be assigned to a portion of this case and it would be inappropriate for you to discuss the case with me at this time." I made a comment complaining about how corrupt my family had discovered the Calcasieu Judicial system and DCFS to be. His response was," You really have no hope once they tie you up in this system. They can cover up more junk than you ever thought of and faster than you can imagine." He said it was practically impossible to win against them. My response to him was, "I would believe that if I did not know who was involved." To which he asked, "Who is that?" I then replied, "God. He is very much involved." He then said to me, "It will take God for you to win in a case like this." At the conclusion of the conversation, I replied, "Because of our God, we will win in the end. My name is Gerald Price and you will hear from us again." I was not trying to sound arrogant. I was simply speaking faith.

I was watching the proceedings through a rectangular window outside the courtroom. I was not allowed in the courtroom on this day. Consequently, I knew Judge Bradberry had no intention of placing the children with my wife and me. In my mind, I rationalized, if he intended to award us custody of our grandchildren, he would have ordered our presence in the courtroom. I positioned myself so I could watch my daughter's face. I knew if I did this, I would be able to interpret how the judge was ruling. I watched as her head fell and tears began to fall. She then raised her head and caught my eye through the window and sadly shook her head. Unknown to me at the time, at that very moment, Walt Sanchez was reading Mrs. Semien's journal for the first time. Jaime later told me as Bradberry was speaking, she could hear Walt saying under his breath as he sat beside her, "This is about to get good! This is about to get real good!" Judge Bradberry had based his entire ruling on the recommendation of Mr. Larry Dilks and said so as part of his ruling. He chose to ignore all of the lay witnesses; he gave no weight in his ruling to the opinion of Dr. Ahavah. It seemed also that he chose to completely ignore the unified testimony of our family. The testimony of Dr. Charles Murphy in which he had testified he believed that Gabe likely self-inflicted his injuries was completely ignored. Judge Bradberry ordered that Jaime submit to Dr. Dilks's recommendation that she enroll herself in a psychological treatment center, Brookhaven Retreat, located in Seymour, Tennessee. The recommendation was for a program that would last for a full year at a cost of one hundred thousand dollars to be paid by our family. He advised her that if she did not do so, her children would be placed in the state's adoption program and she would lose them forever. At the end of the judge's ruling, Mr. Sanchez stood and said, "Your Honor, I have new evidence." He approached the bench, briefly explained the origin of the journal, and began to read out loud to the court the portions of the journal that quoted Gabe as saying, "I am going to do to you what I did to Jaime. I am going to hurt myself and say you did it." The state's attorneys immediately began to shout objections, saying, "We have not seen this evidence!" to which Mr. Sanchez replied, "I got it from them, Your Honor! They have had this journal for a full year and have failed to disclose it in these proceedings and the information in it goes to the heart of your ruling!." He stated his intention to file a motion for a new trial. Judge Bradberry was instantly angry and responded by saying, "Get it on my desk as soon as possible." He promised that day to get to the bottom of who was responsible for withholding such crucial evidence and assured everyone that there would be grave consequences. This was the most explosive moment to date and the most meaningful for our position.

After the hearing was adjourned, we all made the trip over to Walt's office, which was just a short walk from the courthouse. We assembled together in Walt's conference room. Sitting at the table, our family and his team, he said to us, "Do you know what this is? This is reasonable doubt. This is the closest thing to a Perry Mason moment I have ever experienced in my thirty-year career!" My response to him was "Walter, what happened today was God shot his arrow right up in the middle of your courtroom." I was referring to the sixty-fourth psalm. I was remembering the times I had opened to this psalm in prayer many times before and had believed it to be a promise from God that I could hold onto. God never fails and He is never late! There was a great sense of victory that day. I looked across conference table at Jaime and reminded her of the promise of God by simply looking at her and quoting, "In the end, I win." We thanked Walt and headed for home, but we were far from finished.

TRUE COLORS

On December 20, 2011, I attended a hearing in criminal court. This was the first proceedings in criminal court since the bond hearing at the start of all this trouble. On its face, this was a hearing for Larry Dilks and Mrs. Ann Landry to testify as to the necessity of having the children testify via closed circuit television as apposed to live testimony when the case actually went to trial. Our attorney had a different purpose for the hearing, which was to get both of these witnesses on record testifying as to whether or not they had received copies of the journal provided by Mrs. Semien. Our side knowing full well that in a sworn affidavit, Mrs. Semien had already testified to the fact that she had routinely made copies of her journal and provided the copies Mrs. Landry and Mr. Dilks on multiple occasions. It was a cold and rainy day, just five days before Christmas that I entered the courtroom, carrying an umbrella with me, and sat in the back.

I listened carefully as Mrs. Landry and Mr. Dilks each perjured themselves, denying ever having received copies of the journal from Mrs. Semien. Walt had subpoenaed each of them to provide for the purpose of this hearing, copies of all documents and or pictures provided to them by Mrs. Semien. They each declared that there were no documents in their possession responsive to his subpoena. Mr. Dilks denied having any knowledge of the contents of the journal. He also stated that now, after having reviewed the journal, that its contents would have made no difference in his recommendation to the court. He called the journal "irrelevant." That in itself was a shocking statement, given the fact that the content of the journal was completely contradictory to the assumed facts of the case upon which Mr. Dilks based his recommendation to the court in the family proceedings. In my mind, it was an extreme and clear indicator of how far Mr. Dilks had gone in his arrogance in believing that his recommendations carried so much weight and had so much influence and power that he could not be questioned. He claimed not to have received the journal from Mrs. Semien, so Walt, believing that he was in fact perjuring himself, requested that he, accompanied by Cynthia Guillory and Carla Sigler who were the prosecutors from the District Attorney's office, would visit Dilks's office to look for the journal and verify his testimony. Judge Clayton Davis who presided over the hearing so ordered and they did in fact visit Dilks's office during the midday break and returned that afternoon. They did not find the complete journal, but only the first thirteen pages. Assuming that Mrs. Semien was not lying, this made a strong and compelling case for perjury and criminal activity on the part of Mr. Dilks. One could only conclude that Mr. Dilks had somehow disposed of the completed journal.

Mrs. Landry, on the other hand, acknowledged having the journal, but simply denied having received copies of it from Mrs. Semien. She claimed to have received a copy of the journal from DCFS. This was a direct contradiction of the account provided in Mrs. Semien's affidavit. The astonishing thing is that anyone, professional or laymen, could have a copy of this journal, read it, and pretend to come to the conclusions that Mrs. Landry indicated in her reports concerning Jaime's guilt or treatment for the children.

I have nothing but respect for Judge Clayton Davis; he seems to be a very likeable man and I have all confidence he is a fair judge. Nonetheless, I remember thinking it inappropriate for the two prosecutors, Mrs. Guillory and Mrs. Sigler from the District Attorney's office, who being apparently familiar with him brought him chocolates for his enjoyment during the hearing. I suppose, after you have seen what I have for the last two years, you tend to become suspicious of everything. That just seemed to cozy to me.

There was a day after the revelation of Mrs. Semien's journal in which Walt rehearsed a conversation to me which had taken place during a meeting at the District Attorney's office. I'm not sure if it was Carla Sigler or Cynthia Guillory he was referring to when he said the assistant DA had said to him during the meeting, "Walt, any deals that are made are going to include jail time for Jaime." Apparently, their conversation had alluded to a possible deal. His reply to this was "Any deals that are made are going to include all charges dropped against my client and retribution for losses." When your attorney in a criminal case can, with confidence, make such an assertion to the prosecutor, it makes you more confident that things are beginning to turn to your favor. When I consider how horribly bleak things looked in the beginning, then I know that God's process is at work as I begin to see things turn.

Walter filed a motion for a new trial on October 18, 2011, based on the revelation of the foster mom's journal. A hearing was set to be conducted on April 5, 2012, responsive to his motion. The motion in its content makes reference to the affidavit of the foster mom. In addition to DCFS, Mr. Dilks, and Mrs. Landry, Mrs. Semien had also provided copies of her journal to Mrs. Melanie Smith Daley, the children's then state-appointed attorney. She affirms that she made copies of the latest updates in her journal for each of these participant's convenience and records upon each respective visit. Mrs. Landry's and Mr. Dilks's denials of her accounts are very troubling. Mrs. Daley has not made a court appearance since being removed from the case. She is cited specifically in the motion for the new trial as being in violation of *Louisiana's Rules of Professional Conduct Rule 3.3 Candor Toward the Tribunal* It is noted in the motion that Mrs. Daley argued strenuously in court that there was no other explanation for Gabe's injuries, than that Jaime had committed them, while all the while having in her possession the journal which contradicted that position completely.

It should further be noted that the foster mom, Mrs. Karla Semien, is a respected worker in the foster children's program who has to date taken more that sixty children into her home. Her journal was thorough and detailed. When compared to the testimony of the state witnesses, it was obvious that they had perjured themselves. Mrs. Semien's journal and her sworn affidavit outlines the times and dates and tells of specific conversations with the state witnesses. Her journal is extremely compelling.

This case is fraught with incidents of questionable behavior by those representing DCFS, the sheriff's office, CASA, and the District Attorney's office. When you know for an absolute fact that you are innocent and from that perspective, you watch as a group of professionals are so obviously working off the same page of music producing harmonious, yet false testimony, it is horrifying. You suddenly realize they have to be meeting and developing strategy to all be telling the same story while we who know the truth and know it to be totally different than their allegations.

[Excerpt from Brandi Green's Interview with Steve Fontenot]

SF: Did they tell you to lie?

BG: Well I mean, it was several times that we had mock trials and we were told if we were asked a certain question, how we need to respond.

SF: And who led these mock trials?

BG: Lee Schmidt. We also had a meeting with the Sheriff's Department, DA's Office, Ann Landry. We would have what they call MSTs, which is Multiply Systematic Therapy where we'd sit down and we'd talk about things. C.A.S.A. is there. Everybody meets. And it's supposed to be to discuss the child but, you know it always would go into other things. And I'm thinking to myself, I'm not about to raise my hand before God and I'm not about to lie about nothing that's going on with this case. If Walt put me on the stand, I'm telling the truth. And to really be honest with you, I don't have anything to lose. I'm already gone. They've made my life a living hell for five months. Since November, I've been going through this with OCS. All because I would not do what they wanted me to do when it came to this case.

SF: And what was it they wanted you to do with this case?

BG: Make that girl into a monster and I couldn't do it. Look at the baby and see if he's lethargic or if she's giving him Benadryl of see if he's sleeping or sleeping all the time. You know I'm like, nothing is wrong with this baby. The baby is well taken care of.

Further into her interview, she tells of a meeting in which Mike Primeaux was present. It was apparently a meeting between the sheriff's office and DCFS to discuss the current conditions of the case and an obvious meltdown in Gabe's behavior. In Mrs. Green's rendition of this meeting, when the details of Gabe's total breakdown became known, Mr. Primeaux called Elizabeth Zaunbrecher to inform her of the latest developments. Brandi claims that when Detective Zaunbrecher became aware of the details of her reporting, Brandi immediately came under an attack from Mrs. Zaunbrecher. Mrs. Semien had advised Brandi of extreme problems she was having with Gabe. Brandi recapitulated how Mrs. Semien referred to Gabe as a "devil child." In the days that followed this meeting, Mrs. Zaunbrecher launched a series of e-mails, wherein she suggested that Mrs. Green had somehow done something wrong in her report and needed to be reprimanded. She openly criticized Mrs. Green for her statements, wherein she quoted Mrs. Semien when she referred to Gabe as a "devil child." She seemed to suggest Brandi had somehow referred to him as a devil child herself. She apparently had chosen to ignore the obvious implications of Mrs. Semien's description of Gabe's bizarre behavior and the fact that it mirrored my family's description of his behavior while in our home. Mrs. Zaunbrecher was obviously attempting to influence the agency's handling of the case. At this point, she seemed to be searching for some redemption for a case that was soon to go very bad for the sheriff's office. Ms. Green saved and filed copies of the e-mails from Mrs. Zaunbrecher wherein she strongly criticized Brandi. These copies according to Brandi were later mysteriously removed from her office. She tells of returning to her office after her dismissal from the case to retrieve the hard copies and found they had been removed.

In the end, Ms. Green was told that she was not performing her job, removed from the case, and placed in the food stamp office. She was certain that she was being moved because of her unwillingness to report as she was instructed rather than what she actually saw in working with our family. Her testimony provides further details of that same meeting between DCFS and the detectives. She tells of them discussing the details and of Mr. Primeaux's frantic recommendation to have him moved to the crossroads facility for treatment. The detective's failure to report this incident as well as the overall contents of the journal, in my view, was an obvious violation of Jaime's civil rights by law enforcement officials leading the investigation. Within a few days, I sent an e-mail to Walt and posed this question: "If a law enforcement official in the course of a criminal investigation encountered evidence that contradicted his belief that the person he was investigating was guilty and he subsequently failed to disclose that information, was that officer, in fact, guilty of violating the defendant's civil rights?" His response was a single yes. Ms. Green in her phone interview with Steve Fontenot had stated, "I couldn't help but wonder if he (Mike Primeaux) was concerned about Gabe or was he simply worried about the fact that there was a large hole in his case."

A few weeks later, my wife called DCFS and requested a meeting between ourselves and their representatives. We were to meet with Dawn Becton, who we understood managed the foster home program for DCFS, and Leigh Schmitt, who was a supervisor for DCFS at the local office. We arrived at the appointed time and were taken into a large open room with a table set up in the center. We assumed that we were videotaped, monitored, or both. Our hope was to convince someone on their side of the truth. We felt if we could find someone within DCFS who would believe us, it could only help to have someone in our corner. After a few minutes of discussion surrounding the case, I remember sitting at that table and hearing Mrs. Becton say, "We are not going to change our minds or be convinced." This is the point when you begin to feel a new feeling of helplessness and frustration when you realize you haven't found an opening but rather you are still up against the wall. What I did not know at the time of that meeting was the fact that DCFS, at that very moment, was in possession of Mrs. Semien's journal and that its content was current through the incidents that led to Gabe being moved to Crossroads and that in all likelihood, both Mrs. Becton and Mrs. Schmitt had seen and had full knowledge of Mrs. Semien's journal. While by this time, the journal had been copied to their office numerous times, we on the other hand still had no knowledge of the journal or its content at the time of this meeting. During the course of the meeting, I rehearsed to them of Gabe's history of self-infliction and bizarre behavior. I told them, "He will continue to repeat this wherever he goes because that is who he is." In that moment, I thought of the rumors I had heard of Gabe being sent to Crossroads for thirteen days and said to her, "Ya'll are having problems with him now," to which she simply smiled and looked away. Mrs. Becton and Mrs. Schmitt were apparently complicit in the effort of DCFS to cover up this information and the journal's content. No matter how many times I think of it, I am always shocked to think that we have officials with extreme authority affecting the lives and future of children, yet have no scruples about lying and deception to attain their purpose.

On Monday, March 19, 2012, I drafted the following letter addressed to the District Attorney, Mr. John Derosier. Before drafting the letter, I considered the fact that everyone concerned was now aware of the content of Mrs. Semien's journal and that Mr. Derosier would certainly by now have full knowledge of the journal and its content. Consequently, I felt that the timing and content of this letter to be appropriate.

> *Mr. DeRosier,*
>
> *As you are aware, my daughter, Jaime Day, is under indictment for multiple felonies in Calcasieu Parish, relevant to child abuse in a case involving Gabriel Hanks. We in the family and my church community have known since the beginning that she is totally innocent of these charges. Jaime is, in fact, a victim of the consequences of attempting to be a mother to an extremely mentally ill and self-inflicting child. This was common knowledge among our family, the neighbors, our church family, professional counselors, and child psychologists throughout the community, all of whom were actively involved with trying to get help for Gabe for a long period prior to Jaime's indictment.*
>
> *Had the case been fully investigated by law enforcement in the beginning, this fact would have been evident. I believe that the evidence currently in hand makes it clear that our family has been telling the truth all along. The question that we in the family and our entire church community have for you is, what will you now do? Our grandchildren have been wrongfully incarcerated for two full years. Our hearts have been broken and my daughter's reputation has been destroyed. We have suffered many harmful things at the hands of OCS, the counselors, and child psychologists surrounding this case. Our thoughts are, surely, our elected officials will not stand by and allow this wrong to continue. We prayerfully await your response*

I originally had hoped to visit personally with the District Attorney, so prior to delivering the letter, I paid his office a visit. I walked in to the office on the sixth floor of the ten story building at 901 Lakeshore Drive and asked to speak to see Mr. Derosier. I was asked, first of all, what was the nature of my business? I explained I was here to discuss the Jaime Day case and that I was Jaime's father. It was then explained to me that Mr. Derosier's office was actually on the eighth floor. But someone would see me. Assistant District Attorney Mrs. Cynthia Guillory came out and introduced herself to me. She said, "Mr. Price, I'm Cynthia Guillory. I will be prosecuting the case. Can I help you?" I replied, "No. My questions today are more of a general nature regarding the operations of the District Attorney's office and they are for Mr. Derosier. I am sure I will have questions for you later." She curtly turned and walked back to her office. I then went up to the eighth floor and ask the receptionist to speak to Mr. Derosier. A nice lady came out to meet me and explained that Mr. Derosier was not in. She also explained to me that he could not discuss the case with me without counsel present. She explained that to do so would be against the law. I responded by stating to her that I was not represented by counsel in this matter, I should be considered a concerned citizen with questions regarding the handling of the case. I ask that he call me and left my number. I was resolved to send the letter. In the end, I elected to hand deliver the letter, so on April 2, 2012, I returned to his office during their lunchtime and left the letter in a sealed envelope addressed to the District Attorney at the front desk. There was no attendant present at the moment, so I simply slid the letter under the glass partition, leaving it in plain view for the receptionist to see when she returned. I afterward wished that I had sent it in certified mail, but I am certain Mr. Derosier got the letter. Just outside the door in the open area where you exit the elevator, there is an emblem mounted on the wall representing the District Attorney's office. In its center, there is an image of a pelican, the Louisiana state bird. Around this emblem are the words, "Union, Justice, and Confidence." I wondered at that moment, when was the last time Mr. Derosier stood where I was standing and read those words or considered their meaning. As of this date, I have not received a response from him in regard to the visit or to my letter. That day, as I rode the elevator back to the first floor, I thought it to be poetic justice that Mr. Sanchez occupied the top floor of the ten-story office building while the District Attorney was on the eighth beneath him.

February 2, 2012, was a Thursday. About halfway through the day, my phone suddenly rang and it was Jaime. I could hear her struggling to breath and I could hardly recognize her voice nor understand what she was saying until I finally heard her say, "My house is on fire!" I rushed to my truck and raced to her home approximately fifteen miles from my job. When I arrived, the fire trucks were still there and I saw Channel 7 News packing up to leave. In a really freakish accident, my shocking system for the two large Boxer bulldogs we have in her backyard had somehow ignited a fire to a partial bale of hay we used to provide bedding for the dogs. The hay, after catching on fire, had started the end of the house to burning. Jaime and Kathan were the only ones home at the time. Apparently, the fire caused the dogs to get extremely excited and their barking got Jaime's attention, which is when she discovered the fire. The damage was only to the end of the house and we easily recovered. It burned through the wall and there was significant smoke damage as well as structural damage to that end of the house. The insurance money for the damages was adequate to give her home a facelift in anticipation of the boys return with a little leftover. I had been praying about financial needs and I could easily see how this fire was an answered prayer. God is always in control.

THE WHISTLE STOP

On Saturday, March 24, 2012, my father-in-law, Mr. Bill Roberts (the children's great-grandfather) passed away. It was a great loss because Bill had been a father to so many of us for so long. He was always a kind and generous man. Other than Bishop Nugent, no other man had impacted my life so much. He had gotten me started in industrial construction, using his influence to get me accepted in the Iron Workers Local Union. Bill and I deer hunted together for many years. Having no contact information for DCFS on weekends, we were unable to contact them to request that Kolten and Kyler be allowed to attend the funeral. We left a message on the voice mail of Mildred Holmes in which we advised her of our request. She returned my call on the day of the funeral ten minutes before the ceremony was to start to advise me that the no contact order prevented the boys from coming. *Yeah, right,* was my thought.

Jaime attended a FTC (family team conference) meeting on Tuesday, March 26, 2012, in which she was appalled but not surprised to learn that in the face of all of the opposing evidence, DCFS still intends to petition the court to have our grandchildren placed in an adoption program. One would think that there would be an effort to backpedal on their part once they were exposed, but there was simply no retreat in these people. We have learned that once they set a course, there is no give in them, even when facts fly in their face against their position. They are relentless in their effort to win. I can only say that if any citizen believes that DCFS is an organization committed to the protection or betterment of children's lives, they are simply uninformed.

A few weeks passed, and on April 4, 2012, Walt called to advise that he had attended a pretrial meeting with Judge Bradberry. In the meeting he was advised that the judge would consider the motion for new trial based on briefs provided by both sides rather than hear the case in court. Walt was very optimistic that the ruling would go in our favor. He further advised that the state's side had not contested the existence of the evidence provided by the journal, but rather had simply acknowledged its existence. Their explanation was that the evidence had been overlooked. As Walter would later declare in his appeals to the court, their silence on the matter was deafening.

Later that same day, we visited the boys at the Whistle Stop. We had a good visit. We brought the boys Easter suits and shoes. I regret that I have not kept a log of each of these visits to the Whistle Stop. Their content would be most useful in conveying this story. The visits at the Whistle Stop were always monitored. They watched and listened to our interaction with the boys, through a two-way mirror and via an electronic listening system. Monitoring was usually conducted by three parties: CASA, DCFS, and the Whistle Stop staff. CASA was represented by the same retired DCFS agent, Ms. Gwen Thompson, who so troubled us concerning Kathan at his birth. CASA is a child services organization whose representatives are on record as being "the voice of the children." According to the chief administrator for CASA, Mr. David Duplechin, a worker's role is to represent the children's wishes regardless of the worker's personal position. I know this because Mr. Duplechin and I met privately to discuss my concerns about Ms. Thompson and her obvious bias in this case. Mrs. Thompson has shown herself to be completely biased against Jaime and aligned with the state throughout these proceedings and events. Her aggressiveness to become a part of the state's success in the court proceedings as opposed to being primarily concerned about the future and well-being of the children was very telling. If she had shown herself to be honest while biased, one might be willing to indulge her. But when she willingly deceived listeners and or twisted facts each and every time she testified, I then realized she was simply committed to assisting the state in another win and apparently impressing her usefulness upon them. This was obviously why they kept her on board as a mandatory reporter. As a social worker and a mandatory court reporter, Ms. Thompson is in fact required by law to report suspected child abuse. I reference the following article of Louisiana Law.

> *(Ref. Louisiana's "Failure to Report Children's Code art.609;Rev. Stat 14:403(A)(1)") to report any suspected child abuse and can be subject to a fine of up to $3000.00, imprisoned for up to three years or both for failure to report. On the other hand, "art. 609;Rev. Stat. 14:403(A)(3)" makes anyone who knowingly makes a false report to the effect of child abuse subject to a $ 500.00 dollar fine and no more than six months imprisonment.*

It is my belief that the penalty for either should be equal, especially given the potential for corruption in these types of cases. One thing was obvious, and that is that Ms. Thompson was falling over herself in her attempt to cast us in a bad light.

Prayer was always a part of our Whistle Stop visits. As the end of each meeting began to draw near, we would gather and ask the boys what prayer request they had. For Kolten and Kyler, the answer was always the same: "We want to go home" or "We want to go home and be with our mama" or "We want things to be normal again." These are the type of comments that would be crucial information in family court to the judge in order for him to determine the best path forward and where to place the boys. Judge Bradberry would certainly want to know what the specific wishes of the children were, and it is the responsibility of the CASA representative to advise the court of the boy's wishes. None of this was ever reported by Gwen Thompson. To be technically truthful, she would in fact mention in a minor way, in her written report, that the boys had stated they wanted to come home. However, her reports were not read in the court proceedings and when testifying in court, Ms. Thompson made no mention of the children's wishes and prayers to come home. This, I find to be astonishing since the absolute truth was that the boys were emphatically stating their desire to come home at each visit. Mrs. Thompson on the other hand was reporting to the court that they were afraid to come home for fear of retaliation. This was a claim for which there was simply no basis. She then would be openly hostile to the notion of sending the boys to anyone in our family. She alleged they would not be safe with my wife and me. She hotly contested any notion of returning the boys to our home. She had no tangible evidence upon which to base her position other than the fact that it was the position that DCFS had taken. Ms. Thompson was obviously rubberstamping the state's case for them.

What was interesting was that DCFS's case workers and Ms. Thompson together attempted to make us in the family to believe, that in the context of the visits, we were not permitted to speak to the children of their mom or to even preempt any conversation that might lead them to speak of their mom. They would specifically instruct us not to discuss Jaime with the boys. If they felt a conversation was leading to Jaime becoming part of the discussion, they would interrupt by walking into the room to set us in order. This, in itself, was an act of disobedience to the court on their part. According to the instructions from the court, they were only allowed to observe the visits and should never make any form of tangible contact during the meetings.

We were accused of leading the conversation to get the boys to talk about their mom. DCFS would then testify in court that the children never spoke of their mom and that the children were afraid to go home for fear of punishment for telling on their mom. When I consider Ms Thompson's role at Ann Landry's office and now her lack of forthrightness surrounding the Whistle Stop visits, I cannot come to any favorable conclusion as to her character or motives. These court sessions were so very telling in their content. It was apparent to me Ms. Thompson was in essence extending her career as a DCFS worker and using CASA as a vehicle to accomplish that feat.

Today is April 17, 2012. Our motion for a new trial was submitted two weeks ago. The motion carefully outlines misconduct and false testimony by the state, DCFS, the state attorneys, and all of their witnesses. In the state's response to our motion, no address was made to these allegations. Their response basically said we never ask for the journal and now a year had expired since the children were adjudicated. Consequently, in the state's opinion, the request for a new trial was unmerited and should be denied based on time limits. Our attorneys then submitted a final address, which addressed the fact that the state did not respond to the allegations of fraud in the court proceedings in their response to his motion. He states that their silence on this matter is deafening and petitions the court to vacate the adjudication of the children and return the children to their mom.

On April 23, 2012, we visited with the boys at the Whistle Stop. We had a good visit. We played board games and ate a meal. These visits typically last two hours and occur on alternate weeks. Our visits were moved from Saturday to Wednesdays some time ago by DCFS. The reason provided to us was that the boys had basketball on Saturday. Basketball has since ended and we have made request to move the meetings back to Saturdays. Our reason is that the midweek visits impact the boys' school schedule and it has a cost impact to us because I have to miss work to attend during the week. The agency has been silent on this request to date. It is my belief that they only pretended to want to facilitate the boy's basketball schedule and the real purpose for moving the visits was to give DCFS control of the meetings and to make certain the agency is the only entity reporting the events of the meetings to the court. The difference is Saturday visits are facilitated by the Whistle Stop staff. The Whistle Stop has ownership to Saturday meetings so they make the ground rules for any of those meetings. Their reports are required in such meetings and are generally unbiased. Midweek visits, on the other hand, in effect, silence the Whistle Stop because they are not required to participate in those visits as opposed to the Saturday visits. This structure I assume is driven by funding. Consequently, DCFS has the latitude to place whatever spin they wish on their reporting and can exclude or include any portion of the facts at will.

We were told that Judge Bradberry has thirty days to rule on our motion for a new trial, and we were anxiously waiting on his decision. Jaime had a meeting last week with Christa Becton, the DCFS representative currently assigned to our case. According to Jaime, she was rude and insolent throughout the meeting. DCFS has in the past requested that Kathan, who at the time was only eighteen months old, participate in sibling meetings between Gabe, Kolten, and Kyler. Our family's position is that if DCFS will allow someone who Kathan is familiar with to attend the meetings, then we would consider allowing him to attend. We have objected to the idea of leaving him with strangers and we do not trust the agency alone with any child. During the discussion on this matter, Jaime described how she commented to Mrs. Becton that her intention was to protect Kathan as long as she had any say in the matter. She further commented on the fact that the right to protect the other boys had been taken away from her by DCFS to which Mrs. Becton smiled with obvious malice and stated, "Yes, we have, haven't we?" This comment had its desired effect on Jaime in that it hurt her feelings. It is difficult for anyone to understand how cruel these people have shown themselves to be unless you have experienced them for yourself. Later, I spoke with Mrs. Becton on the phone. I phoned her to request that the boys' visits be rescheduled to occur on Saturdays. I explained to her that this would eliminate impact to their school schedule. She said she would let us know of their response. We continued to get no response to this request. We now understand the agency's mode of operation. Every request had to be carefully analyzed and their response measured against the agency's overall strategy to win the case. In my view, the betterment and well-being of the children should be paramount in this agency's purpose, but in reality, it seems to be hardly considered.

On April 18, 2012, we visited with the boys again at the Whistle Stop. On this visit, Kolten requested that we bring him a picture of Kathan. Accordingly, we had two pictures framed and intended to give one to each of the boys on the next visit. May 2, 2012, was our next scheduled visit. On this visit, we brought the pictures with us and were told we could not give the pictures to them, but to leave them with the DCFS worker. We have had experiences in the past with providing gifts to the boys through DCFS. Those experiences have taught us never to trust them. Consequently, we declined and kept the pictures. At the close of the visit, I requested a brief meeting with Christa Becton to ask a couple of questions relevant to the meetings and her position on the pictures. She refused to discuss this or to meet with me. She appeared angry and belligerent when she stated, "It will have to wait," saying she did not have time. I should also mention that the boys requested a game to play on the X-Box while we were there. This is a normal request and is part of the everyday operation with children at the Whistle Stop. The actual video games were kept in a separate room from the one in which we held the meeting. We were not allowed to exit the room, except to go to the restroom. There was a list of available games listed on the wall, and accordingly, the boys would look toward the two-way mirror and make their request verbally. On this occasion,

Christa Becton refused the request, saying that they only had about twenty minutes left. It is normally left up to us how we spend our two hours as long as we follow the rules. I think this to be proper, given the fact that we pay for the visits

We played board games and twister with the boys. We brought pizza this week. We prayed together at the end of the visit, and as usual, the boys' only prayer request was to come home. After the meeting, I phoned our attorney's paralegal to update them on the meeting.

On May 11, 2012, a routine meeting with Christa Becton occurred. She always asked a list of standard questions, observed Jaime and Kathan's interaction, and made notes. These meetings are usually over in less that a half hour. The issue of the pictures had become a sticking point with me, so I took this opportunity to readdress the questions regarding them. Mrs. Becton would not discuss the pictures with me accept to say they would address the issue at a later date. I asked for two things. To be advised of whether or not we would be allowed to give Kolten the pictures and to be given an explanation as to the agencies' position on the matter. It was really the explanation response I was hoping to get her to provide to us because I knew it would probably not hold water. I was coldly refused either.

On May 16, 2012, we had another visit with the boys at the Whistle Stop. We were met at the door by Susan Perkins, the Whistle Stop manager. Susan had always been a sweet lady and we knew that she truly only wanted what was right and best for the children. But today, she was doing her job, and she was in a difficult position managing this visit of which DCFS had ownership and made the rules. It was an obviously very deliberate action on her part to be there as soon as we arrived. She immediately advised us that the pictures of Kathan would not be allowed. Additionally, she informed us that I would not be permitted to bring my journal with me. I had in recent weeks begun to maintain a record of all events and conversations relevant to this case. Consequently, I would bring my journal with me to the Whistle Stop visits. It was troubling that suddenly, DCFS would object to me keeping records of all events. I have to admit I had taken some malicious enjoyment out of exhibiting a journal in the course of the meetings given the recent turn of events surrounding Mrs. Semien's journal. Even so, I felt they had no right to prevent me from maintaining an accurate record of the visits. I stated to Susan that we would adhere to their new demands but under protest. I told her that I believed DCFS was violating our rights with these new rules.

The visit with the boys went well. We played numerous games with them. Kyler painted three pictures. He was in a mood to paint. Kolten was acute today in his request to come home. In the early part of the meeting, I stated to him, "I have been looking at pictures of you all day," to which he oddly responded, "I hope when you go back to court, they say, yes, they can come home!" Later, as I played a game with him, he asked me what time it was. I told him it was 3:40 p.m. and that we only had twenty minutes remaining. He replied, "Twenty minutes! I wish we had at least an hour!" I then replied, "I would stay here with you all day if they would allow it." He then replied, "Papa, I would stay here with you forever. I just want OCS to say yes. That is all I want to hear from them is yes, you can go home!"

At the close of the meeting, I approached Gwen Thompson. Ms. Thompson has somehow gotten herself appointed president of the board for the Whistle Stop, this according to Susan. This I find troubling in that it provides her with a broader range of influence in our case. I posed a question to her, "Did you hear and make note of the request to come home by Kolten? I know you have been present in most of these meetings and have heard their numerous requests and prayer requests to come home, so why have you as a CASA representative never reported this to the courts in your testimony?" She replied that she had heard the request in the sessions and had documented them in her report. I then reiterated, "But why has your testimony not reflected these requests?" This is given the fact that her responsibility as CASA is to resound the voice of the children. She made an attempt to sound as though she were truthfully and thoroughly reporting the content of the visits, but we both knew that was not the case.

The following morning, I sent an e-mail outlining the events of the visit to Walt and Ellen. I simply felt that they should be aware of all events. I always had the concern that something that we might think insignificant would turn out to be a huge factor in our case.

DCFS OR GESTAPO?

I suppose an accurate description of me would be "driven." I simply felt pressure at all times to continue to fight and never give up. I sent an e-mail on May 7, 2012, to the director of CASA, David Duplechin, requesting again the bias demonstrated by Gwen Thompson be investigated. I also made sure that he was aware of Kolten's continued request to come home. I suspected that she hedged on what she reported to CASA as well, given all the indicators that she and the CASA organization itself apparently did not share exactly the same mission. I think that I was hoping that he would see that our boys wanted and needed to come home and would do what he could to make certain that the boys and their request were honestly represented by CASA. I kept hoping that I would find an ally on the side of the state that would honestly care about what was right. Below is the content of my e-mail.

> *David,*
>
> *Just a note to bring your organization up-to-date on the status of our visits with Kolten and Kyler at the Whistle Stop. As you know, we have now been continuing the visits for a little more than a year. I would like at this time to report the inefficiency of your agency to truly represent the boys. As discussed in the private meeting I had with you at your office on Louis Street, in Lake Charles, you outlined for me the responsibility of CASA and its representatives. You made it clear it was to*

be the voice of the children regardless of whether or not the CASA representative agrees with what the children's wishes are. There is a constant that has been obvious since our first visit with the boys and that is that they want to be with their family. We pray together at the close of each meeting. Prior to prayer, we ask the boys for their individual prayer request. On each and every request, the answer is the same. It is "We want to come home, we want to see our mom, we want to be with you all every day, we want to come home and things return to normal" or some similar phrase. Additionally, the boys have each expressed in conversation that they miss their mom, want to see her, or something to that effect. I find it inexcusable that none of that information has been disclosed in the court proceedings by your representative. It reinforces my belief that bias is present within your organization. Be assured that the records maintained by the Whistle Stop and the testimony of the children themselves is going to verify this fact. It would be very meaningful to this case if your organization would come forward and truly represent the wishes of the children.

Thank you.

On Friday, May 25, 2012, we had another prescheduled meeting with Krista Becton. Krista has shown an obvious animosity toward me for the last few weeks. Upon learning of the time of the scheduled meeting, I made plans to be present. There is no requirement or rules that state anyone in the family cannot be present. My intent is to document the discussion in my journal and to ask questions relevant to the case. Most important is to document her answers. I asked two questions. The first was if we had resolution to our request to move the meetings with the grandchildren back to Saturday. Her curt response was "The meetings will remain on Wednesday." I then requested an explanation for that position to which she repeated, "The meetings will remain on Wednesday." I then requested to view the documents and forms that she was filling out during her questions for Jaime. She rudely replied to me that I had no right to see the documents because I was not part of the case plan. I turned to Jaime and asked her to request to view the documents. Mrs. Becton also refused Jaime's request and would not allow her to see the reports.

She was very abrupt and was actually refusing to talk to me. At this point, Jaime said to Mrs. Becton, "I have questions for you regarding my babies." Her response was, "We will discuss them on the next visit." Jaime's reply was, "But I have questions today and you are here now," Mrs. Becton stated, "Oh, they are doing fine." Jaime asked, "Did they send me anything for Mother's Day?" She replied with a single cold no. This is the first time since they have been "incarcerated" that they did not make her a Mother's Day card. In short, Mrs. Becton would not discuss the children with Jaime. It is my belief that her actions were in retaliation for holding her accountable with questions recorded in my journal. I felt certain that if we could fully know the law, Jaime's constitutional rights were being violated by her refusal to answer questions regarding the children. We, however, are just laymen; we cannot pretend to know criminal law and ignorance is weakness in this case.

On May 30, 2012, we had a good visit with the boys, but as usual, it was made worse by the antics of DCFS. During the visit, we played board games, video games, and ate pizza. We had good conversation with the boys. As usual, when we ask for prayer requests, the boys stated, "When ya'll go back to court, I hope the judge says yes. My reply was "Yes what?" To which Kolten replied, "Yes, you can go home." I obviously knew what he was speaking of, but it was important in my mind to get the children on record, saying they wanted to come home. As is our usual routine, we stopped about fifteen minutes before the meeting ended to pray.

Approximately ten minutes before the end of the meeting, Mrs. Becton entered the room and rudely and in a mean spirit informed us that a couple of things she had just observed in the visit would not be permitted. The first was a prayer that I had written on a piece of rigid sketching paper. I had taken a marker and jotted a simple prayer down while we were visiting. When I showed it to Kolten, he said, "Yeah, I will put that on my wall." Kolten then asked would I do one for Kyler because he explained, "We both have a bulletin board." I then wrote a simple but different prayer for Kyler. The first one read:

"Dear Jesus, please bless Kolten and Kyler and keep them safe." It was signed Papa and Maw Maw. The second one read: "Dear Jesus, please bring Kolten and Kyler home," also signed Papa and Maw Maw.

We also brought a gift of finger art from Kathan to the boys. Kathan, with Jaime's help, had made a single page picture, depicting a frog whose feet were made up of color prints of Kathan's hands. It was very cute and innovative.

Mrs. Becton stated her position, saying the frog picture could not go home with them because it was "contact between opposing parties." Opposing parties? Was she saying that Kolten and Kyler were opposed to Kathan in some fashion or vice versa? Wasn't Mrs. Becton a participant in attempting to get them to join together in sibling meetings just a few days earlier? She said the prayers could not go with the boys because they violated rule number 11 in the Whistle Stop rules. Please understand. The rule she was referring to prohibited sending written notes to third parties through the children. This would have been laughable had it not been so serious. I was appalled and I have to admit, I was angry, confrontational, and somewhat contentious at this point

I stopped her and said, "Let me please read this to you," which I did (both of them). I then said, "This is a prayer, addressed to Jesus. It clearly does not fall into the category of rule 11 of the Whistle Stop Rules." We knew because we had been provided with a copy of Whistle Stop Rules on our first visit. I then stated to her that to prohibit them to have this prayer would be a violation of the boy's religious rights.

I then followed her from the room to ask if we were going to be permitted to give the boys the pictures of Kathan discussed at the previous meetings. Her response was the same as last week. There was an intense moment where she said to me, "You are just trying to draw these children into the issue between you and me." To which I replied, "No, I'm trying to get you to either allow me to give the boys the picture or provide an explanation as to why not." She seemed to have lost sight of the need to place the children's needs as first priority. The problem that I had with surrendering the picture was, in the past, the agency had defaced or altered gifts we gave the boys so we were trying to avoid that from happening. She remained dogmatic in her position. In the end, I surrendered the pictures to her only to hope that they would receive them and in the same condition we gave them. I hate to mention the elephant in the room, but how is it that the frog picture is a rule violation but Kathan's photos are not? How is it that one is a "contact between two opposing parties" and the other is permissible, but only if we give it to Mrs. Becton first?

Then on an entirely different point and another discrepancy, in this same visit, Kyler painted a picture for Kathan and sent it home by us. Mrs. Becton made no objection to that picture from Kyler to Kathan. So why allow a picture from Kyler to Kathan and not allow one from Kathan to either of the boys. She is obviously very selective about what the rules are and how they apply. The only real difference is the difference in her positions on the issues, and there was simply no rhyme or reason and no consistency to her positions. I realize at this point I am down in the weeds in this struggle with the case workers, and in retrospect, I would be much better off to simply submit to all of their spontaneous rules, but sometimes, that was simply not as easy as it sounds.

I conferred with the Whistle Stop manager to make my case. I specifically asked if she agreed with Krista Becton's opinion that the written prayer violated Whistle Stop rules. She stated that if she were in charge of the meeting, in her opinion, the prayers should be allowed and that they were not a violation of rule 11. We are desperately trying to not be contentious and at the same time hold DCFS accountable for their actions and their statements in these and all meetings relevant to this case. It is obvious that they are not attempting to be honest or transparent toward the court in these proceedings. They will never willingly disclose to the court the true wishes of the children or their constant request and prayers to come home.

After Mrs. Becton left with the boys, we had a brief discussion with Gwen Thompson. She, for today, has put on an air of wanting to be helpful. That usually preempts some underhanded attack against us or some fabrication or distortion of the facts. She advised us that she wants to visit us in the next few days at our home. In the past, the outcome of these meetings is some sort of new evidence that she gleaned from our conversations that she could use detrimentally against us. Let's not forget her role as a state mandatory reporter. We can never forget the way the game is played. She advised us she would call in a few days to set up a time she can come visit. We decided we would decline except if she agreed to meet us at our attorney's office.

GWEN

Today is Monday, June 4, 2012. My wife called earlier to advise that Gwen Thompson will be calling to request a meeting with us at our home. Not long afterward, she did indeed call and made that request. My first question to her was "What is the purpose of the meeting?" She stated to me, "That is a very good question," and provided some answers. She stated she wanted to reaffirm the information regarding our home status. If you are paying attention, then you should instantly realize this request falls outside of her role as a CASA worker but well within the responsibility of a DCFS agent. She mentioned that my wife has been sick. I believe she wants to somehow use that against her. Our discussion led to me explaining very candidly that I did not have any trust in her, given her past false testimony, the fact that she suggested to the court that I was attempting to sexually assault my grandchildren, and the overall failure on her part as a CASA worker to truly represent the children's wishes to come home.

I couldn't resist sharing with her the hope we had of winning this case and God's promise of victory. I told her that we believed that we had assurances from God that it would end well and I told her that she was simply fighting against God. Some may say I was casting pearls before the swine and maybe I was, but I just could not shut up. I had to tell her! She took exception to my claims of having assurances from God, telling me in an irate tone, "You are not the only Christian involved in this case!" I thought, but did not say, *Regardless of whether or not you are a Christian, my confidence in God's promise remains the same.* After a tense conversation, we did agree to meet the following Wednesday at 5:30 p.m. in my home. Afterward, I called Walt to seek counsel on the proposed meeting. He advised that to refuse to meet with them would seed the field for them to have something to use against us. We decided to go forward with the meeting as originally planned.

Mrs. Gwen Thompson arrived at our home a few minutes before 6:00 p.m. as scheduled on Wednesday, June 6, 2012. She spent approximately two hours in my home, discussing our grandchildren and the case against Jaime. She stated that Kolten and Kyler, Kolten in particular, had stated to her in conversations that they had witnessed Jaime harming Gabe. But when she specifically reads from her report what she actually asked Kolten was, "Do you understand why you cannot see your Mom?" To which he replied yes. According to her, Kolten states that he understood it was because Jaime had hurt Gabe. Not the same thing. I believe Mrs. Thompson was on a fishing trip. Her obvious purpose for the meeting was to attempt to cast some doubt in our minds concerning Jaime's innocence or to cause us to make some statement that could be used against us in court. I know for a fact two things. The first is Jaime did not commit the crimes alleged against her. We are all eyewitnesses of Gabe's extreme behavioral problems and self-infliction. The second is that the state has had my two grandchildren for two years and they have had plenty of time to influence what these children are saying or even thinking for that matter. I believe if he is saying anything at all, Kolten was simply telling what he had been told by everyone around him for the last two years.

Additionally, after having time to reflect, I came to a number of conclusions. For me to believe that the allegations made by the state and all of its witnesses were true, a couple of things would have to apply. First of all, I would have to negate everything I saw for myself in terms of Gabe's bizarre behavior and self-infliction.

It was curious that everyone on the state's side was seemingly willing to ignore or discount all of the eyewitness testimony from me, my family, the neighbors, and the professionals who were actively involved with Gabe during the months of his breakdown. Second, I would be forced to conclude that it was possible for these types of atrocities to have occurred in Jaime's home and I not detect them even though I was constantly in the home. Number three, I would have to conclude that all of the eyewitnesses from the neighborhood were in fact lying and or duped. And most of all and the least likely, my own grandchildren would have had to have appeared normal to me while all the while experiencing and concealing these horrors. I am referring to two happy, vibrant, and normal in every way detectable children. Not only did they never disclose that anything as alleged by DCFS was occurring, but gave no discernable indication that anything was wrong beyond what we all were already aware of in terms of his self-infliction and the entire family openly discussed that, including Gabe.

I always had a concern of the possible effect that living in the same home as Gabe and in the midst of his bizarre behavior would have on the children, yet I have learned that we have small understanding of how resilient children can be and they adapt well to their surroundings. However, I do believe if they had witnessed what Child Services claimed, then they would have appeared troubled and disturbed. They would have made mention of it at some point. Gabe is claiming he was hung upside down and beaten daily and starved. First of all, I can say with absolute certainty, that is a preposterous claim. Without any analysis and by virtue of what I know about my daughter and her nature as a human being, she is incapable of harming anything. Everything I know and believe about my daughter who I raised in my home would suddenly be untrue. Remember, Dr. Ahavah provided tests that conclude that she was incapable of committing the crimes that have been alleged against her.

Additionally, it is impossible for these things to have happened and we in the family be totally unaware for all of the reasons mentioned above. My question for Ms. Thompson and DCFS is why is there such disparity in what you now say the boys claim as opposed to what they stated in the videos two years earlier at the beginning of the investigation. I believe they are coached and or coerced if in fact they have said anything. We certainly know that these people are capable of lying about it and two years in possession of children at their age and in their predicament is certainly adequate time to impress upon their young minds anything of your choosing.

MURRY JAILED

June 15, 2012. Today is Friday. I had not mentioned it previously, but probably three months earlier, Murry's bail was revoked and he was placed in jail where he has remained since that time. The reason provided for this was his failure to appear at least twice on scheduled court dates. According to Murry, this was due largely to the incompetence of his state-appointed attorney who advised him he need not appear. Today, Murry appeared at a bond hearing to explain this and attempt to obtain his release. The District Attorney's office argued against his release, now alleging that Murry had violated a no-contact order between Jaime and him and based this "fact" as grounds for denial of his release. While I am hesitant to use strong words, I know of no other way to describe it than to say this is a clear indicator of the dishonesty, incompetence, and corruption surrounding this case. The District Attorney should certainly have known full well that a no-contact order was not in place. The no-contact order issued at the beginning of the criminal proceedings was removed several months earlier in November 2012 in the family court proceedings. They also were fully aware that visitation rights had been ordered for Murry to visit Kathan at whatever schedule he and Jaime could work out between themselves by family court judge Guy Bradberry. The court had made clear there were no restrictions on his visits with Kathan. But in another of their bullying corrupt tactics, they apparently hoodwinked this criminal court judge, Clayton Davis, into going along with them. I think we can certainly conclude that Judge Davis would not knowingly play into the game, but he is probably not completely familiar with all of the facts of the case this early in the proceedings. I think it fair to say that the judge assumes that the DA would not knowingly present false statements to him. So for the District Attorney's office to allege that Murry had violated a no-contact order that court documents clearly verified had been previously lifted amounted to malfeasance in office. The court-appointed attorney for Murry was uninformed and had not done due diligence, to the point he was not prepared to present the true facts to the court in a redirect. Consequently, Murry was ordered back to jail until trial in October.

On June 16, my wife and I were enjoying a couple of hours together on Saturday morning and we opened the morning newspaper to find our story printed again in the local news section of the paper. The subject of the article was Murry's bond hearing. Because we have observed over the course of the last two years the way the local prosecutors have used the news media to influence the case and shape public opinion, we now have a better understanding of the reason for Murry's jailing and the position of the District Attorney. Our next court date was to have been in ten days on June 26, 2012. In the past, the DA's office has found ways to update this story, either on the local cable network or as in this instance, in the local paper at seemingly strategic times that would most likely have a desired affect on the mind of the judge and possibly the overall outcome of the case. The entire case is described in this article in full detail. This seamed puzzling to us until you factor in the possibility that this is likely all part of a larger strategy on the part of the prosecutors. Having the bond revoked on Murry might have never have been deemed newsworthy otherwise. One has to acknowledge that the judge is pressured from a political standpoint because of the public access to the case. No matter how reluctant we are to admit it, public opinion is of utmost importance in the mind of elected officials.

We could only wait and see whether or not our family court judge was willing to be intimidated.

Previous to one of the family court hearings in August of last year and a pretrial conference, Judge Bradberry had advised the prosecution that if they had anything else to submit, they needed to do it. Otherwise, he intended to place these children with the grandparents at the next scheduled hearing. This statement was made in a meeting in his chambers with the prosecution and our attorney present. Whether intentional or not, in essence, the state was thereby advised that they needed to come up with something. On the evening before the hearing he was speaking of, there was a special convening of the grand jury in which the District Attorney laid out new charges against Jaime. Later that evening, it was all over the local TV news, my daughter was being indicted on new charges of attempting to drown Kolten at a family swimming event some three years earlier. These charges were simply false and preposterous, but they gave the District Attorney's office the ammunition they needed to control the judge's ruling. Walter explained to me that these special convening of the grand jury is basically a dog-and-pony show where the District Attorney's office is allowed to make his case with no opposing counsel present. Consequently, he can put whatever spin on he wishes.

The charges stemmed from an incident in the family pool. The state alleged that Kolten had described to them an event where he swam by his mom, and in passing, he kicked her. She then grabbed his foot in an apparent effort to catch him, and in the process, his head went under the water for a moment and he said it scared him. This is was simply a conversation between Kolten and a friend while swimming at the Potts' home and it was overheard by Mrs. Potts. This is the absolute only basis for a felony indictment for cruelty to a child levied against Jaime. The effect of these new charges, while ridiculous in their content, made Kolten, in effect, a victim in the course of a possible felony, which became grounds to not release him from state's custody until the investigation was complete. They were also "miraculous" in their timing as it relates to the DA needing ammunition for his case. The DA's petition to the court was that Kolten should not be removed from state's custody until the new charges had been investigated. Obviously, if Kolten could not be replaced, then neither would Kyler as there was a consensus that they should not be separated to which we also agreed. In the modern world of slow-moving litigation, this action automatically added many months to a timeframe for removing the boys from state's care. It was also simply a way to tie the hands of the judge who had in our opinion given them a heads-up by advising them of an intent on his part to place the children back in our care.

Jaime had a meeting on June 21, 2012, with Krista Becton from DCFS. She now receives her meeting notices via regular mail. This is a change from the phone call contacts that were done for nearly two years previously. I find this change curious, but I have no explanation for it. According to Jaime, Mrs. Becton's questions in this meeting were more pointed and laced with hostility. She asked again what progress Jaime was making toward compliance with Larry Dilks's recommendation for treatment for fictitious disorder. Jaime's standard answer was "My attorney will address that in court." She then asked, "Do you take responsibility for the fact that you have not been able to see your children?" to which she again replied, "My attorney will address that in court." According to Jaime, this seemed to aggravate her. She asked, "Did your attorney instruct you to say that?" To which her answer was "That is just my answer." She then wanted to discuss the recent newspaper write-up. Mrs. Becton feigned ignorance of the status of the no-contact order, all the while asking questions she already knew the answer to. Jaime has learned to be very discreet when dealing with DCFS.

Five days from today, we would be having a hearing in family court. On the surface, the hearing is for the state to make their case before Judge Bradberry to have our grandchildren placed in a permanent adoption program. February marked two full years that my daughter had not seen her two sons who she loves with all of her heart. For those two years, the state had successfully kept those boys incarcerated in a effort to preserve a perceived testimony against my daughter. To date, Judge Bradberry still has not responded to our motion for a new trial. We are prayerfully hoping that this next hearing will be the day we have all been waiting for.

We attended the hearing on June 27 as planned. DCFS has attempted to have the children placed in the adoption program for many months. They have been very clear on this point. To their disappointment, Judge Bradberry denied all of the state's motions. Ms. Gwen Thompson was her usual self in that she made a courtroom performance stating her concerns for the children if placed with my wife and me. She was very vocal before the judge, saying we would not support the children in what she says are their allegations against my daughter. I am persuaded that if my grandchildren are now saying anything akin to what Mrs. Thompson implies, then it is because of suggestiveness or coercion by someone on the side of the state during the two years they have been in their care. Judge Bradberry again extended his time frame to rule on the motion for a new trial to July 27, 2012. He has had since early April to rule on this motion and appears to be extremely hesitant to rule on this matter. He did, however, make himself very clear that the boys were to continue the biweekly visits with us. This was after it was realized that our regular biweekly visit had not been scheduled for the next day even though it should have been automatic by now. Mildred Holmes, the DCFS supervisor, claimed it was an "oversight."

Walt approached us at the end of the hearing and said to me, "Keep praying, I believe the winds are turning." My reply was "You can count on that." If there is one thing that is certain, it is that God is our only real hope. As we were exiting the courtroom, in the elevator, one of the attorneys for the boys said, "Boy, I didn't know they started football season so early." To which Walt said, "What do you mean?" He then replied, "He punted. And why did he again not rule on your motion for a new trial?" Walt's response was "Because it was not denied," to which the other attorney simply nodded. I certainly hope they are right in this. Still waiting

THE BOYS COME HOME

On June 28, we visited with the boys on our biweekly visit. It was a routine visit, I suppose. We ate pizza and played games with the boys. As is always the case, we brought them a gift. This time, it was simply a pair of plaid shorts apiece. We have pretty much inundated them with clothes, but that is the only thing that is allowed. The thing that troubled me was the way Kolten has ceased to mention his desire to come home. Up until two visits ago, he was very vocal in his expressions of wanting to come home. His prayer request was always the same. "I want to come home." When asked on Wednesday about his prayer request, he leaned in my ear and said for God to protect Kathan. I said to him, Kathan doesn't need protection. This was a knee-jerk response driven by my perception that someone was suggesting to him Kathan needed protection.

I ask Kolten, "Your prayer request have always been the same each week until last week. Is something wrong?" He lowered his head and did not respond. I was persuaded that someone either from CASA or from DCFS had initiated a discussion with him, advising him that he was doing something wrong in talking about going home. Not sure who would the actual person might be who would have that conversation with him, but I have the usual suspects. The person with the most direct access to the boy's thoughts and emotions was Ann Landry.

I have a fight-back tendency in me, which is often to my own detriment. While attempting to believe God and be still, I often develop strategy in my mind to react to some of the manipulation we experience from DCFS and the DA's office. This causes my wife anxiety and often creates heated discussion between us. We are really starting to feel the wear of this two-year long battle. We pray that God intervenes soon. We continue to lift this whole thing up to him in prayer each and every day.

On July 11, our regular scheduled meeting with the boys was canceled due to a death in the Potts family. It should have been rescheduled, either on the weekend or moved to the next week. We were told that the meeting would not be rescheduled and we would not see the boys for an additional two weeks. We interpret this as a deliberate ruse to keep us away from the boys as much as possible. It is also a violation of the instructions of the court.

Krista Becton is no longer assigned to our case. We are told that she is no longer with the agency. We are always suspicious when there is a change in the case plan. We are hopeful when a worker leaves the agency. We always hope it is a case of someone's conscience bothering them. In our minds, we hope for these typesof people to become potential witnesses. I called the new assigned worker at her office but got no answer. I left a message, hung up, and called Mildred Holmes. She answered the phone and I asked her to consider a makeup visit. I explained how crucial that I felt the meetings were. Not to mention that they are court ordered. I recorded both the message I left for the new worker Christina Phillips and the conversation with Mildred Holmes. I then forwarded these conversations to Ellen Anderson. I had decided to record all contact with them as much as possible. Mildred and I agreed she would check into scheduling a makeup visit and would call me back by Friday. The curious thing is she pretended she had to check with the foster mom. I am certain that DCFS actually determines when the visits will occur. The foster mom is obligated to comply as part of her responsibility. We'll see what happens when and if she calls back.

The Rev. Jeff Arnold preached camp meeting this week at the Tioga campgrounds. His message I felt was completely on time. I felt great ministry in his message. He preached about "The Before God." His message was built upon the many times that God has proven both in life and in his word that when He leads us into something albeit something that is painful or trying for us, we can be assured God went before us and has already provided deliverance, blessing, and provision before the trial started. I felt my family could identify well with that message.

Mildred Holmes called on Friday, July 13, to notify us that we would have a visit with the boys on Wednesday, July 18, 2012. I am grateful and hopeful that we will also be allowed to visit on the following week. The thirteenth should be a makeup for missing last week's visit. Mildred was very cordial as was I. We are hopeful that we will hear from the judge within the next ten days. When Wednesday finally came, Sherri and I decided to bring hamburgers from Cotton's Famous Hamburgers for the boys' lunch. We thought we would first eat at the restaurant and then get the boys' meal to go. When we arrived at the Whistle Stop' Susan was outside. She said the power was off to the building. Mildred Holmes arrived shortly and informed us that the meeting would be canceled. Dana asked if we could consider having it in another location. Mrs. Holmes very curtly said no visits in public places. You have to have been under the duress of a predicament like ours to appreciate the significance of having someone tell you that you cannot be seen in public with your own grandchildren. The dismissal of this visit made our next scheduled visit, for Wednesday 7/25/12, one day before Judge Bradberry was to rule on the motion for a new trial.

For the last few days' I have felt a strong apprehension building. While I am certain that we have good lawful standing as a basis for a new trial, I have also watched over the course of the last twenty-eight months as the court has ruled in a way that has facilitated the protection of the state's case above all else.

The most significant indicator of this has been the fact that our grandchildren have remained in foster care. This is all while the state claims to have the interest of the children as a first priority. My wife and I are able to provide them a good and stable home life, one that is structured in Christianity. It is a home that they are already familiar with and one that the children have stated repeatedly that they would love to come to.

I have had plenty of time to reflect upon the effect that what I call "incarceration" has had upon our grandsons. I considered that first of all when the state took these children, they were obligated within a very short period to tell the boys why they could not go home. Then I considered their very young age and how impressionable they would be at the ages of four and six. I then thought about Mrs. Landry's effect on our children. This is the same counselor that alleged that I had attempted to seek sexual gratification with my grandchildren in her office while she observed! You have to ask yourself, what was her motive for such a derisory and inflammatory accusation?

I considered the sibling visits that she facilitated on a scheduled basis with Gabe and our two grandchildren. Then I realized that from a counselor's view, the first step for a path forward with these boys would probably be to lead them on a path of recovery from the abuse the state alleges that the boys witnessed and from the social impact that such an event would have on them. I would think that the first step in that process would be to have the boys acknowledge that the events occurred in the first place. My reasoning was confirmed by referencing Mrs. Landry's letter addressed to Brandi Greene dated September 20, 2010. This letter was provided to DCFS to serve as a progress update, treatment plan, and recommendations for Kolten and Kyler. On page 5 of that letter under the heading "Treatment Recommendations," she provided the following recommendations;

> 3. *Assist Jason with understanding and processing his feelings related to the emotional abuse inflicted by his parents and*

any feelings of guilt that he may have about the abuse of his brother Gabriel.

4. Assist Jason with talking about fears that he may have about the present or future.

OCS Goal: Reunification
Treatment Goal: Long Term:

Provide Jason with a safe and nurturing therapeutic environment in which he may process the incidents of abuse and his participation in them, in his home to enable him to discuss and process feelings of abandonment, grief, loss, guilt etc.; and in which he may be able to adjust to his current placement.

The operative words here I think are *assist* and *therapeutic*. So our grandsons who never actually witnessed anything, except the actions of an extremely mentally ill child, have for the last two and a half years been surrounded by a world in which they would find no acceptance without conceding this alleged abuse. It is chilling to consider that this therapist who is reputably in the business of helping children recover and who at least in this case is so completely wrong will become a key witness to the court in this case and that, after she has had two years to advance her own perceptions upon these children. Basically, be brainwashed or consider yourself an outsider would be the message to the child. You have to have been there to realize the weight of her recommendation in these family court proceedings. My fear is that over a long enough period the children would not remember the actual truth, but only what had been persistently forced into their psyche. All of this is done in the name of playing on the team of the State of Louisiana. The significance of the use of the word *therapeutic* should not be lost on us. This is Mrs. Landry's endorsement of a plan to keep herself involved and thereby continue to get paid.

Additionally, while we can never know for certain, but I can't help but believe that someone in power has used behind-the-scenes methods other than those used in the media and the obvious ones to influence the rulings of the judge. It is obvious that while he has been careful to rule within the law, it has always been in a way that seemed to preserve the hopes the state has for a conviction and always seemed to give their side the benefit of the doubt. I would say that in this court, evidence against the state would have to be 100 percent conclusive before any type indictment can be brought against them, while on the other hand, when a citizen is accused, he is in modern times assumed guilty until he can prove otherwise. Neither is there any apparent meaningful consideration for the actual needs and request of the children in any of the court proceedings to date. We prayerfully hope that changes this week.

It was 9:00 a.m. at Phillips 66 Refinery in Lake Charles, Louisiana, on July 25, 2012. Today we should have another scheduled visit with our grandchildren at the Whistle Stop. We have not yet been notified by DCFS of the meeting. I placed a call to Mildred Holmes and sent her an e-mail reminding her. Sometime later, we received a call from Christina Phillips advising us of the visit. We have become so financially strapped from the impact of events over the past two years that we struggle sometimes to have the cost of the visits and provide some token gift for the boys. We hope to have a pleasant visit today and then on to tomorrow's hearing on our motions for new trial and the return of our grandchildren. Hoping and waiting.

Our church for thirty years has conducted a weekly prayer meeting on Monday nights to pray for our city. Primarily, we pray for the lost, but many other needs have been met within the congregation through the prayers of the saints. On Monday, July 23, 2012, we were at prayer meeting as usual. There was something very unusual that occurred on this night. Oftentimes, at prayer meeting, some of us will walk and pray while others will simply find a place to kneel. I was walking and I saw Bishop Nugent moving toward me. He took my hand and began to pray and violently shake my hand back and forward. This went on for what seemed like ten minutes or more. Knowing what I know about this man, I determined within myself, "I will not let you go until you release me." Something broke in that moment, and he later said to the congregation that as he was walking, the spirit showed him a thread suspended in the air. He said the spirit spoke to him, saying that the thread was all that remained holding this case against our family. We believed a victory was won in the spirit and we would see the fruit of it at the hearing scheduled for Thursday.

It is Thursday, July 26, 2012. I remember in the previous hearing, sitting outside the courtroom, watching my daughter through the rectangular window, hoping to glean from her reaction what the ruling of the judge would be. I did not have the courage to do so in this hearing. I remember this feeling even as I sit here writing of it, I find it indescribable. I am afraid and I hope against hope that today will be the day. One thing I know, there will be extreme finality to whatever the judge rules today. I sat with my back to a wall alongside my wife. I stood and took only one peek through the window, then returned to my position against the wall. I could hear the judge's muffled voice through the wall as he handed down his ruling. Even though I couldn't understand the words, I was anxiously hoping that they would deliver good news.

After about thirty minutes, I suddenly noticed increased activity in the courtroom and people started exiting at a fast rate. Suddenly, the doors opened and Jaime emerged, surrounded by her attorneys. She was leaning on Walter Sanchez and sobbing uncontrollably and so loudly that I could not initially tell if there was good or bad news. Suddenly in the midst of the confusion, I understood one thing she said. She was virtually yelling, "Ya'll got the boys! Ya'll got the boys!" I think of the long journey that got us here and the many disappointments, the endless nights going to sleep, wondering what our grandchildren were thinking about and how they were being treated. The horror of witnessing the dishonesty and manipulation that had been the mode of operation for this organization that calls itself an agency for the protection of children. In the days that followed, I would think of the hours of prayer over the course of 883 days (two years, five months, and two days) and the many times I had lifted up the prophetic promise of God to him in prayer. What seemed like a never-ending nightmare had suddenly come to an end in one moment. Yet it had taken nine months from the time that the journal was introduced in court until a ruling was made in regard to it, while our grandchildren remained in foster care. Things move very slowly in the judicial system.

Judge Bradberry ruled that his previous ruling of Kolten and Kyler being indeed children in need of care be vacated and that they be turned over to us, the grandparents. His ruling also included the total release of DCFS from the case. He further addressed why such crucial evidence as found in Mrs. Semien's journal was withheld from the court and our family during trial and promised to fully investigate this matter. He ordered that Kolten and Kyler's attorneys be released from their assignment to represent the boys. Additionally, he ordered a hearing to be held on September 27, 2012, for DCFS to show why they should not be held in contempt. But most importantly, he ordered that Kolten and Kyler be delivered to us at the courthouse by noon that day! Only a couple of hours away.

We made our way up to Walt's office to wait for someone to bring the boys from Oakdale. They had been there for two and one half years, staying in the home of Scotty and Roxanne Potts. A storm came up while we were waiting and I decided at Walter's prompting to move my truck close to the front door of the courthouse to wait. You could actually view the entrance to the courthouse from Walt's glass-enclosed office. As I was getting out of my truck, my eye caught that of Mr. Steve Berniard, attorney for the state, as he entered the courthouse. He seemed to pause and look over his shoulder at me. I wondered what he must really think about all of all of this. I wondered how many times he had represented the state and found himself on the wrong side of right and wrong. I wondered what kind of man he was.

Suddenly, I saw the boys with Mrs. Potts walking up the sidewalk. I cannot in words describe what I was feeling in that moment as I watched them run toward me. Immediately, Christina Phillips from DCFS converged on the scene, holding an envelope which contained the boys' social security cards and birth certificates. Apparently, the significance of the ruling Mrs. Phillips had just heard had been lost on her. She was anxiously trying to instruct Mrs. Potts that she should leave. She addressed someone in the crowd and stated that she needed to make certain that we understood that there was to be no contact between the boys and Jaime. She alleged that a no-contact order was still in place. Becky Jacobs was present and advised her, "You've been released." I supposed she missed the part in the judge's ruling concerning the agency being released and his previous ruling being completely vacated. We have won a great victory and we feel that our God has shown who is in control. He has demonstrated that He knows from the beginning to the end and can keep is promises. We still have the criminal proceedings to deal with, but we are confident in the future and our God.

PARENTS AGAIN

Unquestionably, Walt Sanchez is one of the finest criminal attorneys in the State of Louisiana and he seemingly has never wavered in his commitment to fight for Jaime. Nonetheless, at this point I had become concerned as to how far he was willing to travel down a road of bringing litigation against the powers that be in our local District Attorney's office and law enforcement. It was now obvious to me that each of these agencies had fully extended themselves and, if found at fault, would be very vulnerable to litigation. Out of this concern, I called Walt and arranged a meeting. This meeting took place in his office. Both of his assistant attorneys, Becky and Tom, were present.

In opening. I suggested to Walt that my concern was that he had to "live to fight another day" in this world of litigation that he lived in. I ask the question, what was the point beyond which he would not go in seeking justice in this case? He responded by saying, "That is a fair question." In answer he said to me, "I will go as far as the law allows and as for as long as I have something to work with." He said to me, "I will start pulling the thread from where we are now and then follow wherever that leads" At this point, we knew that the journal was in place and we could start with our attention on DCFS. I felt better, but still it was difficult for me feel completely reassured given the gravity of what we were facing.

My concern grew on this issue months later, when on the day of one of our final hearings in family court, just minutes before things got underway, Walt led me around a corner, out of hearing from everyone else in the sitting area outside the courtroom and began to enlighten me on latest developments. He told me that he had been meeting with John Derosier. In those meetings, he had demonstrated to Mr. Derosier the extreme problems the state had with their case. He explained how Mr. Dilks, through his own testimony, had testified in court that there was no verifiable data to support his diagnosis and prognosis of Jaime. That he had basically built his theory of her condition simply from an assumption of guilt. Basically, he was saying, "We know she did it, so this is the only explanation for it." Walt talked to me about how my daughter's constitutional right to parenthood had been violated through fraud. He further explained to me that he suggested directly or indirectly (I couldn't be sure) to Mr. Derosier that he could offer he and Tony Mancuso "a way out." I took that to mean a way to escape untarnished. He seemed to suggest that the only ones probably at fault were DCFS and all of the expert witnesses. My position at that moment was that they were all guilty and should be held accountable. But then on the other hand, caution and reason said to me, I did not possess the skills, experience, or knowledge Mr. Sanchez did in managing a criminal trial. For an attorney, it has to be about what you can prove, not what you believe. I still found it frustrating for two reasons. It bothered me that it was obvious incompetence on the part of the sheriff's investigators in the beginning that brought about the indictment and they were certainly guilty of false arrest. I believed that they should be held accountable on this point. Secondly, I felt that the actions of the DA's office were egregious once the evidence had unfolded. Once the foster mom's journal was revealed, it became apparent that the case against my daughter was flawed and that she was most likely innocent.

In the days following, I composed an e-mail and sent it to Walt. I called it my synopsis of events from my view. I provided an outline of all of the agencies or persons who I felt should be held accountable and listed each of their actions, which I believed unlawful. This included media, Calcasieu Parish School board, Sheriff's Office, DA's office, Melanie Daley, DCFS, and all of the state witnesses. I was very adamant that my feeling was that none of the guilty parties should ever be allowed to bring this much harm to any family again.

It is troubling the things that have occurred and the unforeseen impact this case has had on each individual member of my family. I think of my daughter and all of the long nights over the course of two and one half years in which she could not help but wonder if she would ever see her boys again and whether or not she would spend the next twenty years in prison. Now the court has placed both boys in Sherri's and my care. And we suddenly find ourselves with another complete world of responsibilities, some of which we were hardly prepared to meet.

We were advised by Walt that even though Jaime had access to Kolten and Kyler with no restrictions, he still preferred that she not go into the general public with them and that we should not leave her alone with the boys. I am sure this is difficult for her, given all she has been through and the fact that she is innocent. Walt's concern was that he did not want to rub the District Attorney's nose in it before the criminal proceedings were complete and he did not want to provide them with any ammunition with which to advantage their case. One thing we knew for sure is that there were no limits beyond which our enemies would not go to win this case. We had to remind ourselves that while we had won a great victory in family court, we had not yet to come face-to-face with the criminal charges in court against the DA's office.

New and somewhat unexpected problems began to occur when we began to make decisions concerning the immediate future for Kolten and Kyler. We had to decide where they would attend school. I felt it necessary to build some structure into their lives. We gave them house rules. We required that they make their beds each morning and that they keep their room clean. We developed ways to guide them into good thinking as it related to showing respect for authority at school. We required that all homework be complete each day before any playtime. Additionally, we got them involved at our church, with Sunday's school, and children's ministry. As we began to apply these things into their lives, it seemed that resentment began to grow on the part of my daughter. In a matter of a couple of weeks, it had increased to the point where she was openly accusing me of being on a power trip and trying to take over as the parent. The other thing is she never wanted to leave the boys' side. She began to refuse to go to her own house. The problem was that I didn't have a large enough home to accommodate her. All of our beds were taken and she had a two-year-old she had to manage. She had a home to maintain and desperately needed a job. She was trying to attend McNeese University for nursing, and I was paying all of the cost to maintain her home. Somehow, we were quickly becoming the enemy in the heat of all the pressure. It seemed outrageous at first, but in retrospect, I realize that all of Jaime's reactions should probably have been expected.

The position I took was that for as long as the courts and God had placed the responsibility of providing care for the boys with my wife and I, we would do it with all of the energy and ability we possessed. I was determined to impact them as much as possible in a positive way for as long as I could, if only for a short while. Also, knowing myself, I knew that for as long as Kolten and Kyler lived under my roof, they would have to abide by my rules. In the middle of all of this controversy, I still understood that only my daughter knew the things that she dealt with inwardly. Only she could understand how her inner person reacted to all of the horrendous trouble that had occurred in all of our lives. When you consider this, you can only have compassion on Jaime.

On the decision of where to place the boys in school, we had three choices. All of my children had been educated in Christian education. For all of the years of our kids growing up, they had attended Lake Charles Christian Academy. This was Livingway's private Christian school based on the church grounds. The school had closed for the first time, this year, thus our three choices. Number one was to send them to the public school system. We ruled this out immediately because we were afraid of the idea of state access to the boys given our past with the public school system. Our second choice was the new and local charter school. We primarily wanted to start them in Christian education, but we knew that our budget would not afford the local Christian school, Hamilton Christian Academy, so we defaulted to sending them to the charter school. To our shock and surprise, while going through the enrollment process, we discovered that the principal and teachers, who had perjured themselves in family court against us, had moved from Fairview Elementary school and would now make up the staff for Kolten and Kyler's grade level at the charter school. We decided immediately that we would not risk more fraud from these folks, so we were resolved to enroll them at Hamilton. We went to them and explained our financial situation. While we knew we couldn't clearly see how we would be able to pay the cost for private education, we felt that we were obligated to try. God has ways that are far above us. One of our friends, who attended our church, had recently become the finance manager for the school and was able to assist us. By the time we got there, she had already had some discussion with the principal and given him a little bit of the history. There was a consensus that was detectable coming from them that no matter what, they wanted those boys at Hamilton. We were so very thankful and felt that even though we could not see very far in the future, we were doing the right thing and we were resolved to trust God for the rest.

The date is August 31, 2012. Walt filed a motion for sanctions against DCFS this week. In the motion, he outlines the case to date and the proceedings in family court. He brings a railing indictment against DCFS for willingly and unlawfully withholding documents having a direct impact on the case and these same documents being in contradiction to the state's case against Jaime. I also note that within the content of his motion, he twice makes reference to what he deems as ethical conduct by the District Attorney's office in providing him the journal in discovery. He praises the DA and states, "If it had not been for the ethical conduct of others, this willful misconduct of DCFS and its agents would never have come to light." I, on the other hand, still remember a trumped-up new charge that was brought against my daughter by the District Attorney's office on August 18, 2011, alleging she had attempted to drown Kolten in a swimming pool. This was an obvious attempt to reinforce DCFS's case against Jaime at a time when their case was in question. Also, it was well after the DA's office, had Mrs. Semien's journal in their possession. It seemed to me that in light of the content of the journal, the state would have been prepared to talk about dropping all charges rather than levying new ones.

It seemed apparent to me Walt was attempting to gain some favor with the DA in his motion. I reasoned that his overall strategy would have to be to have the District Attorney's office aligned on his side against DCFS rather than having them all aligned against us. His motion requested that the court order that DCFS compensate Jaime for all attorney's fees and expenses associated with the case. He wanted the court to consider all costs over the course of the last twenty-nine months. Walt cited an article that provides for imposing sanctions against any party participating in the kind of wrongful conduct DCFS has obviously indulged in withholding evidence in this case. It is my belief that when the pressure mounts against DCFS, all sorts of new revelations will fall out of the closet, implicating the Lord only knows who.

On Friday, September 7, 2012, Jaime received a call from Walt's paralegal. She called to inform Jaime of a new motion being filed by the assistant District Attorney's office. In the motion, the DA was alleging that Jaime had broken the conditions of her bail and petitioned the court to jail her until jury trial. Her hearing date was set for October 3, 2012. They alleged she had been in contact with Murry via telephone calls and visits to the jail. They further alleged she had broken the terms of her bail by having contact with the alleged victim. It is difficult to determine whether Mrs. Cynthia Guillory, who filed the motion, is guilty of baseless bullying or if she is simply so incompetent that she doesn't know the facts. For her to make a charge like this one for which there is simply no basis and apparently without reviewing all of the documentation available to her in this case is unthinkable. As she did in the case of Murry, she is attempting to have a judge jail Jaime for violating a no-contact order imposed by Judge Mike Canaday in criminal court but lifted by Judge Bradberry in family court in November of 2010. Obviously, he would have to make this adjustment, if Murry was to be allowed to visit with his son. Additionally in our hearing on August 26, 2012, Bradberry had vacated his previous ruling of Kolten and Kyler being children in need of care and had released DCFS from the case. Walt had advised Jaime that consequently, she had unlimited access to the boys. So we ask ourselves, what is really going on here? We see that the District Attorney is able to bring false representation to the courtroom and persuade a judge to jail a man wrongfully. I am not certain which is applicable, but it is certain that either this District Attorney's office is malicious in their willingness to hide facts from a judge in an effort to impose their will upon their victims or there is such gross incompetence and lack of communication within the office that they cannot be trusted to pursue justice within their own system. Not certain which applies.

I sent a text message to Walt yesterday, September 10, 2012, asking him to call me. I wanted to question him regarding this last motion from the state to have Jaime jailed. As I was leaving the parking lot at Phillips 66 at the end of my day, my phone rang. It was Walt calling me in response to the text message from

8:00 a.m. that morning. It is very difficult for me to ascertain where we actually stand in all of this.

I initially asked him where he felt we stood on the issue of the state's latest motion to have Jaime jailed again. Walt assured me that the state would not actually follow through on this motion. He advised me of a phone conversation between Cynthia Guillory and himself in which he assured her that if they should go through with this motion, then he would go through the motions to have the DA's office removed from the case. The explanation for how he could accomplish this is held in the fact that counsel for DCFS was allegedly not informed of the existence of the journal nor of its content. Their then counsel, Steve Berniard, had since become employed by the District Attorney's office, thereby making the DA's office a potential witness against DCFS. This conflict, we hoped, would be justification to have them removed. The case would then go to the attorney general's office. Walt went over the details of lawsuits that will follow Bradberry's ruling on his motion form sanctions. His comments made one thing apparent to me. He plans to aggressively file suits against the state (DCFS), Mr. Dilks, and Mrs. Landry. It is still bothersome that he is not mentioning the sheriff's office, media, or the school board who all were complicit in the effort to incriminate an innocent woman.

On September 18, 2012, Jaime received a text message from Walt's paralegal, Ellen Anderson, informing her that the hearing to hear motions for sanctions had been continued to October 23. The reason provided was that all of the pertinent DCFS workers were on assignment in New Orleans assisting with the food stamp program. I find this most suspect. It seems to me there is a concert effort to delay through the date of the hearing set on October 3 to attempt to have Jaime jailed.

THE BISHOP'S ILLNESS

It was Sunday night, September 30, 2012. We had a powerful service at Livingway on that night. Bishop Nugent had led much of the service and was in the vein of the spirit. There was a great anointing on him as is usual. After service, he went by the student center, a restaurant facility owned by the church across the street from McNeese University in Lake Charles. Barbecue dinners had been prepared and were for sale that night to raise funding for our building program. We were currently about to enter into the construction of a new family life center. After picking up lunch for him and Sister Nugent, the bishop went home to relax and enjoy his food. Shortly after eating, he was relaxing in his recliner, and suddenly, he realized something was wrong, and in a matter of a few moments, he went into a seizure. He later described feeling himself slipping out of control and the only thing he could bring himself to say was "911" to Sister Nugent. She could hardly understand him and thought at first he was playing a joke on her. He was rushed to St. Patrick's Hospital. Once a diagnosis was done, he was transported to a Lafayette hospital where a qualified neurosurgeon could be found. It was thought at the time that he possibly had bleeding on his brain. The next day in Lafayette, a tumor was discovered on his brain. It was decided that he would undergo laser knife (stereotactic radio surgery), which utilizes a pinpoint beam of radiation to treat small tumors. We were told that the procedure would require five or six treatments. All of us were certain of one thing: we were not prepared to give up the bishop at this time. To think that the man we all, as a church family, had come to love as our father or the man who had led us in great revival for thirty years might be at risk was unbearable. Prayers for him began to go up across America.

Today is October 16, 2012. Jaime received a summons to appear in court on a separate incident on Thursday of this week. She and Murry were witnesses to an automobile accident last year, and apparently, there are some criminal proceedings that are an outfall of that accident. She is very apprehensive about appearing in court for any reason. Murry received a subpoena as well, and he will be transported from the parish jail to testify. Murry has now been incarcerated wrongfully for over eight months. You can be certain that there is a strategy in the minds of the prosecutors in keeping him in jail. He has also been advised by his state-appointed attorney that his trial date for October 29, 2012, is still in place. In all of the "out of court" back and forth between Walter and the DA's office, Cynthia Guillory had advised Walter of her intent to continue Jaime's case. We can only guess, but I suspect that they hope to get a plea bargain or a conviction in Murry's case, thereby reinforcing their case against Jaime. Again, I am appalled at the unscrupulousness of this group of prosecutors in their effort to get a conviction. They are probably convinced at this point of her innocence, but for political gain are willing to press forward for a conviction.

We are at a very pivotal moment in these proceedings. Along with the possibility of the entire case being turned over to the attorney general, there is also the possibility of our landing in federal court with charges levied against numerous players on the state's side, including the District Attorney's office. If only the public could know and believe how this game is actually played.

On the afternoon of Wednesday, October 17, 2012, I received a call from Jaime. She had called to inform me of a new continuance in place for the state in regards to the hearing for sanctions that was to be held on October 23. According to her, she had just received a call from Ellen informing her of the latest change. Ellen said that the state had petitioned the court for all minutes of the proceedings in family court over the course of the last two years. There is an implied attempt to discover something said in the previous proceedings that would vindicate them in regards to their withholding the information contained in Mrs. Simien's journal. Well, this is understandable. If you are the defendant in any criminal proceedings and you are not prepared to defend yourself, then by default, you will seek a continuance as would any good attorney. We can only pray that the state will not be allowed to continue to manipulate the process.

Up to this point, my references to Mrs. Simien's journal have been based on the portions of the journal that are included in Walt Sanchez's motions regarding Jaime's trial. When I began reading through the complete journal starting the day Gabe first met Mrs. Simien at Memorial Hospital, I was intrigued by the obvious repetitious cycle that I saw in my mind's eye as I read her story. She described beginning at February 26, 2010, a sweet and polite little boy and described everything as great and pleasant. But as I continued to read, the subtle changes of bad manners and rudeness appeared. Later on, she told of receiving a note from the teacher, telling her of the teachers concern over changes in Gabe's behavior. As I read from one month to the next, you could see the obvious cycle of his behavior until finally, he was an out-of-control child who was screaming and threatening to "do to you what I did to Jaime" and claiming to hear voices telling him to hurt himself and to burn her house down. This was the point in time where he was so out of control that he was moved to Crossroads for treatment. It was the exact time period and incidents cited in Brandi Green's recorded phone conversation with Steve Fontenot. It was also an eerie reminder of the same cycle occurring in our lives just a few months earlier.

My cell phone rang at around ten minutes after eleven a.m.. It was my wife calling and the first question she asked me was

"Have you talked to Jaime?" When I replied no I had not, she then informed that Murry was being released from jail. Today is October 29, 2012. She said that apparently a new no-contact order was being imposed on Jaime and Murry. Also, Murry was going to be allowed visits with the boys, but they were apparently only going to be allowed at the Whistle Stop. Immediately, I felt the apprehension arising, thinking of what possible new attack the state was mounting. Obviously, they were not ready to concede loss or admit their mistakes. I can't imagine them not trying to impose the same restrictions on Jaime as Murry. If so, that would mean she could only see her children under the controlled environment of the Whistle Stop. We have prayed and fought now for almost three years, and it seems that this nightmare will never end. I am resolute in my determination to hold on to the promises of God.

On Friday morning, November 2, 2012, Jaime was called to a meeting in Walt's office. She was informed that Murry would be attending the meeting. The purpose for the meeting was to go over the details associated with the fact that Walt was now agreeing to represent and include Murry as his client in a civil law suit against DCFS and its witnesses. Walt had moved forward and was making preparation to file civil suits against the State of Louisiana, Larry Dilks, Ann Landry, and Lake Area Psychology in Lake Charles. Since civil law was not Walt's forte, he brought in a new attorney to the team. His name is Stephen Spring of Spring and Spring LLC in Baton Rouge. Mr. Spring had apparently had some success with these types of lawsuits, and Walt felt that he could use the experience and guidance in the proceedings. The other thing we learned today was that Ms. Melanie Smith Daley has been suspended and disbarred from practice. No explanation has been provided to us explaining why this action was taken, but as Walt once said, "Their silence on the matter is deafening." While unlikely, I can't help but consider the possibility of her being disbarred for her actions in our case. I may never know for certain, but I believe she coerced and coached the testimony of the teachers who claimed Gabe to be an exemplary child and student, knowing full well nothing could be further from the truth.

FIRING BACK

It is very difficult for me not to be excited and happy to arrive home from work on November 6, 2012, to learn that Mr. Larry Dilks was served that day with a lawsuit against him for malpractice and for having provided false testimony in the criminal proceedings. I am at this point very grateful for a brilliant attorney and thankful that he had the foresight to orchestrate that previous criminal hearing wherein Mr. Dilks and Ann Landry placed themselves on the courts record, testifying of limited or nonexistent knowledge of the journal. Mostly, I am excited that we are now on offense. Our God promised, "In the end, I win."

The following day, Jaime texted me to notify me that she was picking up some paperwork from Walt's office. When I arrived at home around six o'clock, Sherri had a large pot of Louisiana gumbo cooking on the stove. I fixed a bowl and settled in my recliner in the den to watch a little TV and relax. Jaime walked in and handed me a copy of a federal lawsuit filed on Monday naming the State of Louisiana, Office of the Governor, Department of Children and Family Services, Lawrence S. Dilks, PhD, Cecilla Ann Landry MSW and her company Ann Landry, MSW, LCSW, RPT-S, LLC along with a long list of state workers from DCFS as defendants.

The suit requested that the court grant compensation for past, future, and present hospital expenses, physical pain and suffering, mental anguish and suffering, lost wages and diminished earnings, emotional distress, loss of enjoyment of life, and such other damages caused by the defendants. Within the content of the suit, Walter lays out the events of the case starting from Jaime's arrest and accounting for all of the wrongful conduct committed by the defendants. The suit accuses them of a conspiracy to defraud Jaime and Murry of their rights as American citizens. After all of the many times I have faced these people in courtrooms, at the Whistle Stop, and in their respective offices over the course of the last thirty-three months and considering the bullying, Gestapo-like methods in which they imposed what I can only describe as lies and dishonest propaganda on our family, I could only wish that I could be there to see their faces when they were served the suit.

There was one disappointment as far as I was concerned and that is because a principal player in the attack against our family was as far as I could see was not being held accountable, and that was Gwen Thompson. No one contributed more than she to commit this travesty against my daughter, yet as a volunteer, she was apparently immune to litigation against her. Also, one thought continued to trouble me. I ask myself why? What motive would these people have for wanting to send a woman from an insignificant family like ours to prison? I thought to myself, why did they not, when the journal was discovered, simply present it as new evidence and let the thing run its course? After all, it wouldn't be any loss to any of the individuals named as defendants, unless they had something to lose that was not so obvious. The only thing that makes sense is that there is another party and that party would have to be superior to the frontline players and they would obviously need to have a motive. The only motive that made sense to me is, if you are a prosecutor and you have committed yourself in the public eye to a high profile case like ours, you might very well be willing to do anything to prevent yourself from appearing incompetent or wrongful in the media. So for my part, I would have to point to the District Attorney's office and law enforcement as the strength behind this madness.

To my thinking, the only way anyone would undergo such a risky proposition as these state workers have, with no apparent motive, would be if they were directed to do so and believed they were well protected and some sort of guarantee of the future was made. As I told Walt in our discussion about his choices of who he would name in the suit, I believe when he starts pressuring these lower tier parties, a lot of unexpected things are going to fall out of the closet. I would expect that when the folks at the bottom of the list of defendants get under the pressure of a civil lawsuit that they will not protect the hidden parties who had the most influence. One thing I have observed for a large part of the last three years is that it is obvious that these people have been operating in concert in such a way that would be impossible without someone leading as a conductor.

Today is Wednesday, November 28, 2012, a cool front came through again yesterday and the temperature is falling to around forty at night. Jaime's next court date, which is in regards to allegations that she violated the conditions of her bail, has been moved to the end of January. No court date has been set either for the criminal proceedings or for our motion for sanctions against DCFS. This February 28, 2013, will mark three full years since the trouble first occurred. During all of this time, Jaime has not had a job. She is attending McNeese University for nursing and cleans a house every once in a while. My income has supported my house and hers for all of this time. The waits are always disconcerting. So often we wait months for a court day, only to have it continued until a later date at the last moment.

THE FINAL SEASON

On January 30, 2013, the first criminal proceedings were conducted in which the state is being represented by Mrs. Lori Nunn. She is a recently hired prosecutor from Baton Rouge who has been assigned to the case in the face of all the recent developments, including our lawsuit. In this hearing, the state filed a motion to set a date for a pretrial conference for April 11, 2013. They also filed a motion to withdraw their previous motion to have Jaime's bail revoked and have her jailed until trial. It appears that the state has realized some serious problems with their case and I find that very encouraging.

Bishop Nugent is scheduled to have surgery today, February 5, 2013, to have the tumor removed from his brain. The cyber knife procedure has not been successful. The church has committed to a schedule of prayer and fasting beginning this past Monday, trusting that God will bring him safely through it. A few weeks ago and unknown to me, he had another seizure and was admitted overnight at St. Patrick's Hospital in Lake Charles. The next morning, I awoke while checking my messages and saw where I had missed a call from his son Darrin at 3:00 a.m. When I called, I learned that he was to be transported shortly to Lafayette. I drove to the hospital only in time to visit for a moment before the ambulance driver showed up to load him for the trip. As we stood around the back door of the ambulance, I realized that nobody was to be riding with him on the trip. I thought to myself that he shouldn't have to ride alone, so I asked the driver if I could go along. He said, "Sure, if you want to," so I said, "I'm ready now," and stepped into the back door for my very first ambulance ride. If I had any notions that an ambulance might be designed to provide comfortable transportation for a patient, they were soon squashed. I learned that an ambulance is probably the roughest ride you will ever make in your life. I later told someone, "Might as well have been riding on the back of a two-ton flatbed." On the way, I called Sherri to inform her where I was and make arrangements for her to drive to Lafayette to pick me up. We arrived safely in Lafayette with no further incidents. Bishop Nugent's family was there, having already made the trip and were waiting on us when we arrived at the hospital.

The day finally came when the financial pressure overcame my family. When the trouble began, we had borrowed every dime we possibly could to pay legal fees in Jaime's defense. Suddenly, I found myself paying the bills for two families with forty percent less income, plus the additional debt for legal fees, not to mention the additional cost of providing the needs of two boys. After three years of fighting this battle, I solicited the services of a local bankruptcy attorney. Gerald Casey, after review, decided the best path forward for me was chapter 13. He later determined that I didn't qualify for 13 but that chapter 7 would be the only thing I could do. My intention was to pay everyone everything I owed, but I simply couldn't continue on this path. It was miraculous that after three years, I still had managed to keep most everything current, but the pressure finally overcame us.

As I sat in Mr. Casey's office, we had a conversation concerning our case. I shared the highlights of the case with him and discussed how it had impacted our family's finances. Through our discussion, I learned that he had been in criminal law in his early years. As we sat in his office, he said something to me that resonated soundly within my heart. He said, "I'm sorry, but I do not believe in capital punishment and you shouldn't either. What they attempted to do to you and your daughter, they are doing every day to many people. Are they sending innocent people to prison and killing some of them?" He then answered his own question, "Absolutely." I have always believed in capital punishment until that moment. This was the first time I had ever been reluctant to embrace the concept that punishment for the crime should be equal to the crime. I still do believe this in theory, but when the people we trust to pursue truth, justice, and the right thing are found to be corrupt with lust for power, political advancement, and the desire to preserve their own careers, then we can no longer trust them to execute the laws upon which we as a nation are built. As a consequence of the actions of leaders, many of the less significant players in the system seem to have come to a resolution that "this is the way that the game is played" and have long since seared their conscience and have no remorse over the consequence of their misrepresentation of facts or lying to affect a desired end in criminal law. I have found our officials to be more corrupt than the criminals they prosecute.

On February 22, 2012, a hearing was held in the case involving Murry and the supposed no-contact order he had allegedly violated and consequently was jailed for eight months. The judge ruled no restrictions would be on him or his right to see his boys. For the first time in three years, Murry was allowed to see his children. They spent the entire weekend at my home playing games, watching videos, and we all attended the house of God together, both Sunday morning and evening.

Murry confirmed what I had always believed. I knew that there had to be some strategy in the minds of the prosecutors when they opted to jail Murry and I always believed that the purpose was to pressure Murry into some sort of plea deal. That there was a strategy pretty obvious given the fact that the DA knew Murry had done nothing unlawful yet had him jailed anyway. He confirmed to us that during his tenure in incarceration, they had repeatedly attempted to get him to make a plea. According to Murry, the deals were being offered to him from the District

Attorney's office. He described an offer in which he was promised he would immediately be released and given custody of his children. This I learned during a heated conversation with Murry over his responsibilities versus liberties with the boys. He angrily and in a threatening way said to us both, "I sat in the DA's office and they looked at me and said, 'All you have to do is agree to testify and you'll be home by Friday and we will get you custody of your children.'" I quickly replied, "You're not going to do that Murry, because if you do, you will have to actually go to work and start paying for their living and you know you have never done that." There was something else he said at that moment that eventually would become significant. He looked at me and said, "The reason I didn't was because I know the truth."

It's not surprising that the District Attorney's office would attempt to get one defendant to testify against another in an attempt to get a conviction on their prime suspect. This is a normal practice in modern-day criminal prosecution. What is troubling is that at this point the prosecution is looking at the same evidence as we are. They certainly understand that even from their own point of view, Jaime is in all likelihood innocent of all charges. Even so, they steam forward in an extreme effort to get some sort of win out of this case. What is appalling is the tactics they were willing to resort to in Murry's alleged no-contact violation. To think that our elected officials would fabricate a charge and have an innocent man jailed in an attempt to further a case that they already know that they are on the wrong side of, to say the least, is horrendous!

It's March 5, 2013. I spoke with Walt this morning. He advised me of two upcoming significant hearings that I should attend. One is set for the doctor who treated Gabe to testify concerning his observations as an expert witness for the state. He is an elderly man and the state is having his testimony video recorded in the event he should expire before trial. The other will be held two weeks later on March 27, 2013, and is the sanctions motion.

Walt informed me that the state had asked that he continue this hearing. He said that his response was "respectfully no."

At first, I was puzzled to learn from Walt that the state intended to steam forward with the trial. He assured me that the District Attorney intended to go forward and that it would probably happen in August 2013. I had recently rationalized that they would never allow this case to go to court due to the obvious fraud involved. But when I considered their options, then I understood that to try the case in spite of the facts, fit perfectly with the mode of operation I had learned about our system. It was clear now that a defendant's innocence or guilt had little to do with the decision to prosecute. It had everything to do with political posturing. The question is simply "Can we win?" If you are a modern-day prosecutor and winning appears unlikely, then which scenario will best serve you politically becomes the question. Simply put, they would rather try the case and lose than to openly admit after all the publicity surrounding our case that they had simply been wrong. Not only wrong, but fraudulent. Consequently, I suppose, it seemed to them more sensible to prosecute, and when they lost to simply yell to the press, with a straight face, "We believe the defendant is guilty as charged!" Let us not forget who controls the media, so in the end for them, it is how it is portrayed in the media. I remember at the very beginning, at the time of Jaime's arrest, we attempted to get some relief by way of the District Attorney through our attorney. His response was that he wanted to be cautious because a lot of eyes were on this case. Even that early on, it was apparent that the major concern was public opinion.

On March 13, 2013, two noteworthy things occurred in court as it relates to our case. The first was that the hearing to record Gabe's doctor's testimony was reset for April 10, 2013. When we appeared at court this morning, Judge Davis ordered that it be rescheduled due to the overloading of his docket for today. The second thing is more significant. The hearing for sanctions against

DCFS for fraud was continued. I saw Walt at the courthouse that morning at which time he informed me that the state was attempting to have the hearing reset. Walt advised me that he was attempting to prevent that but was uncertain which way it would go. Later in the day, I called Ellen and she verified that DCFS had indeed been successful in having it continued. The hearing will now be held sometime in May. Apparently, there was a meeting today with all parties, including the judge, to discuss the matter. It is eye-opening to discover how much more accessible the judge is for the state in these matters as opposed to a public defender appointed to defend a common citizen who has no money for defense. One of the things I have learned is that not all men are created equal in the American justice system. One example of this is an attorney with a certain level of credibility and respect in the courtroom has a much greater chance of impacting the outcome of these type of meetings than let's say a three-year law graduate that is working out of the public defender's office. So you generally have a greater chance of facilitating an outcome from a discussion in chambers if you are represented by a reputable attorney. Having said that, Walt was not able to prevent having this thing continued again even with his influence and local status.

THE BISHOP RETURNS

On Thursday, March 14, 2013, Bishop Nugent appeared at church. This was his second appearance since the brain surgery he had undergone. It was the first time he felt strong enough to sit at the front, whereas on the previous time he had arrived at the last moment at sat quietly in the back. This night would prove to be different. Pastor Massey wanted him to say a word to the congregation, but out of concern for his physical strength, he stepped down from the rostrum and carried a microphone to him. As he approached the bishop, he said, "You don't even have to stand," then he simply handed him the microphone. It was nothing short of phenomenal when instantly, rather than address us, the bishop began to prophecy to the church. During his recovery, his voice has always seemed weak when he would speak, but as he delivered the word of this prophecy, his voice was strong and powerful.

> *Have I not chosen saith the Lord. My word is neither common. My word is not commonplace. But I have spoken in the midst of this place and said I have chosen you. I have appointed you for this hour saith the Lord. For behold in certain places, in certain spots there will be revival such as you have not seen before. I've chosen this place, saith God, that I might pour out the miraculous and the glory and power of God might be manifested. In the midst of famine there shall be plenty. In the midst of harvest, saith God, I shall pour it out in the midst of this church. I chosen you not because of your beauty, I've*

not chosen you because of your wealth, but I have chosen you because I choose whom I will saith God and I've chosen this place that I might shine forth and show my glory in the midst of this generation saith God.

We have known since the beginning that Livingway was destined for great revival. In fact, we have experienced nothing but revival all the years that we have been here. Nonetheless, what we believe is in the mind of God and what this church has in store at this critical time in history is unsurpassed, unprecedented, and unheard of since biblical times. You see, this is not two stories running parallel, but rather, this is one story. The origin of our trouble came from the spirit world. As Bishop Nugent had advised us early on, "We will fight this battle in the prayer room and act it out in the courtroom." It was not an attack against my family only, but rather one aspect of a war launched against the people of God.

THE LOVE OF MONEY

On Sunday morning, April 7, 2013, there was a special article in the Lake Charles American Press covering DCFS's adoption program. The article touted the fact that DCFS had successfully entered seventeen children into adoption during the month of March. It went on to say that DCFS in Louisiana saw a record number of 652 children adopted by 468 families in 2012. It further stated that there are currently 638 children immediately eligible for adoption in the state of Louisiana, 80 of which are located in the Lake Charles region.

What the article did not disclose was the amount of revenue generated by this number of children to DCFS from government agencies. To the casual citizen, the article paints a picture of a wonderful organization that has one sole interest and that is the betterment of children and providing a future and hope to them. When I consider the Gestapo methods that I have witnessed in this case and the deception and bullying that we have been subjected to, then I know that there is more to consider. According to the DCFS News Room, November 21, 2012, issue, located at Louisiana.gov>DCFS>News which is an electronic business news report produced by DCFS and is available to the public, Louisiana DCFS received $ 1.4 million in incentive awards for those 652 children of 2012. To be precise, that was $1,455,596 awarded from the federal government. This is a separate incentive, that is to say, above and beyond normal funding and is provided by the federal government. It is a result of the federal Adoption and

Safe Families Act of 1997 and a reward for DCFS's successes in the adoption program. This federal act allocates $4,000 per child as an added incentive to placing children in adoption. $8,000 is allocated for each child above the age of nine. It is in essence a bonus check for getting more children adopted.

Then there is the federal Social Services Block Grant (SSBG), which supplies funding to the state of Louisiana for social services in a single grant. DCFS is the direct recipient of that money. Louisiana's allotment for Federal Fiscal Year 2011 from this grant was $24,753,353. Now understand that funding is available to DCFS for each child who is eligible for funding according to the standard shown in the SSBG Intended Use Report. According to page 15 of this report, the funding is available for "All children determined by DCFS to be in need of this service."

Excerpt from SSBG Intended Use Report

State Fiscal Year; July 1, 2011–June 30, 2012

State Objectives;

1. *To provide adoptive services to children available for adoption*
2. *To Provide reports to the court on adoption petitions filed in the State*

Eligible Categories WRI: All Children determined by DCFS to be in need of this service

Simply put, the more children they can place into the adoption or foster care programs, the more money is available and who gets placed in these programs is solely or largely up to DCFS and at their discretion within the guidelines of state law and generally subject to court review. All of this is federal money, and we are not even talking yet about state and local funding for these programs. Total funding, which according to the SSBG report includes all federal, state, and local funds, is revealed in a schedule of values shown on page 23 of this report. Total expenditures for DCFS, for the report period of the fiscal year of 2012, from July 1, 2011, through June 30, 2012, was a whopping $239,708,010! This is the total sum of expenditures for DCFS for one year. Of this amount, only $2,207,086 is allocated for administrative services. The amount includes $37,808,021 for the adoption program. Based on the 652 children DCFS claims to have placed in adoption last year, that tabulates to a staggering amount of $ 57,987.76 per child. Also, an unbelievable $139,428,026 was allocated for foster care! Small wonder DCFS immediately pushes to place children in foster care. In addition, there are strong discrepancies between the SSBG Usage Report's total number of children in foster care and adoption as claimed by DCFS in this report when compared to what the same organization reported in their very own Newsroom article. In the SSBG report, DCFS affirms to have 5,760 children in the adoption program and an additional 8,165 in the foster program. On the other hand, DCFS's Newsroom article dated November 21, 2012, makes the following claim.

> DCFS is working each and every day to make connections between potential families and more than 600 foster children who are available for adoption," said DCFS Secretary Suzy Sonnier. "This award reminds us of our success in the last few years matching families and children and of the work we must do to recruit new foster and adoptive families to provide safe and nurturing homes to the more than 4,000 children currently in our foster care system. No child should exit the foster care system without a family."

So what is the true number of children in the foster care and adoption programs and what is the true explanation for the discrepancies? Are the numbers in the SSGB Intended Use Report deliberately inflated to increase the amount of the allocation which converts to more revenue in the hands of the agency?

All of this raises grave questions as to where the money actually goes and what is the true motive for DCFS's aggressiveness toward placing children in foster care or adoption. They will quickly tell you that their first option is reunification with the family, but that is hardly the truth from our view and based on the experiences we have had with them. At the end of the day, there has to be some explanation as to why an organization who on its face is an organization dedicated to improve the lives of disadvantaged children but behind the scene's is committed to winning at any cost and has solely given itself to the tactics observed throughout the course of our case. I conclude as the word of God declares, "The love of money is the root of all evil."

What is most alarming is that while they paint themselves to the public as being saviors of abused children, in reality, they were willing to maliciously and criminally conceal the fact that they had discovered for themselves that my daughter and our family had been telling the truth about Gabe. When Gabe himself confirmed that it was in fact he who self-inflicted his injuries, one would suppose that they must have realized the compromising position they were then placed in and were willing to go to any lengths to conceal that fact from the courts. Those lengths included failing to place the needs of the children above their own selfish interest. While our grandchildren were willingly misdiagnosed and received what can only be described as treatment detrimental to their well-being.

GORDON WINSLOW

Sunday night, April 7, 2013 was a special service at Livingway. Evangelist Gordon Winslow was the guest speaker for the evening. Brother Winslow has ministered at our church numerous times through the years. He has a phenomenal ministry of operating in the gifts of the spirit and is known nationally throughout our organization as a prophet of God. Some time ago, possibly more than a year previous to this night he was ministering in the congregation at Livingway and as he simply followed the leading of the spirit, he declared suddenly, "There is a woman here that has been fighting in court for her two children." He paused and said, "They are going to lose the paperwork." That was all he said. We didn't understand what that could mean but believed most certainly that it pertained to Jaime who was present on that day and in a desperate fight for her two children. When the journal from the foster mom became a part of this story, then we understood this prophecy.

The message that Brother Winslow brought to us on this Sunday evening was that God was declaring "enough." That there were those in our church who had suffered long enough and deliverance was coming tonight. The overall message was just simply that. God had watched the enemies of the people of God oppress them for long enough, and tonight would mark the end of many of our struggles. As the service drew toward a close and as is our custom, the entire congregation moved forward around the altar and began to worship and pray. Kathan, who is my my youngest grandson, had sat with Sherri and I that evening and was now sitting on the front step of the altar. A large man to my left began to worship boisterously, so out of concern for Kathan, I reached down and moved him to my right. When I raised my eyes, Evangelist Winslow was standing before me and nodded to me with a smile. I wasn't sure whether he was assuring me that, yes, he had a word for me or if he was simply saying I did the right thing in moving Kathan. He then said to me, "I want to pray for you." He paused and said, "God told me to." He then laid his hand on my head and began to pray. He said to me. "God says that he's going to restore your house. He said he is going to reward your faithfulness." I believe the word of God. It is enough.

Wednesday, April 10, 2013, brought a change in the wind as it relates to the criminal proceedings against my daughter. As I had long since believed it would, the District Attorney's office is seeking resolution to this case. It is my belief that they, understanding the seriousness of their predicament, are now offering to plea bargain with Jaime. Having started with a whopping thirty-two counts of cruelty to a juvenile levied against Jaime, at a hearing yesterday in criminal court, the special appointed DA made an offer to reduce the charges to one count of simple cruelty to a juvenile with a guilty plea. As a parent, I find myself in a very difficult spot. As I explained to Jaime, for myself, and given all of the known circumstances of this case, I would never plea guilty to anything I had not done. To do so validates, at least in some sense, the charges brought against Jaime and I believe it exonerates the Sheriff's office, DCFS, and District Attorney's office of wrongdoing. As for me, I would face my enemies, trusting God and believing that right would prevail in the end and then we could make everyone accountable for their actions. On the other hand, I am not the one facing prison.

On Thursday, the following day, Murry had a scheduled court hearing. The purpose of this hearing was for the District Attorney to offer Murry a plea bargain. The offer was to be the same as had been offered to Jaime, one count of simple cruelty to a juvenile with a sentence of zero to ten years. Lori Nunn, the new prosecutor, had the paperwork all prepared, but Judge Clayton Davis refused the offer from the state. He dismissed it as premature and stated flatly that Murry's case could wait until there was final resolution on Jaime's case. I took that as a very positive sign. In my view, the District Attorney's office is desperately reaching for any hope they may have of coming away with anything that will help them save face in the public eye. An admission of guilt on any charge from either of them, no matter how much reduced, would be their saving grace. Every time I think about it, I am further appalled that the whole process for the state is about political posturing rather than whether or not the defendant is innocent or guilty.

SENATE BILL 109

The Lake Charles *American Press* on Sunday, April 14, 2013, carried a front-page article covering the story of Jerry and Amanda Spaetgens. They are a young family from Iota, Louisiana, who had lost their three-month-old daughter to Sudden Infant Death Syndrome (SIDS). Jerry, according to the *American Press*, is a respiratory therapist and had tried to revive his daughter but was unsuccessful. Two days after their daughter's funeral, DCFS began an investigation into these people's lives and placed them on a "care plan." Under this plan, they were not allowed to be alone with their other two children without approved adult supervision, meaning that DCFS would have to approve such an adult. I think it fair to say that their investigation could be better described as an invasion. It is appalling that in the good ole USA, an individual could simply be suspected and immediately be stripped of their rights and treated as though their guilt were a foregone conclusion. You should understand the way the process works. DCFS receives a report, then after a brief inquiry into the report, if they feel justified, they take their suspicions to a judge, who will sign an order for them to act, usually based on the agency's recommendation. For example, in our case, for the agency to take Kolten and Kyler from our home, the DCFS worker brought with them a signed order from a judge stating that Kolten and Kyler were being starved, tortured, and burned. Nothing could have been further from the truth, but it immediately became our task to prove it was a false allegation, not the other way around

as we have been told all our lives and as the constitution of the
United States affords American citizens. In cases like ours and

in the case of this family from Iota, an innocent family then
watches while their lives are ripped apart. Their family was
forced to move in with relatives during the entire course of this
investigation, which lasted eight months. In their interview
with the *American Press*, the parents talked about being denied
their parenting rights and roles. Mrs. Spaetgens, in the article,
mentioned not being allowed to take her own children outside
to play or to take them to see Santa or drop the kids at school
without having someone there to supervise the event. Her
description was hauntingly familiar and would have related well
with my daughter's experiences over the course of the last three
years. All of this occurred because of the suspicions of a doctor
who had a history of working with DCFS and had expressed a
suspicion that the baby could possibly have died of shaken baby
syndrome. I instantly sympathized with this family having lived
my own nightmare with dealing with this ruthless organization.

This was very reminiscent to me of the day that the agency
had taken our youngest grandchild from the hospital under the
preposterous allegation of abuse in the hospital by my daughter
on the second day of the child's life. From our family's view,
everything about that incident was suspicious. We reasoned,
since we knew that no such abuse had occurred, then how is it
that DCFS had managed to come up with a "report "of such
abuse. Did they have someone from the hospital working with
their organization providing them with such false allegations,
thus empowering them to move at will? At the time I still could
not imagine a motive for DCFS's intense aggression or their
determination to take our newborn grandchild. It wasn't until
I had knowledge of the strong financial incentives that were in
place for DCFS to place children in adoption and understood
that all of their funding is based on quantities of children, that
any of this made sense. The article in this recent case stated that

Mrs. Spaetgens had begun her own investigation and found similar cases throughout the US and some in Louisiana. It went on to say that she had found one similar abuse claim at the same hospital by the same doctor. I couldn't help but think of Mrs. Spaetgens's other two children and wonder what plans DCFS had been formulating for them.

In response to the horrible events that have occurred in the lives of this family, Sen. Dan "Blade" Morrish, R-Jennings has produced a bill that seeks to prevent parents from being falsely accused of child abuse. Senate Bill 109 would require that more than one opinion and physical exam be performed in any case where child abuse is suspected or alleged. Currently, only one is required. When I factor in my personal observation of this organization and its expert witnesses, then I am certain that such a bill is necessary.

I arrived at the courthouse at approximately 12:50 p.m. The date was April 22, 2013. I was there to attend a pretrial conference to hear a plea offer from the District Attorney's office. The prosecution had been instructed by Judge Clayton Davis in the last hearing to prepare their best offer by the time of this conference. After a brief wait, Judge Davis entered the courtroom and the customary "all rise" was sounded by the bailiff. Lori Nunn, the recently assigned District Attorney, along with Detective Mike Primeaux, was seated at the front, to the right, at the prosecutor's table. Walt was to the left and Jaime and I were seated behind him in the area for observers. There were a couple of brief matters that were addressed by Judge Davis and then he came to the matter at hand, the Jaime Day case. Walt requested a meeting in chambers to discuss the plea bargain being offered by the state to which Judge Davis agreed. Jaime and I remained seated and whispered, discussing various aspects of the case while Walt, the judge, and Assistant District Attorney Lori Nunn retired to chambers. When they returned, there was no discussion. Judge Davis simply said "So we have decided to go back to the original date of August 20 for trial." The prosecution began, "Your Honor, we would like to note for the record that we brought a plea offer for—" Judge Davis interrupted her and said, "I see no reason to include your offer in the record. She is not accepting your offer so there is no need." She quickly objected and stated with more emphasis that she would like to have her offer on the record. Judge Davis turned to Walt and asked, "What do you say, Mr. Sanchez?" To which Walt replied, "That is up to you, Your Honor." Judge Davis then stated, "I see no reason for the plea offer to be in the record." End of discussion.

After the proceedings were dismissed, Walt met with us outside the courthouse on the sidewalk and briefed us on the chambers meeting. Their offer had been for a guilty plea of one count of cruelty to a juvenile; they would recommend a five-year prison term. When Judge Davis asked what Walt's response was to the offer, he explained to him, "Your Honor, I have a factually innocent client. You know I don't try many of these, but I intend to try this one." What Walt said next should not have been surprising. He told us that in the discussion in chambers, he had made mention of the journal at which point Mrs. Nunn informed them of her intent to have the journal suppressed as evidence in the criminal trial. Judge Davis at that point interjected, saying, "I am not going to inform the jury of the journal's existence, but how do you intend to prevent the testimony of all of the lay witnesses surrounding the journal?" This was a very good question because by now numerous people had specific knowledge of the journal and its content, and Mrs. Semien who authored the journal was one of our key witnesses for the defense. My question to Walt was, is it possible for her to succeed in having the journal suppressed? To which he shook his head and replied to me, "When Mrs. Semien testifies, then the journal is in because it is part of her testimony." I felt very assured that Walt knew what he was talking about. But as one might expect, I was further appalled as I realized I was experiencing firsthand what I stated in the preface of this story, when I said that participants of our current judicial system were not interested in what is the truth. Here they are, perfectly willing to suppress extremely compelling evidence that directly contradicts their case in order to obtain a conviction. They are willing to do this with total disregard to the harm their false allegations have brought on an innocent woman, her children, and her extended family. By now, they can no longer believe with any conviction that she is in fact guilty, but that simply does not factor in to determine their path forward. It is as the retired security guard at the courthouse stated to me early on, "Anything for a conviction," that is the policy.

After reading the *American Press* article on the young family from Iota who had lost their child to SIDS, I did a search of all the people in Louisiana by the name of Spaetgens. I made an attempt to locate their family and was almost immediately able for find a cousin to Jerry Spaetgens by just going down the list dialing each Spaetgens until I got an answer. I explained to the girl that answered that my family was involved with a case similar to theirs and would like to speak with someone from their family. On Tuesday April 23, 2013, at exactly 1:30 p.m., my cell phone rang and it was Amanda Spaetgens calling. I had a very enlightening conversation with her. Afterward, she called Sherri and continued the conversation. Amanda is spearheading the effort to have Dan Morrish's Senate Bill 109 passed and was to be traveling to Baton Rouge in a couple of weeks with a group of supporters to further this effort. We agreed that the following week, we would make plans to meet with her family to compare notes. A number of families have come forward with similar stories of corruption in the DCFS organization. I purposed to collect more details as they became available.

Men's conference 2013 was a special time for me. I had phoned Bishop Nugent some weeks earlier to offer to drive for him if he indeed intended to attend the conference. Historically, he had always been a part of the annual Tioga,

Louisiana, event. He and I had agreed that if his recovery was well enough along that we would travel together. I must admit that I had an ulterior motive in that I was covetous of the time spent with the Bishop. One can always hope to be given some unique insight or perhaps a word from God if you spend much time with him. Besides that, there is no man I would rather spend a few days with than him.

We left on a Thursday morning and made the ninety mile trip to Tioga, arriving in the early afternoon. It is my usual custom to fry fish for the event and we usually have a large group of men from Livingway attend. This year was no exception. Friday morning, while most of the men attended morning services, I and a couple of other guys spent our pre-lunch time preparing sixty pounds of catfish fillets along with hush puppies and French fries for every one to eat. It was a wonderful time of fellowship, which I immensely enjoyed.

It was the message of the evening delivered by Reverend J. A. Osborne that made the trip most complete for me. He preached a message from the story of Jacob, Rachel, and Leah. He titled his sermon, "In the morning, it was Leah." For me, it was one of those messages where you might say, "I felt like I was the only one there." Rev. Osborne was hilarious in his opening remarks and had the entire audience roaring with laughter. He then expounded on the horror of the event that had befallen Jacob in the fact that Laban had deceived him and caused him to marry Leah, the homely older sister, to his beautiful Rachel for whom he had worked seven years for the right to marry. It was a powerful message on how that he would never have chosen Leah yet he found himself married to her. And then he brought out the fact that even though he was allowed to marry Rachel in return for an additional seven years of work, it was Leah who was the fruitful one in his life. It was she whose son's names had the most meaning. She had the most sons. And she produced Levi from whom the entire Levitical priesthood would come and Judah, the tribe through which the Messiah would come. In contrast, Rachel, whom Jacob had in fact loved while despising Leah, had produced much less fruit in his life. The message was simply the thing that befalls us in this life that we least enjoy. That thing that we might even hate because it brings us the most disappointment or pain will likely produce the most fruit in our lives.

This morning, I was in prayer. Even though we have had custody of our grandchildren now for almost ten months, our trouble is far from over. Our finances have been devastated. I met with our bank yesterday to discuss our chapter 7 bankruptcy. There is a potential to lose mine and our daughter's homes and automobiles. The attorney fees have well exceeded two hundred thousand dollars and Jaime is still facing the possibility of spending years in prison. The pressure is tremendous. So as I sat in prayer in the front room of my home, I began to worship the Lord. As I worshiped, the spirit came down and I found myself in the only real shelter that I have access to. In truth, it is the only real shelter available to man. As I sat there and worshipped and prayed in the spirit and the power of the Holy Ghost overwhelmed me, I said within myself, this is the one thing that cannot be taken from me. This is the one place where I can hide and nothing can touch me. I am so thankful for the presence of God!

On April 30, 2013, Amanda Spaetgens traveled to Baton Rouge and spoke before a Louisiana State Senate Committee in support of Senate Bill 109. I read her Facebook post after the hearing in which she stated,

> *I truly believe that I had angels with me and I felt the prayers. I felt a strength I had never felt before. As I began to speak, I noticed the previously noisy room was quiet as I spoke. Everyone was hearing our story! Amazing the power I felt today. Despite an opposition towards the bill our testimony and Dan's plea to the committee assisted in getting this Bill pass through the Judiciary Committee.*

Oh, if we can only get past the politics and the rhetoric that is being used in this system! The Lake Charles *American Press* carried an article on Sunday, May 12, 2013, titled "Senate Approves Morrish Child Abuse Bill." According to the article, the Senate had unanimously approved Senate Bill 109. The article expounded on how the bill would provide an option for a parent to pay for an independent medical exam in the event a health care practitioner issues a mandatory report of child abuse. According to the *American Press*, there was an immediate opposition to the bill coming from John Wyble, executive director of Louisiana Court Appointed Special Advocates for Children, saying, "The measure creates additional layers of trauma to children who have been abused. A second exam can be very traumatic." He concedes, "The bill is well intentioned, but we have to maintain focus and attention to the children." So should the public extrapolate from this that DCFS cannot be mistaken and should the obvious fact that they often get it wrong and innocent people's lives are destroyed be ignored or does it make more since to find a solution that addresses both sides of the issue.?

Well, not wanting to prejudge Mr. Wyble or his intent, yet from the perspective of someone who has been there, Mr. Wyble's statements are very reminiscent of the ones I heard repeatedly used by the agency during their fraudulent claims against my daughter. In their extreme drive to win at any cost, it was obvious that the pretense of "putting the children first" was a weapon they had no scruples about misusing. A prime example is the state was adamantly apposed to having our grandchildren testify in court. They claimed that such testimony would be too traumatic for the children. Accordingly, they pressed the court to have them testify via a pre-recorded video. What this does for them is remove the possibility of a cross examination by the defense. When you remember that the two most influential expert witnesses in this case for the state have been caught in fraud and that these two witnesses are experts in the fields of psychology and child counseling respectively and that they had sole possession of the psyche and thought process of our grandchildren for more than two years with absolutely no influence from the family, then they being able and willing to coerce and influence them into a testimony conducive to the state's case is certainly possible and/ or likely.

Another example would be when CASA's Gwen Thompson appeared in court or at a FTC (family team conference), she has been quoted as declaring with an air of appall and strong emphasis, saying, "These children have been in foster care for two years now and this family has done nothing to attempt to provide a future for them! They should be allowed to get on with their lives! This is just not fair to the children!" While this sounded good and I am sure had its intended effect on at least some of the hearers, it was an obvious attempt to propel the children toward adoption. All the while, the reality was, Mrs. Thompson was fully aware, that everyone in this family had done everything in their power, everything that was ask of them by DCFS, the courts, or anyone associated with this case in our attempt to successfully restore our homes. We had exhausted all of our prayers, emotions, and finances in a constant fight to regain the possession of our grandchildren and provide them with a good home. So here is the real picture, a team of professionals pretend to have the best interest of the children at heart while they blatantly ignore our efforts to provide exactly that. Additionally, they willingly ignore the children's constant request to come home. This simply exposes the extreme aggression toward winning and the methodology they are willing to use. It also lends itself to the notion that there might possibly be a not so obvious motive for their aggressions. Stunning!

May 22, 2013, was significant in that it brought about the passing of Senate Bill 109. The bill passed in the Louisiana House of Representatives by a vote of 88-1. It is now headed to Governor Bobby Jindal's desk for signature. This bill would serve to protect innocent families from wrongful allegations by DCFS. It would provide better restraints on a system and an organization that in its origination was designed to protect children, but as is usually the case when men are provided power without regulation, in the end, it brought about corruption and failure. In the future, when an allegation of abuse is brought by DCFS, there will be a requirement of at least two medical opinions before action can be taken against the family. A family will be given the prerogative of soliciting a third party to provide a medical opinion.

SANCTIONS

The second thing this day brought was the sanctions hearing. Unlike previous visits, my wife and I have made to the family court with Judge Bradberry presiding, in today's hearing, there were few people present. This is as opposed to a normally very crowded courtroom where it is often difficult to find a place to sit. On this day, Judge Bradberry was to hear arguments for and against the motion to impose sanctions on DCFS for their actions or lack thereof in the matter of Mrs. Semien's journal. Today, we were allowed to sit in the courtroom and listen to the proceedings. Murry and Nita Hanks were also present at this hearing, each represented by their respective counsel. Nita arrived in chains, escorted by a Calcasieu sheriff's deputy having been transported from jail. I suppose, she, being the maternal mom of Gabe, was the justification for the need to have her present. I was uncertain of the reason for her most recent incarceration.

I have always been fascinated by the courtroom, and today was no different. The basis for our motion for sanctions was the Louisiana Code of Civil Procedure Article 863 which provides specifically "for the imposition of sanctions against a party or an attorney who signs any false pleading filed. The signature of an attorney or party shall constitute a certification that he has read the pleading; that the pleading is well grounded in fact to the best of his knowledge, information, and belief formed after reasonable inquiry; that it is warranted by existing law or a good faith argument for the extension, modification, or reversal of existing law; and that the pleading is not interposed for any improper purpose."

The defense for the state was led by a duo of attorneys, Mr. Tom Sanders and Mr. Nick Pizzolatto. I listened intently as they took turns laying out their case for why sanctions should not be imposed on their client. The synopsis of their entire case rested on three principles. Yet it seemed that they did not have a single strategy but rather three separate things they would sling against the wall and hope that one of them would stick. First of all, Mr. Pizzolatto opined that this case was the wrong forum for sanctions, and consequently, the article for sanctions should not apply. From my view, his was actually the only position on the state's side that held any validity in this case. I took the time to research this law, and even with a laymen's understanding of the law, I could see the strength of his argument. Specifically, he argued that no pleadings had been filed by his client, therefore CCP Art. 863 did not apply. There was no argument from Mr. Pizzolatto that his client had not committed fraud, but rather that this case was simply the wrong forum for sanctions, given the fact that no signed pleadings were involved.

Secondly, Mr. Sanders alleged that their was no clear evidence that their client had in fact had possession of Mrs. Semien's journal or that they had intentionally withheld it from discovery. This was a preposterous position given the known facts of the case.

The last one was the real kicker. Mr. Sanders moved for Walt to testify. Walt agreed so he found himself in the precarious position of being both counsel and witness in the same case. Mr. Sanders made an attempt to show Walt as incompetent. His argument was a continuation of a previous argument in this case, namely Memorandum in Opposition to a New Trial filed by Steve Berniard on behalf of the State in March of 2012. Mr. Berniard had argued in that motion that Jaime Day (represented by counsel) had plenty of opportunity to retrieve the journal from DCFS and had failed to do so. An ironic and noteworthy point is that Mr. Berniard had also acknowledged in the same motion that the District Attorney's office had in fact obtained the journal from Mrs. Ann Landry who in her own sworn testimony said She got the journal from DCFS. In the face of all of this, DCFS continues to deny ever having had possession of the complete journal. DCFS was apparently willing to excuse themselves of the responsibility of "candor toward the tribunal."

Mr. Sanders also attempted to suggest to the court that Walt had the information found in the journal at a much earlier point in time than stated by him or if he didn't, it was only due to his own lack of due diligence, as though to say, "We were guilty, but you didn't catch us at it so it's your fault." They made reference to court records from 2010 that record Walt questioning Dr. Charles Murphy. The questions Walt ask Dr. Murphy in the record seemed to infer in the mind of Mr. Sanders, that at the time of those proceedings, Walt was in possession of at least the knowledge of the content of the journal, which if true, would fly in the face of Walt's claim of receiving the journal and knowledge of its content for the first time in early November of 2011. The thing that Walt was actually in possession of at the time of his questioning Dr. Murphy was knowledge that someone close to the case had suggested that Mrs. Semien at that time in 2010 was concerned about Gabe having made overt threats against Mr. Semien. This concern, we eventually discovered, was born out of an incident recorded in the journal, where Gabe had intentionally scratched his own face up pretty badly and had told one of the other foster children that he intended to report it to DCFS and say that Mr. Semien had done it to him.

For Walt to have this limited information was an entirely different thing than having the entire journal or knowledge of its specific content. All in all, Mr. Sanchez made an excellent witness. As part of his testimony, he made new reference to the December 20, 2011, hearing where Mr. Dilks and Mrs. Landry testified as to their possession of the journal. In Walt's testimony, he declared again that Mr. Dilks's testimony in that hearing constituted perjury on the point of if and when he had possession of the journal and knowledge of its content.

When Walt's turn came to redirect, he was simply superb. He again made a very compelling case of the fraud committed by DCFS. He made it clear that they not only had possession of the journal all along, but that Mrs. Semien in a sworn affidavit had provided testimony of their specific knowledge of incidents recorded in the journal, including dates, times, and conversations Mrs. Semien had with all parties during scheduled visits to their respective offices. It was during these visits that she had made copies of the journal for DCFS, Mr. Larry Dilks, and Mrs. Landry. Walter successfully reiterated to the court the moral and legal responsibility that DCFS had in terms of providing "candor before the tribunal" in cases set before the court. At the conclusion, he raised his voice and practically shouted to the court, "Your Honor, these are the very people that you relied on to provide you accurate and truthful information in deciding the future of Kolten and Kyler Day!"

At the end of the hearing and as our crew boarded the elevator, I was remembering how Walt had received the journal in a banker's box of discovery on November 3, 2011. I asked him the obvious question even though I knew the answer, "Walt, where did the District Attorney's office get the journal?" To which he replied with a chuckle, "They got it from Ann Landry, who say's she got it from DCFS." And DCFS denies ever having the complete journal, while Mrs. Semien claims to have provided it to all three. Follow that trail and you will find many walls of denial and obstructive lies. Judge Bradberry had promised to rule shortly, which we took to mean in the next few days. Walt's comments to me were that he couldn't be certain whether or not the judge would award sanctions, and even if he did, we would likely lose those in the Third Circuit Court of Appeals. He said the federal lawsuit would likely be the event that would produce any actual compensation to us. He said that the thing we should be glad about is the amount of exposure we were producing of the criminal activity of DCFS. I continually remind myself, God is in control, and in the end, He will determine the outcome of any of these events.

THE LANDRY REPORT

The afternoon of June 19, 2013, I was in my office reviewing some of the old files from the case. I came across a letter from Ann Landry to Brandi Green, which served as a report on Gabe's condition and a recommendation for treatment. It was dated September 20, 2010. One thing we can conclude with certainty is that Ann Landry had specific knowledge of Gabe's self-inflictions while in the foster mom's care and of his threats to self-harm himself at the time of this report. Her recommendation in this report coincides perfectly with the content of the journal that Mrs. Semien claims to have provided to Mrs. Landry. In her sworn affidavit, she specifically cites August 4, 2010, as a date she copied an updated version of the journal while on a visit in Mrs. Landry's office with Gabe.

[Excerpt from Landry's Report]

Treatment Recommendations:

OCS issues specified in Initial Referral Form:

1. *Can Gabe learn coping skills to deal with his abuse? Yes, with ongoing therapy as well as a strong support system. His support system needs to include his foster parents, physicians, OCS staff, and school system.*
2. *Can Gabe be considered safe around himself and others? Again, this will depend strongly on those listed in # 1. Gabe has used the threat of self-harm and the*

use of actual self-harm to gain attention. Self-harm has also served Gabe as a way to express his feelings and as an attempt to get relief from his pain, real or perceived.

I forwarded this excerpt to Walt in an e-mail, and in less than ten minutes, he responded, exclaiming it to be a great point. He copied his response to Ellen, advising her to find the report and make sure that there was a copy of it in the file for both Landry and Green. He stated that he would be intending to use it as an exhibit in trial and at closing.

It is troubling to consider how an individual upon whom the family court system relies upon for information and expert opinion could have this knowledge and in the face of the extremities of a case like ours fail to report it to the court. In her position, she would most certainly realize the significance of this information to the judge and to the case in general. She would have to understand the importance of knowing that Gabe's current behavior mirrored with absolute perfection the testimony of my daughter and family. But this expert willingly withheld this obviously crucial information in her testimony. So I ask, what was her motive?

I mentioned to Bishop Nugent at prayer some time ago that Melanie Smith Daley had been disbarred and he made a motion with both hands as you would twist something in your hand from each end. He said to me, "God is turning it around." I know in the end, God will prevail. We would be thankful if final resolution to the whole matter were simply that we had gotten our grandchildren back. The main thing is that the Lord worked the miracle to bring them home, but I don't think for one minute that he is finished. I truly believe God had a very large plan and we have only witnessed its beginning.

THE GEORGE ZIMMERMAN CASE

On Saturday July 13, 2013, the George Zimmerman case was decided by a jury of six women in Sanford, Florida. Trayvon Martin, a seventeen-year-old boy from Miami, had tragically lost his life in an altercation with Mr. Zimmerman who was serving as a community night watchman in a gated community. Crowds waited outside the Seminole County Criminal Justice Center until roughly ten o'clock p.m. to hear the verdict after more than fifteen hours of deliberation. Mr. Zimmerman had been placed under a second degree murder indictment in the death of Trayvon by an apparently politically motivated state attorney by the name of Angela Cory. The overwhelming consensus among legal professionals was that she acted under public and political pressure.

As in the case of certain types of storms, the tragic death of Trayvon could probably be best described as the coming together of specific and certain elements at the precise moment so as to create an explosive result. In this case, it brought about the early end of a young man's life. Setting aside all of our outside opinions, the truth is that this case and all of the facts of the case were carefully examined by a jury, and consequently, Mr. George Zimmerman was found not guilty of any of the charges levied against him. We all are bound together by a common thread, which is our American citizenry. By this common denominator, we are responsible to respect the outcome of this trial whether or not it was to our liking. The thing that is troubling for me and the reason I mention this case at this time is the circumstances that brought about the indictment in the first place.

The details say that under extreme political pressure, a specially appointed and apparently overzealous state attorney Angela Corey bypassed the normal avenue of a grand jury indictment and simply indicted Mr. Zimmerman on the evidence, which was sketchy and circumstantial at best. This was the same evidence that her predecessor in this case had reviewed and determined there was not sufficient evidence to warrant an indictment. In addition, during trial, it was discovered that at the time of the indictment, she had in her possession and withheld exculpatory evidence that would likely have cleared George Zimmerman. Her apparent reason for withholding this evidence was that the evidence was contrary to the charges she was attempting to bring against Mr. Zimmerman. Then, in the course of the trial, it became apparent that the state did not have a sufficient case against Mr. Zimmerman to convict him. Consequently, there was an attempt to throw a lesser charge of manslaughter on the wagon at the last minute. Anything for a conviction! So for me, here we have another perfect example of what our American justice system has become. As I sat transfixed and watch this thing unfold on television, I listened to the Fox News "experts" talk about how a prosecutor is obligated to be first and foremost in pursuit of justice under the law, derived by the evidence. They pointedly exclaimed, "It cannot be about just winning." But here we are in 2013, and in at least two separate Southern State Court venues that I know of, we find a willingness to deliberately and maliciously withhold evidence either on the part of the state itself or its expert witnesses in an effort to affect the outcome of a trial. To prosecute any individual in America solely because of public opinion or under the influence of political pressure or under a pretense of believing in their guilt while withholding evidence to the contrary is simply wrong. We have a lot of wrong in the American justice system.

NEARING THE END

It's July 22, 2013, and summer is well underway in southwest Louisiana. Sweltering heat and high humidity are the everyday expectations. I phoned Ellen Anderson from my office today to confirm that the criminal trial set for August 20 had been continued. Jaime had mentioned a few days earlier that it appeared she would not be going to trial in August. Ellen confirmed two points. The trial was reset for November, and a hearing would be held in August to review the additional indictment of abuse against Kolten in the swimming pool incident. There are days when I truly feel the frustration of living with the weight of this trial hanging over the heads of my family. It seems so very long ago that we sat in Walter Sanchez's office for the first time and paid him his initial retainer. I often wonder, "When will it ever end?" and then I remind myself that God in His wisdom has a perfect plan with perfect timing. When a man or woman determines to place their trust in God and resolve themselves to wait on him, it is certain to succeed. Success may not come in the fashion that we first imagine, but God never fails and the outcome is always to our benefit. We just have to remember that just as children generally cannot determine what is best for them in deciding their own future, so we obviously do not have enough insight or wisdom to chart the course of our own lives.

The last few weeks have been eventful. Our new trial date has been set for November 4, 2013. Jaime called a few days ago upset at the wording in a new subpoena for her to appear for a hearing on August 20, 2013. In it, the District Attorney lays out justification for his indictment and describes how that the incident in the pool was an example and an indicator of the extreme aggression that Jaime had toward children. Now consider this. The District Attorney has made an astronomical stretch to get an indictment out of this swimming pool incident. Even one of the boys' state-appointed attorneys, after reviewing the evidence, said, "If anyone can be indicted on this evidence, then we had all better go home and hug our children because none of us are safe." He knew as well as all of us that the incident in the pool was a description of what has occurred at hundreds if not thousands of family swimming events where the whole family is playing in the water. I remember as a child countless times when swimming with friends and family how as boys we would have war, which amounted to us wrestling, having chicken fights, and even holding one another under the water. We played rough. I suppose we were all guilty of felonies and simply did not know it. Then consider that while we cannot be certain as to exactly how long the District Attorney had possession of exculpatory evidence in the form of Mrs. Semien's journal, we do know they did have it. We know for a fact that they have had it since before November 3, 2011, and possibly as early as August 2010. These guys are really grasping at straws to attempt to "stuff the journal under the mattress," then try to achieve a felony conviction on a minor swimming pool incident in which a mother was simply responding to a child's playful teasing and the only evidence of that event is a conversation between children overheard by a foster parent two years after the fact.

Secondly, DCFS has made a new attempt to involve themselves into our lives. On August 7, 2013, an investigator from their office appeared at Jaime's door, alleging to have a report that she was using mind-altering drugs, staying up for days selling and obtaining street drugs and thereby endangering Kathan's well-being. She was requested to submit to an immediate drug screen to which she complied and tested negative for all possible narcotics or pharmaceuticals. Her prescription medicine was detected in the quick test, but was of course of no consequence. We cannot at this point with any certainty know who made such of a report or for that matter if anyone actually did.

Jaime and Murry have been separated since the day of their arrest. Murry had immediately distanced himself from her and moved to the side of his family and law enforcement when they initially began to pressure him to do so. In recent months, all indications were that he had moved back to our side since Walt had agreed to represent him in the federal lawsuit against DCFS. Their divorce became final on August 8, 2012. We have reason to suspect that Murry is involved with these latest allegations, given recent threats he has made against Jaime to make such a report to DCFS. If so, then this would be the outfall of the antics of a jealous ex-husband. I remember a day last year when I sat with Murry in our backyard and said to him, "Murry, you don't know whose side you are on. You are like one of these lizards that I often see back here. You change your colors based on your surroundings." At the end of the day, he just seems to always do what he thinks will most benefit himself.

After the finalization of our bankruptcy, we realized that whether or not it was to our liking, we would not be financially able to allow the boys to return to Hamilton the following school year. After agonizing over this for weeks, the decision was made that they would enroll in public school for their third and fourth grade years respectively. So on August 14, 2013, they had their first day of school at Dolby Elementary in Lake Charles, Louisiana. Both boys seem to like their new school. Sherri attended orientation with the boys and she says she is very encouraged by what she sees. I have always been a big proponent of organized Christian education while finding great reason for pause when confronted with the notion of exposing children to modern-day public school systems. Whether we realize it or not, there is a very aggressive movement in America to impose modern values on children and the public school system is the vehicle of choice for this movement. These values are often in direct opposition to the word of God.

Walt has been seemingly unavailable for my calls for some time. I have called numerous times in the last two or three months and he has not been available, neither has he returned any calls. I reason that you can hardly blame him since he hasn't received any payment from us in at least eighteen months. However, on the other hand, we are the clients and can hardly be expected to remain in the dark.

On Friday, August 16, 2013, I was finally able to reach him in his office. The conversation I had with him seemed to validate the essence of my inference in this entire story. My first question to Walt was in reference to line items I had noticed on his most recent invoice. Apparently, Walt had been in recent meetings with Lori Nunn and Judge Davis. They had met to discuss whether we would opt to have a jury trial or to simply allow Judge Davis to conduct the trial. Walt advised me that we have that option, but he was not inclined to place the case totally in the hands of Judge Davis. He said, "I believe that Judge Davis is a good man and a fair judge, but he is also extremely politically charged and I can't completely trust him not to decide, 'I am going to convict her of something,' as if to say, he might feel obligated to not leave the prosecutors empty-handed." I may not be quoting his exact words, but the spirit of what he was saying was that he would not risk Jaime's future on the hope that Judge Davis would be totally fair and impartial. It was clear to me, that as an extremely experienced trial lawyer like Walt Sanchez, having spent thirty years working in the Calcasieu Parish Fourteenth District Court that he believed that one should expect or, at the very least, realize there was a possibility of a judge making a deal or providing favors to prosecutors in a criminal trial. This is exactly the spirit of our observation of this "Darker Side of Justice" shown apparent in this story.

Walt also reassured me that the District Attorney's office was not interested in dropping the case. He said to me that they had now made it abundantly clear that they would rather try the case and lose than to back out now. I submit to you again that their decision is not based on a confidence of winning, the evidence or belief in Jaime's guilt, but simply a question. Which position cast them in the best light politically? Walt said to me, "We are going to trial in November. I am literally spending hundreds of hours in reviewing all documents in preparation." He encouraged me to continue to scan the file and forward anything I think noteworthy to his office.

It weighs heavy upon one's mind to arrive home from work to discover that your nine-year-old grandson has been subpoenaed to testify in a criminal trial proceeding against that child's own mother who is your daughter. This is precisely the occurrence on Thursday, August 22, 2013. Lori Nunn had issued the subpoena, which read State of Louisiana verses Jaime Brooks Day, Case: 15589-VC-2010, To: J.K.D. c/o Gerald and Sherri Price. We were summoned to appear in the 14th Judicial Court on the fourth day of September in the year of our Lord 2013 at 9:00 a.m., for the purpose of testifying in this cause. The hearing scheduled for the previous Tuesday had been cancelled due to the fact that Mrs. Potts had been hospitalized and was unavailable to testify.

At this moment, there are crossroads of emotions that arise within me. My first concern is for Kolten and how having to go back to court and sit with strangers and answer questions relevant to all of this trouble will impact him. The next concern is how much of his testimony is real and how much of it will be the result of Ann Landry's and Larry Dilks's impositions upon him. We are obviously anxious as to what impact Kolten's testimony will ultimately have on Jaime's case. As a practice, we simply have not discussed the case with the boys. I did tell Kolten that they wanted him to testify and told him not to worry about it just answer any questions the best he can. I told him, "Just tell the truth."

I phoned Walt's office to inform him of the subpoena. As usual, he was not available, but he rang me back around mid-afternoon on Friday. When he called, I advised him of the subpoena and learned that he wanted to set up a meeting between Jaime and Kolten prior to the court date. The following Monday, I shot him an e-mail advising him of the date scheduled for this hearing.

On Saturday, August 31, 2013, I drove Jaime, Kolten, and myself to Walt's office for this meeting. It turned out to be a stressful day. Being Saturday, the entrance doors to the building were locked as they always are on the weekend. We called Walt and he made the trip down the elevator to let us in. He was dressed casually in a sports shirt and shorts. After the elevator ride to the tenth floor, we made light conversation in Walt's office for a short while, allowing Kolten to get comfortable. Kolten was especially smitten with Walt's large mounted binoculars through which you could view the city for several miles in two directions. After a few minutes, Walt asked Jaime and me to excuse him and Kolten for a while to allow them to talk. We waited in the kitchen. When their visit was over, he brought Kolten out and Walt and Jaime went back into his office for a meeting to discuss the case. As expected, he advised Jaime to not discuss their meeting with anyone, including me. The problem with that is that first of all, I know too much about the case. I know what we should hope for, what we should dread, and what we should probably expect. I also know my daughter and could easily read the mail when I saw how distraught she was after the meeting. When we arrived back at my home, as Kolten and Jaime were exiting and heading in the house, I rolled my window down and asked Jaime to talk. My intent was to discuss an issue concerning the home she currently occupied, which belongs to our family, but Jaime assumed I had a question about the case. She said to me that she couldn't discuss her meeting with Walt, but in tears, she blurted that if Kolten testifies, "I'm done." She then looked at me with brokenness and tears and said, "But I say now and I will say till the day I die that I

did not do the things that I am being accused of!" She didn't have
to tell me that, I knew for certain she was innocent of the crimes
she was being accused of.

This is the point at which I made a mistake. In a knee-jerk
action, I called Walt from my cell phone. He never answers my
calls anymore, so when he immediately answered, I was surprised.
I opened the conversation by making what was in reality a
misquote. My intent was to qualify what I was about to do and
that was to direct Walt's attention to Ann Landry's report and
recommendation to Brandi Green. I intended to point out that
Kolten did not have a testimony against Jaime for two full years,
and it was only after many sessions with Ann Landry and the
constant sibling meetings, which she facilitated, that he began to
suggest he had actually seen Gabe harmed. But the only thing that
registered with Walt was that Jaime had discussed their meeting
with me when I suggested to him she was concerned about Kolten's
testimony. He was instantly livid and began to yell and curse on
the phone that what was discussed in that meeting could only
remain attorney-client privilege if it was never discussed outside
of that meeting. He yelled, "Monica Lewinsky's mom was forced
to testify in criminal court because she had specific knowledge
relevant to the case through conversations with Monica and they
were able to impeach the president of the United States!" Jaime
had not actually discussed the meeting with me, except that one
general statement, and she said nothing to me that I would not
have deduced anyway given her demeanor after the meeting.
Nevertheless, he was extremely angry.

I still do not know any details about what Kolten said to Walt,
but imagine the position we were in. We hugged Kolten and said,
"You did so good! We're so proud of you!" Not wanting to harm
him in any way, but at the same time, we realize the weight his
testimony would have in a court of law before a jury. I am fully
persuaded that if Kolten is actually saying that he saw Jaime harm
Gabe, then that is a consequence of his having been programmed

by the state's team. If not, then nothing else in this story makes sense. None of the known facts add up. All of the self-infliction and the bizarre behavior the family witnessed, the repetition of that same behavior in foster care, the record in Mrs. Semien's journal, Gabe's own recorded threats and admissions, none of it makes sense if Jaime is in fact guilty. And finally, the facts I know personally, through my own observations, are all nullified.

This one thing I do know. No matter how great the pain, no matter how dark the night, no matter the fierceness of the wind blowing against you in the ship of life, if God made a promise to you, then it is certain that he can and will keep His promises. We will often measure in our minds whether or not we should expect for God to keep His promises based on our performance. It is as though we have a mentality that says to us that God has a constant measuring tool on us to determine whether or not we are worthy of His blessings. I believe that is a gross mistake. God is not impressed with our strengths, nor surprised at our failures. He knew everything there was to know about us when He made the promise. He said to my family, "I have a plan and in the end I win, I will lead you to victory if you will trust Me." I have to remind myself that He is an eternal God and sees all the way to the end of the road. He is not limited as we are in that we can only see yesterday and today. If in fact we are not vindicated of all charges in this case, it will not mean that God has failed to keep His promises. It will only mean that God's plan has not yet been fully implemented and He is not finished. We may have to wait until eternity to understand, but we must trust God!

PRETRIAL HEARINGS

Wednesday, September 4, 2013, finally came around. At 8:45 a.m., we arrived at Walt's office. Almost as soon as we got there, he was ready to leave, so we rode the elevator back to the ground and walked over to the main courthouse. We entered the doors in the rear, and the scenario was much the same as the last time we were in Judge Davis's courtroom. Lori Nunn and another young woman from the District Attorney's office were to our right along with Mike Primeaux as Jaime, Kolten, and I sat immediately behind Walt. The major difference was that a television monitor was set up, the intended use for which was to view the prerecorded video of Kolten testifying concerning the alleged swimming incident

Lori Nunn walked over to the bench where we were sitting, greeted Kolten, and asked if she could speak with him for a little while. Walt turned around to reassure Kolten, saying, "Kolten, go with Ms. Lori, she is a nice lady. She just has a few questions for you." Kolten obligingly got up and followed her out of the courtroom. After their visit, she returned and announced to the court that she would not be calling Kolten to testify. In a couple of moments, Kolten reentered the courtroom and announced he had just been visiting with Mrs. Roxanne Potts. It should not have come as a surprise to learn that she was present. The prosecutor had apparently wanted to compare notes between Mrs. Potts and Kolten to verify that their stories were similar. It was fairly obvious that after questioning Kolten, Mrs. Nunn was not inclined to put him on the stand.

Mrs. Nunn's next move to have all present sequestered. We were then ask to leave and directed to a small room to the side of the courtroom where there was a table and a television. There was a deck of cards on the table so we played cards and chatted with Mrs. Potts while we waited as though we didn't know she was a state witness to testify against Jaime. In a few moments, another of the state witnesses entered the room. This time, it was Murry Day. Here he was again, the chameleon, prepared to testify for the state against Jaime. One of the things that is very telling in all of this is the letters Murry wrote Jaime during his incarceration. In those, he alludes to his deep love for her. He acknowledges her innocence and talks openly about them resuming their lives once all of the trouble is over. He tells how sorry he is that all of this has happened to her and declares that he knows she is innocent and a great mom. All of this is so completely opposite of what he was willing to testify for the state in exchange of a guarantee that he would not serve any jail time.

But in the end, Murry never actually testified that day, which according to Jaime was one of Walt's strongest arguments at the hearing. Walt asked Judge Davis to consider that the state had opted to not have their own witness testify, which was indicative of how uncertain they were in their position on the pool incident.

I was mildly disappointed not to be allowed in the courtroom. I had wanted to record each testimony, but that was not to be. But after the hearing, on the way down the elevator, Walt gave me a knowing glance with a nod, and it was easy to discern that he was pleased. As we exited the courthouse onto the street, Walt asked to speak with me, so we took a few steps out of hearing down the sidewalk. He first of all apologized for losing his temper on Saturday. He then explained to me that we had just won a large victory. He said that Judge Davis had basically thrown the swimming pool incident out. He had opined that the evidence was not sufficient to define whether or not a crime had been committed and he could with no certainty establish what had happened if anything. So the swimming pool incident became inadmissible. Walt said to me, speaking of Lori Nunn, "She's very frustrated at this point. This attempt shows how desperate they really are." He went on to say, "We have a concern that Murry is flipping over to the other side, but we have an answer for him regardless of what he does." He did not elaborate, but I could clearly see he was right on to suggest that Murry was now a witness for the state. As far as I could see, this was another answered prayer. I could easily see the hand of God in it all. For the District Attorney's office to come to a hearing that morning with two witnesses prepared to use against our family neither of which actually got to testify is "God in action." Our God is faithful and He has our future mapped out completely. In parting, I looked at Walt and reiterated to him my confidence in God. I said, "Walt, for all of the reasons I told you early on, you will win this case." I pointed upward and said, "He is in control. You are His instrument, but at the end of the day, it is God who is in control." He said to me, "Please continue to pray for me." Even as I write this, the thing that comes to mind is, just as the three Hebrew children in the fiery furnace couldn't with absolute certainty predict what the outcome would be to their predicament, neither could I know with certainty what God's definition of winning was. I do know that it is possible for us as men to misunderstand or misconstrue God's purpose, promise, or plan for our lives.

We have reached the middle of September. Today is the eighteenth and it has been one hundred nineteen days since the sanctions hearing in Judge Bradberry's court in which he promised to rule shortly. We have no explanation as to why there is such a delay in the ruling. It is at this point if you are in our shoes that you become suspicious of everything. You wonder if it is possible that there are behind-the-scenes politics delaying his ruling and thereby providing a benefit to the District Attorney's office. Certainly, it would be deemed harmful to their case for the public to suddenly be made aware of the State of Louisiana being caught in fraud in this case and sanctions to the tune of a quarter million dollars being imposed on them. It is intriguing that since the DCFS was caught withholding evidence in this case that nothing of the case has been in the media. There is certainly an explanation somewhere as to why the delay in Judge Bradberry's ruling, but we may never know what that explanation is. We go to trial in forty-seven days on November 4, 2013, and the trial is expected to last two weeks.

Sherri's phone rang today, September 23, 2013, and it was Murry. He was calling to inform us that he was on his way to a meeting with the District Attorney's office. He was going to sign a deal. He told her that he didn't feel that he was getting equal consideration in regard to visits with the boys. My first question is, what has that got to do with what you will tell the District Attorney if you are Murry? Besides, he has never been denied seeing the boys anytime he calls. He simply doesn't call more than once every couple of weeks. Some may be surprised at the level of intelligence it took to come to this resolution, but I am not. The truth is that for months, we've known he was working on this deal, so to pretend he suddenly came to this decision is absurd. I'm reminded of his earlier statement when he was originally offered a deal in which he declared he didn't go along with them because "I know the truth." I wonder what "truth" he intends to tell them now.

The testimony of the school staff during family court proceedings has always been troubling. As I have already indicated, we knew their court statements to be blatantly false, but could never conceive in our minds a reason why a teacher or anyone on a school staff would deliberately lie against anyone. We still don't have an explanation as to why other than our assumed one of them being intimidated by the state, but we have discovered numerous indicators of the lie itself. Walt asked Jaime to spend a few days in his office going through all of the files in search of anything that would be helpful to the case. On October 1, 2013, which was the first day she started this process, she discovered something I thought interesting.

During the child in need of care proceedings in Judge Bradberry's court, the school principal and one of the teachers, Mrs. Bass and Mrs. Devillier respectively from Fairview Elementary, testified that Gabe was an exemplary student during his tenure there. The truth is that Gabe was a very problematic child for the school. As a normal part of the school's operations, anytime a student exhibits poor behavior on a repeated basis, the school will send home a report of that bad behavior for the parent to sign and return. Gabe received one of these reports on numerous occasions each week. Jaime, in her simplicity and never suspecting there would ever be any need to distrust the school, had always signed and returned the forms as requested with exception to the last one she received. Since Gabe did not return to school after the time the Home Bound program started for him, she was left in possession of the last report. Included in this report is a statement from Gabe's teacher saying that "In spite of Gabe's best efforts to ruin it, they had a pretty good day." The report went on to describe problematic behavior on Gabe's part for that day. When Mrs. Bass, the school principal, testified that Gabe had always been an exemplary student and was then presented with the copy of this final report in court, she reversed herself and said, "Oh yes, that was the one bad day he had." So unless you believe that Jaime is a ball face liar on this point and that Gabe was an exemplary child at school every day except his last day at Fairview, then you have to believe that the principal and teachers are being untruthful. Additionally, it is impossible for anyone like me, who has experienced Gabe for themselves and been eyewitness to his bizarre behavioral habits and self-inflictions to then believe him capable of simultaneously attending school and impressing teachers as being exemplary. It is much easier, I think, to believe the teachers have been influenced by someone else. I think it would take someone in a position of authority to convince them to be less than honest and persuade them it was for the right cause.

She further alleged that Jaime had taken Gabe home from school on certain occasions. According to the counselor, Jaime did this of her own volition, citing Gabe as being likely to harm himself or someone else. This was a point that Jaime has always denied. Her claim was the teachers called her to inform her they were sending him home because of his conduct and it was the school's position that Gabe was a potential harm to himself and others. In the counselor's written statement to sheriff's detectives, Mrs. Bass, the school principal, affirms clearly that Gabe in fact stated to her that if he had to remain at school would hurt himself

[Excerpt Calcasieu Parish Sheriff's Office Report]

Mrs. Bass stated that Gabe had his head down looking at the floor. Mrs. Bass Stated Gabe made a comment that if he had to stay at school he would hurt himself. Mrs. Bass stated when Gabe made that comment he kept his head down all the time.

In Mrs. Bass's courtroom testimony, she alleged that it was Jaime who had stated to her that Gabe would harm himself or others, but here she is clearly testifying that Gabe threatened harm to himself if forced to stay at school. This is hardly exemplary. Below is a copy of a report from Fairview elementary documenting an example of Gabe's behavior at school on December 17, 2009.

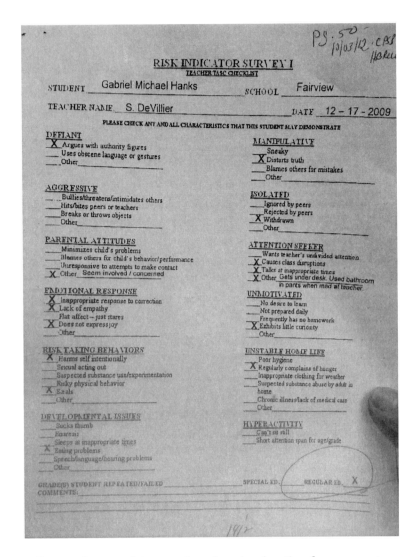

RISK INDICATOR SURVEY I
TEACHER TASC CHECKLIST

STUDENT Gabriel Michael Hanks   SCHOOL Fairview

TEACHER NAME S. DeVillier   DATE 12 – 17 – 2009

PLEASE CHECK ANY AND ALL CHARACTERISTICS THAT THIS STUDENT MAY DEMONSTRATE

DEFIANT
- X Argues with authority figures
- ___ Uses obscene language or gestures
- ___ Other_____

MANIPULATIVE
- ___ Sneaky
- X Distorts truth
- ___ Blames others for mistakes
- ___ Other_____

AGGRESSIVE
- ___ Bullies/threatens/intimidates others
- ___ Hits/bites peers or teachers
- ___ Breaks or throws objects
- ___ Other_____

ISOLATED
- ___ Ignored by peers
- ___ Rejected by peers
- X Withdrawn
- ___ Other_____

PARENTAL ATTITUDES
- ___ Minimizes child's problems
- ___ Blames others for child's behavior/performance
- ___ Unresponsive to attempts to make contact
- X Other Seem involved / concerned

ATTENTION SEEKER
- ___ Wants teacher's undivided attention
- X Causes class disruptions
- X Talks at inappropriate times
- X Other Gets under desk. Used bathroom in pants when mad at teacher.

EMOTIONAL RESPONSE
- X Inappropriate response to correction
- X Lack of empathy
- ___ Flat affect – just stares
- X Does not express joy
- ___ Other_____

UNMOTIVATED
- ___ No desire to learn
- ___ Not prepared daily
- ___ Frequently has no homework
- X Exhibits little curiosity
- ___ Other_____

RISK TAKING BEHAVIORS
- X Harms self intentionally
- ___ Sexual acting out
- ___ Suspected substance use/experimentation
- ___ Risky physical behavior
- X Steals
- ___ Other_____

UNSTABLE HOME LIFE
- ___ Poor hygiene
- X Regularly complains of hunger
- ___ Inappropriate clothing for weather
- ___ Suspected substance abuse by adult in home
- ___ Chronic illness/lack of medical care
- ___ Other_____

DEVELOPMENTAL ISSUES
- ___ Sucks thumb
- ___ Enuresis
- ___ Sleeps at inappropriate times
- X Eating problems
- ___ Speech/language/hearing problems
- ___ Other_____

HYPERACTIVITY
- ___ Can't sit still
- ___ Short attention span for age/grade

GRADE(S) STUDENT REPEATED/FAILED_____   SPECIAL ED ___   REGULAR ED X
COMMENTS:_____

I prayed again this morning that the details of any conspiracy on the part of the state or any of its witnesses would be exposed in open court. I trust God that they will be. I pray regularly that the Lord would give dominion to Walt Sanchez in this case and that he would be provided facts and witnesses needed for a complete win.

I drove home from work on Thursday, October 6, 2013, to discover that there was a pretrial conference the next morning at 9:00 a.m. As we drove through town that morning, Jaime informed me that Judge Bradberry had denied the sanctions and had ruled in favor of the state. This came as no surprise. Jaime and I arrived a few minutes early and went straight to the courthouse. We went through the usual security checks at the entrance and then made our way over to the screen near the elevators to see if we could determine what courtroom Judge Davis would be in this morning. After a brief examination, we were unable to ascertain where we would be meeting so we decided to just hang loose until Walt arrived. Lori Nunn appeared first and made her way to the elevator. Jaime excused herself to go to the restroom, and while she was gone, Walt passed through, leaving instructions with me for us to wait there until he came to get us. After about an hour, Walt returned. He wanted to talk to us, so we went over into the vending area, which was set up with a few tables and chairs for patrons to come and pay premium prices for soft drinks and snacks. Walt had met with Judge Davis and Lori Nunn in chambers to discuss the upcoming trial. It was affirmed during the meeting that Murry had signed a deal with the District Attorney's office to plead guilty to one count of cruelty to a juvenile. In exchange for his testimony against Jaime, the state would recommend no jail time for Murry. This move is not surprising, but it still confounds me that Murry would be so simple as to allow himself to be persuaded to be drawn into this. First of all, he is pleading guilty to a crime he did not commit. He will have a felony on his record for the rest of his life. Secondly, he has to lie in order to be able to provide anything of use to the DA. We have already seen Kati's latest "revised" statement to Primeaux, which provides new manufactured details. But more importantly, what is most problematic for Murry is the content of all of his letters written to Jaime while he was incarcerated. His vows of love for her and repeated acknowledgements of her being falsely accused will not lend themselves very well to his promise to the state to testify against her or to his credibility. He stated to her that deserting her in the time that she needed him the most was something that he greatly regretted.

When Murry was first released from jail, he and Jaime made an attempt at reconciliation, but were unable to ever put it back together. Jaime started seeing someone else and made it clear to Murry that they were through. This is the apparent point at which Murry changed his position and sought a deal with the DA. As Walt sat across from me, sipping a cup of coffee and me with a diet Coke, he said, "I'm really glad that Murry has moved over to the other side. I needed him on the other side."

He began to talk to us about how he would be able to show an apparent conspiracy between Murry and Kati to attack Jaime, which in my mind was for the purpose of obtaining custody of the boys. The problem with Murry having custody is it would certainly be detrimental to the boys given his unwillingness to maintain employment and his questionable personal life. Walt talked to us about the strength of our defense when you couple the content of the journal, which included words from Gabe's own mouth corroborating Jaime's claims of his self-infliction. Then you look at the testimony of Dr. Charles Murphy who was the only psychiatrist who had actually treated Gabe for his self-inflictions and had testified that Gabe was in fact in his opinion harming himself. Then consider the counselors who were in the home every week along with a state certified teacher from the Home Bound Program doing homeschooling for Gabe. Consider the documented fact that while all of this was occurring, Jaime and all of us in the family were constantly trying to push Gabe into the view of these people in an attempt to find the right avenue to obtain help for him. Walt looked across the table at Jaime and said, "I don't have to prove you innocent, I only have to show reasonable doubt of your guilt." Walt used an analogy of fighting in a combat zone. He said, "I have plenty of large ammunition. I am a criminal attorney. I am used to sitting in the trenches with bombs exploding all around me. I don't usually have this much large weaponry to shoot back with. We have lots of large artillery to fire back."

I think it is suspenseful when you realize that at this point the District Attorney's office has no knowledge of Murry's letters to Jaime or of their contents. They will receive those early next week, according to Walt. I think the striking thing about this is that Murry has already signed a deal with them and it will be next week when they discover how broadsided Walt's attack against that testimony is likely to be. You can believe what you will, but I know that God is in control, He has a plan, and He is fully able to execute that plan.

THE TRIAL

We are now in the last quarter of 2013. Today is Wednesday, October 23, and Sherri called around 4:00 p.m. to inform me of a couple of news items. Murry called today asking to see the boys. Given a rash of episodes of violent behavior from Murry, I have asked that he no longer visit the boys at our home, but have agreed to meet him at prearranged locations in public. Accordingly, she agreed to meet him at University Park in Lake Charles. Earlier in the day, Ellen had called Jaime and it came as no surprise to learn that the District Attorney's office had withdrawn their plea agreement with Murry. We can only assume that action was taken based on their review of documents and the letters provided to them from Walt. Once they saw his letters to Jaime, Murry's credibility as a witness against her would drop to the bottom.

We also learned that Murry had recently been apprehended by law enforcement officials and dropped off at Memorial Hospital for evaluation. It seems that his current girlfriend had reported him as being a danger to himself and others. The nearer we get to the trial, the more bizarre things seem to get.

I arrived home from work at around six and started cooking a pot of homemade chili. I turned the television on and tuned to the World Series first game between the St. Louis Cardinals and the Boston Red Sox. Sherri arrived home with the boys a short while later. I ask how the meeting went and she shook her head and said, "Not good." It seems Murry had angrily accused her of some sort of conspiracy against him. He told her he knew that the meeting today was a set up orchestrated by Walt, the District Attorney's office, and ourselves to have him arrested in front of the boys. Apparently, he was expecting to be arrested at the park. He angrily declared that his attorney was having our phone records pulled to prove it. I am reminded of a verse of scripture that says, "The guilty flee when no man pursues." To say that Murry may be a danger to himself and others is probably a true statement.

November 4, 2013, was a cool and clear morning. Jaime and I made our way across town to Walt's office at around 7:30 a.m. There was very little conversation between us this morning; we both seemed to be lost in our own thoughts. Today represents the moment we have spent the last forty-four months of our lives looking forward to. We have long desired to have our day in court. Countless prayers have been prayed literally all across America in support of our family. All of our faith and hope is now in God. We understand that if He does not help us, we will be in great trouble. Our enemies are powerful and have unlimited resources.

We arrived in Walt's office a few minutes before 8:00 a.m. As we exited the elevator and approached the door to Walt's office, the door opened and Steve Fontenot appeared. Steve is a striking figure with his tall frame in a dark suit, accented by a greying beard and ponytail. As I stood in the foyer of his office, Walt appeared. He was looking all the part of a trial lawyer. He wore a dark suit and looked very presidential with a white shirt and red tie.

As we made our way down the elevator, Walt's suggestion to me was that I make hay while the sun was shining. He explained to me that I could be working until I was called by the court to testify. By now, he should understand that nothing was going to keep me away from this trial. We made our way once again along what had now become a familiar walk from Walt's office to the courthouse. After clearing the security check point, I spotted Lori Nunn standing at the information booth. As I approached her, I introduced myself, explaining that I was on her subpoena list and wanted to discuss my not having to be there full-time, but wanted her to know my work was only a few minutes away. She obligingly stated to me that if she needed me, she would contact me through my attorney. This I did simply so that I would have the latitude to come and go as I pleased during the trial. Since I was on the subpoena list for both the state and the defense, I would not be allowed in the courtroom during testimony. This was another frustrating aspect of the trial for me. I didn't want to miss anything.

Today was to be the day of jury selection. I found my place outside the courtroom and simply waited on the process to unfold. I brought along a copy of John Grisham's *The Racketeer* and read to occupy my time. In a few moments, I saw Jaime being accompanied by Walt leave the courtroom and head down to another room for a conference. In a few minutes, they reappeared and I noticed that Jaime was crying. Next, Mike Primeaux appeared in the hall. He is a heavy man who waddles somewhat in his attempt to carry his mass squarely. Today, he was dressed in a black suit with white shirt and black tie with colored prints of children covering it. I suspect the tie is intended to create an impression. A jury pool of around fifty persons suddenly appeared. From these, the final twelve jurors along with two alternates would be selected. A pleasant surprise was to see Tammy Nugent, who is the oldest daughter of Bishop Nugent, appear among the potential jurors. We certainly knew she would be dismissed, but it was just a nice moment to see a friend among so many enemies. A very troubling thing we learned was that one of the questions on the forms filled out by all potential jurors was to "Do you or have you ever attended Livingway Pentecostal Church?" We found this most troubling and wondered if anyone's rights were violated with this line of questioning when qualifying as a juror. By the end of the day, all twelve jurors were seated, and we were scheduled to start the trial on the following morning.

I spent the early part of this morning in prayer, the same as most days. It is Tuesday November 5, 2013 and we actually begin trial today. I seek continually the mercy of God and a deeper repentance within. I prayed today for our case and for the will of God. I arrived at court this morning at 8:40 a.m. I found myself a seat in what I call the lobby area. It is a large open area with chairs around the walls and courtrooms at the corners of the building and a door marked "District Attorney" on the west side of the lobby area. Not long after my arrival, I notice Murry, Dana, and Katy enter the District Attorney's office. Throughout the remainder of the day, I occasionally would see one or the other of them exit to make a bathroom trip. Other than that, they seemed to be in a "lock in" with the DA. In a little while, I noticed a couple of people apparently from the sheriff's office arrive with a box of evidence and something flat and rectangular wrapped in brown paper. I assumed this to be the mattress taken from Gabe's room.

One of the matters at hand was the need to respond to a motion Walt had filed regarding evidence illegally obtained by the sheriff's office. According to testimony from Dana Day, during the course of the investigation, Mike Primeaux had confided in her that he had taken evidence from Jaime's home and hidden it until he could obtain a search warrant. The items were a dog leash and a sock. One thing I can be certain of is that if you or I were in the shoes of Mr. Primeaux and were accused or such an act, we would certainly not have been given the benefit of the doubt. In this instance Mr. Primeaux denied the conversation between between he and Dana Day and the evidence was therefore allowed at trial. You see, there is an assumption that the authorities are the truth tellers and that lay people are potential liars in all court proceedings. It would take more than your word to clear yourself of such a concerning allegation unless you are a police officer or someone on the state's team. In this case, an innocent woman's future was in the balance.

The trial continued to unfold today and the state paraded its witnesses one by one before the court. We were much encouraged by all of their testimony because many of the prosecutor's witnesses were either the same ones Walt had intended to call or we had rebuttal documentation to disprove their testimony. Things really seemed to be going our way and we had not even begun to put on the defense. The teacher from Fairview Elementary testified, fulfilling ours and the state's expectations. And when she was presented with documentation from the school, clearly reflecting Gabe's uncontrollable and bizarre behavior, she alleged it was a fraudulent report. This report was from the school and was in discovery from the District Attorney's office.

The Home Bound teacher, Mrs. Evelyn Vincent also testified. Her testimony was most troubling for my daughter because she was obviously lying about events she witnessed in Jaime's home. The thing that is difficult for most of us ordinary people to believe is that our officials can really be corrupt enough to coerce testimony from a witness especially a school teacher. After all, teachers are the salt of the earth, right? We want to believe that people are what they appear to be. In February of 2010, Evelyn Vincent visited Jaime's home for a session with Gabe just days prior to Jaime's arrest. In her report relevant to that visit, she states that she is relieved to report that previous concerns about possible abuse are unfounded. She does however indicate being troubled about Gabe and his behavior. A revised version of that report dated the same day is presented at trial, but it has additional comments in which she claims to have seen a collar on Gabe and Jaime holding a leash. These comments are the apparent result of a "miraculous" memory. Mrs. Vincent testified that when she returned home that evening and saw the events on the news that she then remembered seeing the leash in Jaime's hand and a collar on Gabe. In the first place, this did not become news until a full month later. Jaime wasn't arrested until March, and these events took place in early February, so she certainly did not see anything on the news on that evening. These new claims would obviously have contradicted the comment in the earlier report of being relieved over concerns of child abuse. But here, she even alludes to having some sort of out of body experience where she felt as though she were dreaming. And finally, Mrs. Vincent was a witness for the state in the earlier trial in family court and made no mention of a collar or a leash being present in Jaime's home at that time. Her story obviously changed after two years had elapsed and numerous interviews with the Sheriff's office had occured.

Then there was another event that cast a shadow on her testimony. She was on the witness stand and it came time for a break. In these instances, the witness is not allowed to leave the courtroom, except in the company of a bailiff. This is to protect the integrity of the witness's testimony. Everyone in the courtroom understands this, especially personnel who have experience in such things. So the forensic crime investigator associated with this case certainly understood that this witness was unapproachable during this break. But Mrs. Elizabeth Zaunbrecher approached the witness during break and was seen whispering in her ear. Mrs. Zaunbrecher was consequently rebuked and removed from the trial by Judge Clayton Davis, but we had only her word on what she discussed with the witness. The damage was done. I am compelled to believe that knowing she would likely be removed for approaching this witness felt that there was something that she deemed worth the risk that she needed to say to this witness. I was horrified to realize what had been attempted in open court, but believed at the moment it would work to our favor. Things really seemed to be going our way and we had not even begun to put on the defense. But that was soon to change in a most dramatic turn of events.

Before there was ever an arrest, before any charges had been levied against Jaime and at a time when Gabe's worst episodes had just really started, she made a video of him. She had been instructed by the professionals at Memorial Hospital to video his tirades. By this time, she was a desperate woman who was not dealing with what most people would perceive as a sick little boy. She was dealing with a child monster that who demonstrated characteristics associated with what professionals called Dissociative Identity Disorder (DID), also known as Multiple Personality Disorder. In the video, she is attempting to get Gabe to demonstrate the antics he had only moments before been displaying. Her methods were terrible and she came across on the video as bullying him. It was the ill-advised actions of a desperate woman who was trying to follow the advice of professionals. Once the trouble came and she was arrested, she wanted Walt to comprehend the magnitude of Gabe's problems, so she of her own volition downloaded the video she had made and carried it to Walt's office and viewed it with him. He was instantly troubled because of the way it presented her as bullying him. Because it had now become evidence, Walt was obligated to present it in discovery, which placed it squarely in the hands of the prosecutors. This video coupled with the state's "expert witnesses" became devastating evidence at trial.

That brings me to the subject of "expert testimony." This is a commodity that can be purchased as one might buy an insurance policy. The opinion of an expert is often sought after in these types of proceedings and depending on what your specific needs are as a defense lawyer or a prosecutor, it can be readily purchased. As in the case of previously mentioned witnesses for the state, the common terminology among attorneys for these valuable resources in criminal law is "whores." In many cases, it is an opinion for a fee. It is as simple as that.

Dr. Scott Anthony Benton is an associate professor of pediatrics at the University of Mississippi Medical Center in Jackson, Mississippi. Lori Nunn sent an e-mail to Dr. Benton on October 23, 2013, advising him of a FedEx package of documents relevant to the case being sent to him for review. In it, she asked him to review the case. She also advised that Dr. Dilks would like to meet and consult with him. Additionally, she advised him of the scheduled trial date.

On Friday, November 1, 2013 at exactly 1:16 a.m., Dr. Benton responded to Mrs. Nunn for what was apparently the first time. In it, he apologizes for not responding sooner and acknowledges he has not had any time to study the case. He explains that he has been tied up in a hotly contested trial. He does advise her however that his coordinator had organized the materials from the FedEx package and that he intended to be "fully up to speed" by the next evening. Below is the full content of his e-mail, which displays his need to get a feel for what his expected role was. He does, however, provide a commitment to testify for her prior to having reviewed any facts of the case.

[Excerpt from e-mail to myself from Walt Sanchez]

Gerald,

As requested.

Sincerely,

Walt

Walter M. Sanchez, The Sanchez Law Firm, L.L.C.
901 Lake Shore Drive, Suite 1050 | Lake Charles, LA 70601
wsanchez@waltsanchez.com | www.waltsanchez.com
t 337.433.4405 | *f* 337.433.4430

From: Lori Nunn [mailto:lnunn@cpdao.org]
Sent: Friday, November 01, 2013 11:02 AM
To: Walter M. Sanchez
Subject: Fwd: St. V Jaime Day : Your CV and reports

Walt- I am forwarding this email from Scott Benton because it answers your question about his "reports." It is entirely possible that he will not prepare a formal report in this case since he is not examining Gabe Hanks but instead his involvement so far is as he describes If that changes I will let you know. His CV should sufficiently establish his eminence for you.

Lori Nunn (Sent from my iPhone)

Begin forwarded message:

From: Scott Benton <sabentonmd@me.com>
Date: November 1, 2013 1:16:53 AM CDT
To: <lnunn@cpdao.org>
Cc: Rebecca Mansell JD <RMansell@umc.edu>
Subject: Re: St. V Jaime Day : Your CV and reports

Ms. Nunn,

I apologize for not contacting you sooner, but I have been in New Orleans on a hotly contested trial with six defense experts for the past two weeks. That trial was not expected to go, but a settlement vaporized. The good news is my opinion was supported by the jury verdict.

My coordinator has organized your materials. I intend to be fully up to speed tomorrow evening. I have a meeting tomorrow in Hattiesburg, MS which involves a 2 hour drive there and back. If convenient to you, I would like to at least hear the facts of the case you intend to present and get a feel for what you anticipate my role to be. Outside of some personal events, I also am available to you most of this weekend. Do you mind if I attempt to call you either on my way to the meeting (0830-1030) or on my way back (timing not as well known, but likely after noon)?

I have searched my files and I do not see that I have ever prepared any reports. I do show a general conversation with Det. Mike Primeaux above his desiring to involve me in this case. I have no independent recollection of this case. If your files reflect that I have written on this case, I hope that it was contained in the FedEx package mentioned and I will study it.

I briefly spoke with Dr. Dilks this week. We have made tentative arrangements to talk on Sunday. I assume from your email that sharing information with him is permitted.

I am happy to provide trial support to the extent able to include observing other prosecution or defense experts. Attached is my CV which is minus only the trial from the past couple of weeks.

I have noted your request or subpoena for my expert testimony in the upcoming trial for which I will make changes in my schedule. I understand that the legal process has some inherent uncertainty and would appreciate timely notice of any continuances or settlements.

I welcome any pre-trial preparation at no cost to you. I can be reached via my mobile at 601-608-8311

Note that the University of Mississippi* has established the following standard fees and expenses for faculty providing expert testimony:

Research: $175/hr
Expert testimony: $175/hr (door to door**–capped at $1750/day)

Expenses:
ground
federal mileage rate
common carrier
actual expense
housing
actual expense (paid in advance by your office)
meals
local federal per diem rate

*UMMC EIN: 64-6008520

**door to door is defined as from time leaving Jackson, MS until return to Jackson, MS and is rounded up to the nearest quarter hour

—

Scott A. Benton, MD, FAAP
Associate Professor of Pediatrics
Chief, Division of Forensic Medicine
Medical Director, Children's Justice Center
University of Mississippi Medical Center
2500 North State Street
Jackson MS 39216
T 601-608-8311 | F 800-571-1469
sbenton@umc.edu
cjc.umc.edu

On Oct 31, 2013, at 11:59 PM, Scott Anthony Benton
MD <sbenton@umc.edu> wrote:

From: Lori Nunn <lnunn@cpdao.org>
Subject: St. V Jaime Day : Your CV and reports
Date: October 23, 2013 at 3:40:34 PM CDT
To: "sbenton@umc.edu" <sbenton@umc.edu>

Scott-

I sent you a box of documents by FedEx yesterday for you
to review, and I would also like for you to observe Gabe's
testimony during trial, and perhaps some other parts of
the trial before I call you as a witness. You do not need
to be here on 11/4 unless you want to come early, since it
will take a day or two to select the trial jury. I expect it will
take me 3 days to present my case, and I will put you on
towards the end.

Would you like to talk to Gabe? Dr. Dilks, a local
neuropsychologist who is highly experienced, evaluated
Gabe and the other family members in 2010 as part of the
custody case in family court. Dr. Dilks would like to meet
you and consult you, and I have his reports if you would
like for me to send them.

I need your CV as soon as you can provide it, and if you have prepared any reports so far, or in years past, please send them to me ASAP so that I can turn them over to the defense attorney.

Lori L. Nunn
Assistant District Attorney
14th Judicial District, Calcasieu Parish
P.O. Box 3206
Lake Charles, LA 70602
Phone 337-437-3826; Fax 337-437-3325
lnunn@cpdao.org

The prosecution put on the video which was very damaging because of the portrayal it created. They also showed the pictures from the hospital and offered the expert testimony of Dr. Scott Anthony Benton who simply testified that in his expert opinion all of the evidence in this case pointed to abuse. The journal and its contents, Gabe's threats to harm the Semien family, and his admissions of self-harm while in Jaime's care were either explained away or ignored. This two-man team of experts testified that all of that behavior was simply indicative of a child being abused. One alarming thing for me was that one might easily believe that Dr. Benton could truthfully testify in regard to previous cases he had been exposed to, but how could he compare them to our case without studying specific information and documents relevant to Gabe and this case. The answer is he had Dr. Dilks to rely on to provide details as he stated in his e-mail to Lori Nunn. This in itself was most troubling because at the time of his testimony, Mr. Dilks was one of several defendants named in a federal lawsuit relevant to his participation and apparent perjury in the child in need of care case in family court. This lawsuit would provide strong incentive for Dr. Dilks to attack the journal and its significance in the criminal proceedings. So here we stood with the trial momentum changing into the state's favor and that based largely on the fact that unsuspecting jurors were hearing prejudiced testimony from a man whose professional future might very well hinge on his ability to discredit the journal and its significance toward this case. This is the same journal that implicated him in a conspiracy to defraud the court and Jaime Day of justice and a fair trial respectively.

Also one should consider the motions filed against Dr. Dilks by Walt Sanchez to have him brought before a state board of ethics review. All of this was in place and certainly an adequate motive for Mr. Dilks to lie or misconstrue the facts. He was essentially fighting for his own career. I would have thought that he would certainly be ineligible to testify as an expert witness in regards to the journal or anything else associated with this case given these circumstances. After all, in Judge Bradberry's ruling, he made much reference to the fact that he had placed all weight on Mr. Dilks's opinion in his first ruling against our family and then vacated that ruling in light of Dr. Dilks, Mrs. Landry, and the DCFS's apparent withholding the evidence of the journal and their apparent conspiracy to deny Jaime a fair trial.

After the prosecution rested, I made my way home to freshen up before we started the afternoon. I had worked for a few hours that morning so I was in work clothes and wanted to change before court that evening. As I was changing, the phone rang and it was Ellen from Walt's office and he wanted to see us immediately in his office. We finished changing and headed back to his office. Walt met me at the door and shut it behind me as I entered. He sat down directly in front of me and looked into my eyes. He said to me, "I had hoped to never have this conversation with you." He was ready to throw in the towel. He wanted to approach the District Attorney for a deal. He said that the video along with Dr. Benton's testimony had sunk our ship and conviction was certain. I listened to this from the exact setting so many other discussions relevant to this case had taken place. Here we were again in Walt's plush office overlooking the city and I was stunned. I remember asking Walt a question on one or our first visits. "Do you believe our daughter is innocent?" I asked. I felt at the time that it was essential that whoever represented her believe in her innocence. I then said, "You should understand we are not interested in a plea." I doubted that he remembered that conversation.

We left Walt's office and made our way once more back to the courthouse. We were about to be exposed to a side of Walt and Steve we had never seen. We were led to the jury deliberation room for a meeting with counsel. Sherri, my mother-in-law Jean Roberts, Jaime, and I represented our family while Walt was represented by his entire team. Tom and Becky were there along with Walt, Steve Fontenot, and Ellen. We were then stunned by what we endured for the next three hours. Walt and Steve were a tag team determined to persuade Jaime to take a deal to plea in exchange for an eighteen-year sentence. It was a good guy/bad guy setup. Walt would attack her with an in your face charge, literally yelling at her that this was her only recourse, and if she did not take it, she would spend the next forty years in prison. He didn't stop there, but told her if she did not take this deal, then she was, in fact, the crazy selfish nut the state had painted her to be. What I found even more troubling was he made a statement, saying, "I cannot believe you are going to do this to me." I thought, *To you?* Who's going to prison here for a crime they never committed? I was in shock to see this new side of Walt Sanchez. On Steve's side, he also had a "yell in your face" method, but his was more of a pleading with Jaime that their suggestion was for her own good. This went on for three hours and I can only liken it to what one might envision an FBI interrogation to be like. There was only one answer that these guys were willing to hear, and they were committed to badgering her into submission. Walt looked at me and said, "Based on thirty years' experience as a criminal attorney, I am telling you that this is only choice you have." My reply may have sounded self-righteous, but you have to understand my mentality at the moment. I stood in the hardest moment of my life to choose between taking the recommendation of the experienced trial lawyer who was handling the case for which I had exhausted my entire living and three years of hardship, emotional drain, and intense prayer or believing a prophetic word from God. Of these, if I chose to take the attorney's recommendation, they would immediately, on that very day, place my daughter in chains and carry her away for eighteen years. I looked at him and said, "Walt, I understand your position and I certainly respect your knowledge and experience. You say you have thirty years' experience to backup what you say, well, I have thirty years' experience in serving the God in whom we trust and my thirty years trumps your thirty." Yet in all of this, I understood that only Jaime could actually make the final decision. I looked at her and said, "I cannot tell you what to do, I can only tell you what I would do if I were in your shoes. You have to live with this and the risks are all yours. Know this: I will support you in whatever decision you make. I love you, baby." I looked at Walt and asked, "You do concede that the decision is hers to make?" He nodded in the affirmative and said, "It is her decision." In a moment, Judge Davis appeared and had Walt meet him outside the room and ordered all family out of the room. Jaime remained another hour, resisting the pressure to plead guilty. She later told me that Walt in an exasperated tone told her, "Okay, you want to finish the trial, I'm going to put on your next four witnesses and I'll see you in forty years." She also said once they returned to the court and were seated, Walt looked at her and said, "Okay, now what do you want to do?" As if to say, you are now in control, you didn't take my recommendation, so you are now calling the shots. And we suddenly find ourselves feeling very helpless.

The pressure from Walt did not stop with Jaime's decision to continue the trial. All of these events were happening on Friday, November 8, 2013, and the following Monday was Memorial Day and a government holiday. Consequently, trial would not resume until Tuesday morning. For the remainder of the weekend, Walt pressured Jaime to reconsider. He advised her he wanted her answer by Saturday morning as though he didn't already have her answer. He was apparently on standby to notify John Derosier and Judge Davis of any change. There was an obvious expectation of her relenting and he was not going to give up. He made multiple calls on Saturday and resumed those calls on Sunday afternoon. Walt advised us that if she did not consent to the plea, we would anger Judge Davis, and she would surely receive the maximum sentence in retaliation for extending the trial.

On Sunday, after I had completed my church bus route and made my way home, I retired to my bedroom for a nap. My bedroom door suddenly opened and Jaime came in, saying that Walt was calling and what should she do? By this time, I was getting really concerned at this aggression coming from Walt. I told her to send him a note and tell him that her decision was final and to please stop badgering her. It was at that moment that the doorbell rang. When I opened it, there stood Walt in a pair of jeans and a sport shirt, asking in a soft tone if he could speak to Jaime. I opened the door and allowed him in. They moved into the kitchen area and talked quietly while I remained in the den idly staring at a football game. After about a forty-five minute conference, Walt stood to leave. They had finalized Jaime's determination to go on with the trial. She loudly and with deep emotion declared to Walt, "These people had taken everything I have. I've lost my children, my home, I kept pictures of that little boy on my wall for as long as I had a wall to hang it on. I will not allow them to take the only thing I have left and that is my declaration of my innocence. I will never plead guilty to something I never did, no matter what the penalty." I told her tearfully how proud I was of her for standing up for the truth. As Walt was leaving, I extended my hand to thank him for all of his support for the last three years. I told him no matter how things ended, I considered him the best criminal attorney in the state.

He placed both of his hands on my shoulders and looked directly into my eyes and explained to me once more how we were risking forty years in prison. He then revealed something to me that was brand-new. He said, "Gerald, I have been undergoing some tests and have been diagnosed with cancer. I have put off treatment until now so I could continue to fight for your daughter." I was moved with compassion and offered to lay hands on Walt and pray for him. He said, "You will absolutely pray for me!" As Sherri and I lay our hands upon him and began to pray in the name of Jesus, Walt broke and sobbed deeply. I thought, *My oh my, what is the Lord going to do here in the final analysis?* Some of Walt's actions during this trial now made more sense. Even so, in light of all the circumstances and recent events, I had to ask myself a question. Was Walt concerned about my daughter or was his greatest concern about winning or going down in the loser's bracket in one of the most, if not the most, high profile case he had ever handled. I honestly wasn't sure which applied.

Trial resumed on Tuesday, November 12, 2013, with Walt calling his lineup of witnesses. The most notable was Carla Simien, the author of the by now infamous journal. She methodically provided accounts from Gabe's stay in her care and at Walt's request read from the journal accounts of Gabe's self-inflictions and bizarre behavior. She testified that he would harm himself and threaten to accuse them as his foster parents. She then read from the journal, quoting Gabe as saying, "I am going to do to you what I did to Jaime." Her testimony was full of accounts of the bizarre behavior of Gabe while in her care, which so perfectly mirrored our own family's rendition of his antics and demeanor while in Jaime's home. Surely, all of this would at least create a reasonable doubt in the minds of the jurors one would think.

Jason Schnake, who was the initial responding officer to calls from Katy Day of alleged abuse, was also among the witnesses for the defense. He testified that none of the circumstances or events described by the media and the prosecution were true. He talked of his attempts to make his superiors understand that what they were alleging and offering him a special commendation for was an inaccurate description of the facts and the things they were alleging concerning a dog leash and confinement were simply not true.

Then Dr. Charles Murphy testified of his sessions with Gabe, saying that Gabe was very manipulative and that there were always consequences if you did not comply with Gabe's demands. A few days earlier, Jaime had shared with me a conversation she had with Walt in which he had reiterated a description from Dr. Murphy of one of his encounters with Gabe. Gabe was near the end of one of his hospital stays, and Dr. Murphy was preparing him to be released. They had a brief conversation in which Gabe seemed like a happy little boy who was pleasant to talk to. But when Dr. Murphy suggested to him he was making good progress and he would be returning to his foster parent, Gabe objected and said he didn't want to leave the hospital. When Dr. Murphy said to him again that he was doing well and would be going home, he then described a transformation in Gabe in which he went from being a pleasant little boy to having the demeanor of a man and said, "If you release me from this hospital, Doc, I will go home and kill myself." What he described was much more than simply a change in his tone, but you could actually see the physical transformation as it took place in him, and when he then spoke, it was as I have previously described, as if a man were speaking from a small boy's body. The prosecutors simply blew it off as Gabe being afraid to go to Jaime's, but according to our understanding, this event took place while he was in his third foster mom's care, not while he was still at Jaime's.

One of the things I find most troubling is that Walt did not have Glen Ahava or any expert on in rebuttal to Larry Dilks's testimony. Dr. Ahava had examined Dr. Dilks's reports and had testified in family court that all of Dilks's test were improperly applied and had basically accused him of coercing the children. He further stated that in his opinion, Dilks could be sued for malpractice. And his was an expert opinion also. The jury was not allowed to have any inkling that Dilks's integrity or professional ability was in question. He was presented uncontested as an expert witness. Dilks further testified that he had read the journal and that its contents did not change his assessment of Gabe being abused. He further testified that the journal while it was authored by a well-meaning person, that person was simply not qualified to properly collect the data needed in the journal to do a proper analysis. In reality, because I know all of the facts, I can say his entire testimony was a lot of hogwash created by smoke and mirrors. The journal was a straightforward account of events as they happened and didn't need any "professional enhancement."

Why did we not have our own professional witness in the criminal case, whether it was Glenn Ahava or someone else is a question that begs an answer. Earlier in the year, Walt had made mention numerous times the need for an additional expert witness. Under the belief that this expert was essential to our case, I approached a church friend asking for help. He provided a check for fifteen thousand dollars, which Walt assured me would be held in an account for the purpose of acquiring this expert. That expert never materialized. We had no counter for the Dr. Benton or Larry Dilks.

After closing arguments from both sides were complete, the jury went into deliberations and we all exited the courtroom to prepare for what could possibly be a long wait. The time was 11:58 a.m. and the date was Wednesday, November 13, 2013. It had been 1,352 days or 3 years, 8 months, and 11 days or if you want to be more technical, 32,448 hours since Jaime's arrest and we had been dragged for that amount of time through what I can only describe as a horrible and seemingly never-ending nightmare.

At 1:12 p.m., Walt received a call from the courtroom and left, believing the jury had a question. I got up from my chair and went into a file closet that was opposite the kitchen in Walt's office to pray. I prayed earnestly for God to provide a good verdict today. I had been in prayer only a short while when my phone rang and it was the bank wanting a payment on one of the many notes that I had become so consistently late to pay in recent months. In a moment, one of Walt's office assistants appeared to advise me that we were all wanted at the courtroom so I advised the banker that I was in court and would have to call them back. I headed over to the courthouse, only this time I could hardly place one foot before the other. It felt as if a press were resting on my heart. I knew by then that the jury was back with a verdict. Hardly more than an hour and they were back! Sherri and I approached the courtroom only to be met by a bailiff who advised us that no one else was being allowed in the courtroom due to overcrowding. We were unable to persuade him to allow us in, so we stood outside the courtroom and received the horrible news from a bailiff that the verdict was guilty! Our daughter who was absolutely innocent had been found guilty by a jury of her peers based on the evidence presented in court by the state, true or false. No words can describe the impact that verdict had on the heart, mind, and spirit of my wife or myself.

We were then allowed into the courtroom to hear the judge order Jaime remanded into custody to await sentencing on December 10, 2013. We were advised to go get the boys and bring them to the courthouse to say their good-byes to their mom. This is something you would have to experience for yourself to appreciate the significance of the event. It is one thing I suppose to go through this if you have in fact committed the crimes for which you are accused. But in a case where the fact is the only thing you are guilty of is poor judgment in trying to do the right thing this is horrific. You hear people talk about being numb or feeling as if someone has punched them in the gut when some tragedy occurs in their life. All of that was present and much more, as I moved like a zombie through the motions of getting the things that had to be done accomplished in the next hour. We finally got the boys from school and picked up Kathan from the babysitter and made it back to the courthouse to say a five-minute good-bye to my daughter/their mom.

CONTINUING TO BELIEVE

On Sunday morning, November 17, 2013, I made my way to the Outpost in Sulphur. I was on my usual routine for Sunday. I typically will arrive at the Outpost in time for prayer before heading out with the bus on my route. Today, I am devastated because of the loss of the case and the fact that Jaime is locked up in the parish jail, waiting on sentencing from a judge who apparently believes she deserves forty years. I cannot describe the weight and the brokenness that has now engulfed my spirit. I began to pray, and as I did I felt myself talking to God from my heart with simple prayers. I said to him, "Lord, you don't have to ever speak another word to me and I will still believe your promise. But if you will, I would love for you to confirm if we are where we are supposed to be and if we are still in your will." I was thinking of the prophecy we had held so dear for more than three years: "I have a plan, and in the end, I win," yet it seemed all of our hopes of deliverance were crushed by a guilty verdict from a jury of twelve ordinary citizens. Afterward, I made the bus route and delivered everyone to church. Pastor Massey was out of town this weekend and today Bishop Nugent was delivering the message from the word of God. He preached from proverbs on hope, and there was a powerful ministering of the Holy Ghost present throughout the preaching. At the close of the sermon, a prophetic word in tongues was given and the interpretation was as follows:

I have a Plan Saith the Lord, that is higher than yours. I have a purpose saith the Lord, that is greater than yours. I have a way already planned. I have footsteps that you cannot see because of your flesh. But I say unto you follow me. Follow me closely saith the Lord and I'll reveal my plan. Day by day and step by step I'll reveal my plan in your life Saith God.

I say to myself, "I don't understand God and I don't pretend to. But I know too much about Him and His Word not to trust Him." Then I ask myself truthfully, "What choice do we have? Is there really an option? Should we not as the apostle of the Lord say, 'To whom shall we go? Thou has the words of eternal life.'"

Walt and I exchanged e-mails on November 21, 2013. I provided the copies of this e-mail below.

Just so I have this correct. The state and its witnesses were caught in wrongful conduct in the family court proceedings. Consequently, they lost in family court and our children returned to us. This fact was withheld from criminal court, thereby allowing the state's expert's testimony to remain untarnished as far as the criminal court and the jury was concerned. So now, they don't have to be accountable at all for their actions given the fact that they were allowed to basically destroy the very evidence that got them in trouble in the first place in the criminal trial. Yes, I think I understand.

> *Gerald Price*
> *From: Walter M. Sanchez [mailto:wsanchez@waltsanchez.com]*
> *Sent: Thursday, November 21, 2013 2:09 PM*
> *To: Price, Gerald (Turner Industries Group LLC)*
> *Cc: Ellen Anderson; Stephen Spring (springlaw@gmail.com);*
> *Steve B. Fontenot*
> *Subject: [EXTERNAL]Civil litigation—to be dismissed*
>
> *Gerald:*
>
> *One issue I do want to address is the pending civil litigation. Based upon Jamie's conviction, neither of these suits have any*

viability. If Jamie had been acquitted, then we would have had the ability to proceed; however, given her conviction, which would be admissible in either trial, there is no meaningful way forward. I have spoken with our co-counsel, Stephen Spring, who agrees with my assessment. Under the circumstances, we will be taking the necessary steps to dismiss the suits in an attempt to minimize the costs which have been incurred to date.

Sincerely,

Walt

Walter M. Sanchez, The Sanchez Law Firm, L.L.C.
901 Lake Shore Drive, Suite 1050 | Lake Charles, LA 70601
wsanchez@waltsanchez.com | www.waltsanchez.com
t 337.433.4405 | f 337.433.4430

As you might expect, I am extremely distraught and disappointed at this turn of events. It seems as if the innocent will be sentenced and the guilty go free.

The sentencing hearing was moved up to December 6, 2013. This was due to the need for Walt to complete some preliminary task associated with his cancer treatment. But the more I thought about the case, the more troubled I became. Walt had called last Sunday afternoon to inform me that Lori Nunn intended to put Larry Dilks back on to testify at sentencing in regard to his sessions with the boys. If allowed to testify, Dilks would say that the boys had also stated that they had witnessed and been forced to participate in the alleged abuse. I was going through my file of the case and came across a copy of Judge Bradberry's ruling. I was astounded even more that Dilks could possibly be allowed to testify as an expert in this case when I read the content of his ruling in what Judge Bradberry called a "companion case."

[Excerpt From Bradberry's ruling in Family court]

This Court made it very clear on its November 4th, 2011 ruling that great weight, the proverbial tipping of the scale, was afforded to Dr. Dilks and his opinions and recommendations. In Dr. Dilks' psychological evaluation of Jamie that I want to point out, it's going to be the one he performed on March 3rd, 2011, at Page 14 of his psychological evaluation, at this time the etiology of Jamie Day's behavior, mom's behavior I think is the word he used, is unknown but the consequences of the disturbance are clearly evident in the photographs, the accounts of the two school counselors, Gabe Hanks and Gabe's two brothers. The records and collateral interview showing cognitive, behavior and social gains of the victim while in foster care are further data supporting this diagnosis.

This analysis is clearly contradicted by the journal in that it in no way describes the sort of cognitive, behavioral and social gains that Dr. Dilks describes. A brief perusal of this journal says the exact opposite. In fact, conversely, this journal describes Gabe's clear and escalating pattern of bizarre self injurious and manipulative behavior that parallels the behavior described by many witnesses that were called to testify in this trial.

On December 4, 2013 just before 10:00 AM, I sent the following email to Walt

From: Price, Gerald (Turner Industries Group LLC)
Sent: Wednesday, December 04, 2013 9:56 AM
To: Walter M. Sanchez
Cc: geraldprice@suddenlink.net
Subject: court Ruling

Walt

Attached is Jaime's letter to Judge Davis. I have also attached a copy of Judge Bradberry's ruling from family court. If Judge Davis has not read this ruling then I respectfully ask that you insure that he does so, prior to him passing sentence on my daughter. You talked at closing about everyone failing Gabe. Gabe is hardly the one who has been failed in this process. If Judge Davis does not know all of the facts of this ruling prior to him passing sentence on this innocent woman then the system,

You, and everyone concerned will have failed to provide her a fair trial and justice will certainly not have been served. In the name of justice and in accordance with the oath that you took to become who you are, please help us now. If not Dr. Dilks will come on and further the manipulative lies he has told until now at her sentencing.

On Wednesday, December 4, 2013, I put together a package and hand-delivered it to the third floor of the Fourteenth District Judicial Center. There is a glass-enclosed receptionist center in the open area just outside the elevator where all correspondence is fielded for either judge who offices on that floor. My package included a letter to Judge Davis from Bishop Nugent, Jaime's letter asking him for leniency, a copy of Judge Bradberry's ruling in family court, and a copy of a new letter from myself to Judge Davis. The following morning at 9:17 a.m., which was now just one day before sentencing I sent the same letters to Dusty L. Higgs (Judge Davis's judicial assistant) in an e-mail asking that she forward them to Judge Davis. At 9:35, she responded. Below are copies of the series of e-mails.

[EXTERNAL]RE: State Verses Jaime Day
Dusty McIntosh dmcintosh@14jdc.org
Thu 12/5/2013 9:35 AM

Received. Thank you.

Dusty L. Higgs
Judicial Assistant to Judge Clayton Davis
14th Judicial District Court
P.O. Box 3210
Lake Charles, LA 70602
(337) 437-3530–Telephone
(337) 437-3332–Facsimile
From: Price, Gerald (Turner Industries Group LLC)
[mailto:Gerald.Price@contractor.p66.com]
Sent: Thursday, December 05, 2013 9:17 AM

To: Dusty McIntosh
Subject: FW: State Verses Jaime Day

Attached are two separate letters I have drafted for Judge Davis's Review. I respectfully ask that these be forwarded to him as expediently as possible. I left a large yellow envelope at the front receptionist desk on Yesterday 12/4/13 which included additional information and copies of these letters. Your assistance is greatly appreciated.

Thanks
Gerald Price

From: Price, Gerald (Turner Industries Group LLC)
Sent: Wednesday, December 04, 2013 9:56 AM
To: 'Walter M. Sanchez'
Cc: geraldprice@suddenlink.net
Subject: court Ruling

Walt

Attached is Jaime's letter to Judge Davis. I have also attached a copy of Judge Bradberry's ruling from family court. If Judge Davis has not read this ruling then I respectfully ask that you insure that he does so, prior to him passing sentence on my daughter. You talked at closing about everyone failing Gabe. Gabe is hardly the one who has been failed in this process. If Judge Davis does not know all of the facts of this ruling prior to him passing sentence on this innocent woman then the system, You, and everyone concerned will have failed to provide her a fair trial and justice will certainly not have been served. In the name of justice and in accordance with the oath that you took to become who you are, please help us now. If not Dr. Dilks will come on and further the manipulative lies he has told until now at her sentencing.

Respectfully yours
Gerald Price

Later that afternoon, as I sat in my office, I began to reflect on the actions I had taken in the last twenty-four hours and a growing concern began to nag at me that I should not allow Walt to be blindsided by my last letter to Judge Davis. It was at this point that I forwarded a copy of the letter to Walt. He called me within moments to ask if I had actually delivered the letter to Judge Davis. I replied in two words, "I did" He then asked how the letter was provided to Judge Davis to which I replied, "I hand-delivered it to his office on yesterday in a large yellow envelope." He tersely said, "Okay," and hung up. Within moments, he called back and in controlled anger began to explain answers to questions I had raised in my letter to the judge. Here is the letter I sent to the Judge.

Thursday, November 21, 2013
14th Judicial District Court
P.O. Box 3210
Lake Charles, La 70602
Attention: Honorable Judge Clayton Davis RE: State Vs. Jaime Day

Dear Judge Davis

While I am extremely concerned about approaching you in regard to this case, in particular in this fashion and for a second time, I have huge concerns relevant to this case. I have in my personal files a copy of Judge Bradberry's ruling against the state in the "State of Louisiana in the Interest of Jason Kolten Day and Dalton Kyler Day." I have provided this to you for review. I felt counsel in our defense should have felt obligated to insure that critical information in this case, (which in Judge Bradberry's own words was considered a "companion" case to the one in your courtroom), was in fact made known to the jury during trial. For whatever reason he deemed appropriate much of this information was withheld from court. Then in the process of trial the same "expert" witness, who was found to be withholding evidence, his opinions contrary to all physical evidence, accused of perjury and under a federal lawsuit for his actions in the family court, was allowed to participate in your court as an expert witness. Additionally he was under a motion to bring him before a State Board Review. With all of these troubling circumstances in place he was allowed to testify as an expert witness for the state against the journal. The journal, being the very evidence that got him in trouble in Judge Bradberry's court, he is now allowed to discredit. I will also mention to you one other thing.

During the course of the testing on Jaime and the boys, we as Jaime's parents were required to spend two one hour sessions each with Mr. Dilks for evaluation. This requirement was mandated by DCFS as part of the case plan and we were advised by Mr. Sanchez to cooperate fully. In these sessions Mr. Dilks attempted to build a platform from which he could create a diagnosis explaining what caused Jaime to commit the crimes she was accused of. This was obviously based on an assumption that Jaime was actually guilty. He first suggested that I should pay for an EEG for Jaime to monitor electrical activity in her brain. He explained to me, that if I would agree to this he would be able to say she probably suffered from blackouts. He asked the question, "wouldn't you rather be able to say that she was mentally ill than to be left with what the state is alleging as the only explanation?" I was appalled and said so. My statement to him was, "if that were the truth then we would say so!! We are all looking for the truth, aren't we?" It was shocking to me that he could suggest that we create an explanation for Jaime's alleged actions in such a flippant way. He seemed to be suggesting to me that whatever he said regardless of the facts would be accepted as reality in the court room. The sad reality was that he was exactly right.

The next thing he attempted was to fabricated statements from me, saying I had said to him in one of our sessions, that Jaime had been abused repeatedly growing up and that I carried much guilt concerning this. No such conversation ever occurred nor has any such events ever occurred!!. During my wife's next session with him, he declared this new theory to her, citing me as telling him of this abuse. She was shocked at this and told him so. She ask him disbelievingly "My husband said that to you?" When she saw me later, she asked me unbelievingly, had I made such a ridiculous claim to Dilks? "Absolutely not was my reply." I called him the next morning and demanded how he could fabricate such a preposterous story. I remembered his making a claim of his own Christianity in court, so I ask him how he could make such a false claim and obvious fabrication and still claim to be a benevolent Christian. In reply he said "that is what you said Mr. Price" To which I replied " You know very well that I did not say any such thing." He then obligingly stated to me "well maybe I misunderstood you" to which I replied "no Mr. Dilks, you did not misunderstand me. You know very well that I never said anything akin to what you are now suggesting." He then recanted this story and landed on the one he submitted to the court saying my daughter had something called Fictitious Disorder which is apparently synonymous to Munchausen Syndrome by Proxy. Again I apologize for such a lengthy letter but I am making a last effort to fight for my daughter and an innocent woman's freedom.

Respectfully yours
Gerald Price

December 6, 2013, will always be a day engraved in the corridors of my memory. Today was the day that my daughter would face Judge Clayton Davis who was set to pass sentence upon her for crimes she never committed. It was cold and cloudy with a strong north wind blowing when I parked my truck in the Civic Center parking across the street from the courthouse. Pastor Massey was in his truck on the phone when I stepped out into the morning chill. We made our way together across the street and up the sidewalk to the main entrance of the Fourteenth District Judicial Center. After checking through the security scanner, we went on to the second floor where the hearing was to be held. People from the church trickled in for the next half hour, including Bishop

Nugent. He and Pastor Massey were both scheduled to speak for Jaime before sentencing. In a few moments, Walt appeared and very sincerely asked to speak to both of them. He walked a short distance down the hall and spoke privately to them both, I suppose to preempt them to speak. I will never be able to form words to describe the pressure and anxiety I was feeling at this moment. It felt as though there were a heavy press squeezing me from within. There were moments when I had difficulty breathing and I simply didn't feel that I could carry on a conversation with anyone. At 9:00, we all assembled into Courtroom G to make final pleadings for her and to hear Clayton Davis's sentence.

Bishop Nugent was called first and he began to speak from his heart. He talked about how the Jaime Day that had been portrayed in newspaper reports and television news was not the Jaime Day we knew. He declared to the court that he had known Jaime since the day she was born and knew her to be a very sweet girl. In a letter sent the day before to Judge Davis, he told of a time when he had himself tried to get Gabe to eat when Jaime was not present. This would have happened while Gabe was enrolled at Lake Charles Christian Academy. He said Gabe growled at him like an animal and refused. Bishop Nugent was obviously passionate about this and it showed as his voice rose in his declaration of her innocence. He said "I keep waiting for one intelligent person to come forward and say they ever saw Jaime abuse a child." That is the point where Judge Davis cut him off and said, "Someone did, Katy Day came forward. She is considered somewhat of a hero around here." Bishop Nugent might have responded to that in many ways, but he understood he was being shut down so he complimented the judge and ceased. He might have responded but did not by saying, she may be a hero among this small circle of prosecutors and law enforcement officers, but for those of us who live in the real world know too much about her to trust her. We know about her history. We know she and her mom were asked to keep Gabe just days before they made the phone call and told the falsehoods that initiated all of this trouble. We know that the reply from Katy was "That crazy kid is not going to be staying in the home with my daughter." She was speaking out of concern for her own child who was then a toddler. If he had known, he might have told the judge at that moment that only a few days before Katy's call, Jaime had in fact asked Dana to take Gabe for a few days to give her a break, but after one day, Dana and Katy brought him back saying they just couldn't deal with him. Judge Davis would never believe the horrible truth and that is that Katy had lied to the police and to the court. She never saw what she claimed. I just think after she told it once she couldn't find a place to stop telling it even though she knew it was a lie. The entire Day family is bizarre to say the least. I don't think if the prosecutors had known about Katy's questionable background, it would have made any difference because they are driven by a common cause to win at any cost.

After Bishop Nugent spoke, Pastor Massey stood before the podium facing Judge Davis and pled for mercy, saying he had never known Jaime to commit any crime in the six years he had pastored at Livingway. Lori Nunn then made a rehash of all of the trumped-up charges and repainted Jaime as a monster. She took about ten minutes making her case for Jaime being a danger to all children and that she should be locked away for forty years.

The last thing that happened was that Jaime was allowed to walk forward in her orange jumpsuit and chains to plead for the mercy of the court. She tearfully pleaded for Judge Davis to allow her to be a mom to her children. Her efforts were to no avail. Judge Davis, in sentencing, cited the video that Jaime had made herself and the opinion of Scott Anthony Benton who wrote an opinion that said the video offered a window into the mental abuse that Jaime had inflicted on Gabe. In his comments, Judge Davis revealed just how unqualified he was to preside over this trial. He relied on Dr. Dilks's testimony that children do not starve themselves. Judge Davis said, "If you accept that and I do, then the defense kind of crumbles." He should have done his research and he would have known better. He could have, as I did do a simple search and found as I did that *"In New York State (NYS), self-inflicted injuries are the fifth leading cause of injury-related hospitalizations for children ages 10 to14 years"* that according to New York State's Department of health website. He would have found that without exception every single act that Gabe committed in self-infliction is found in their list of behaviors to watch for including eating disorders. Or maybe if he had simply read the word of God, he would have found an account where a child was casting himself into fire before Jesus cast the devils out of him. Or possibly if he had ever visited and spent time at a mental hospital, as I have, he would have had a better inkling of just how great the impact of mental illness can be. How it can drive an individual no matter their age to indescribable depths where there is no limit to what they will inflict on themselves. What modern-day professionals call Dissociative Identity Disorder (DID) or Multiple Personality Disorder, the Bible identifies as being possessed by a spirit. Whichever term you prefer, the consequence for attempting to be a mom to a sadistically sick and manipulative child was that Judge Clayton Davis sentenced Jaime Day to thirty years at hard labor in the Louisiana correctional system. He stated plainly that he relied on the opinion of Dr. Benton who took no significant time to study this case, never interviewed or spoke with Gabe Hanks, but simply drove into town and tag teamed with Larry Dilks, whose career and financial future, likely hinged on his ability to discredit the most compelling evidence in this trial. That effort was made easier for him by virtue of the fact that he was talking to an uninformed and unsuspecting jury. The eyewitness testimony and record of the foster mom who kept Gabe for the larger part of the first year after he left Jaime's home held no weight. You will remember I told you early on in this story that expert opinion trumps eyewitness testimony every time in a court of law. One can only conclude that modern-day judges are protecting themselves from future criticism when they follow this practice. They can never be criticized for ruling in accordance with the expert. I learned how easily an expert opinion can be purchased by just following one trial. So can anyone actually believe that the judges in the modern-day judicial system are blind to the fact that in most cases set forward by the state, expert testimony is likely prejudiced? You will never hear of purchased expert testimony provided to a prosecutor in a criminal case that is damaging to his or her case. During the family court proceedings, when we realized we needed the expert opinion of Dr. Glen Ahavah, the first thing Walt explained to me was that there was great risk involved. Simply put, he might not tell you what you want to hear, and once you have possession of his opinion, you are required by law to provide his opinion into discovery. So is the State of Louisiana always right or do they know in advance what their experts will say before they agree to use them? You decide. Remember what lawyers call them.

After the hearing, Walt asked to speak to Bishop Nugent and myself. He wanted to inform me of some latest developments that I thought to be strange. He said that there was an attorney from Baton Rouge who would be handling the appeal process. Once I allowed this to settle in, I found it strange and could not help feeling a little uncomfortable. Less than eighteen hours earlier, Walt had been furious with me over the letter I had sent to Judge Davis. Without specifically intending to do so, I had suggested that Walt had performed inadequate counsel to Jaime and the facts supported that notion. I wasn't attempting to attack Walt, but at this point, I could not afford to protect him. My daughter's life was at stake. During our heated conversation, I told him plainly, "One thing you should understand is that I have come nowhere close to ending my fight for my daughter." I went on to say, "For as long as there is life in me, I will fight for her." In an earlier conversation, he had told me that he could see no value in an attempt at appeal. He said at the time that he felt that Judge Davis had been more than fair with us. And now in less than twenty-four hours, he has an attorney from Baton Rouge who wants to handle the appeals process for us pro bono? I thought, *He's been busy since yesterday.* I pieced together the events of the last twenty-four hours in my mind and was troubled. I could not help but wonder whose interest this proposed new attorney would be protecting. I decided at this point, I needed to go outside of the Louisiana area, seeking counsel for Jaime's appeal. My hope now is that this story will draw the attention of the right people, and God would send them to guide us through this process.

As in my letter to the Fourteenth District Judicial Court when called for jury duty, wherein I said, "We believe now that a high percentage of those incarcerated are in fact innocent victims of this system." How much more true is this for the African American community? I now have a much clearer understanding and can appreciate as to why there is so much anger and resentment coming from the people of color in our nation. I decided as I watched this trial unfold and the merciless process in which an innocent woman's life was destroyed that one thing was certain, if you had no money and no influence and you were accused by this system, you would certainly be devoured by this machinery that modern politicians call justice. Everything from buying testimony to lying under oath and even to coercing witnesses is prevalent. So if you have neither money nor influence and you are black, how much less likely are you to be able to defend yourself? I thought of the lack of respect that the black community suffered, especially in the south from the possessors of this system. I wondered how many of them were just "ran through the mill" on their way to prison or death, while the only true indictment one might have brought against them was that they matched a profile that law enforcement and the local judicial system both despised and found to be easy prey in the course of building their political careers. I can now appreciate the terror that surely must have been in the heart of many minority individuals who had committed no crime and were caught in the jaws of this system with no meaningful representation. The black man's cry is loud in the ears of anyone who will listen and many are the tales of abuse suffered at the hands of law enforcement and prosecutors in the name of justice. If you need evidence, look at the black to white ratio in the jail and prison systems over the last fifty years. I believe it is time to expose this "Darker Side of Justice" for what it is and seek a path forward to prevent political lust from being the fuel that feeds the fires of these injustices.

REFLECTION

It is interesting how multiple children can be born and raised in a family, experience the exact same influence, same instruction in the same environment, yet all of them will generally be different one from the other. I have noticed in other families, as well as my own, each member is unique in many ways. As individuals, we have different strengths, different weaknesses, and a different outlook on life. Our children are all individuals, and in many ways, we have to deal with them as such, applying different principles as is needed. In observing our children, while some seem to do well, others seem more problematic, yet we love them all. We learn as children of God that apparently, it is the same in his kingdom. It seems that God in His infinite wisdom made us all unique, some with more strengths than others, and some with more weaknesses, and in many instances, he deals with us accordingly.

And then of even more importance, we should consider God's will and purpose in our lives. If we began a search for answers as to why the kind of trouble that our family experienced in this story would come into a Christian's life, in the end, only God knows for certain. However, there are some things we should consider. Perhaps we already know the answer. Is there a fault or secret sin residing in you that could be detrimental to your walk with God? Is it possible that trouble is the only remedy for these things? Is God preparing you for a greater work in the future? Has he seen some fruit in your life and is pruning you so you will bear more fruit? Ultimately, we know that God's process will work in you until the day of Jesus Christ if you don't check out. From a different perspective, possibly you are as the Apostle Paul and are appointed to suffer some things for the Name of Jesus. Certainly, we should consider the patriarchs of the Word of God to give us perspective. Obviously, Job had many questions of "why?" throughout his ordeal. Consider Joseph who must have wondered many nights in prison why he found himself in such trouble, but ultimately, became an instrument to fulfill the purpose of God for the entire nation of Israel. Bishop Nugent once said to me, "That is what the entire Word of God is about, the people of God getting in trouble and God delivering them out of it." We must remember that all of these things work together for our own good if we are called of God and if we love Him. Throughout this entire ordeal, I have been made acutely aware that any notion of a Christian life without trouble and trials is simply not found in God's word. We should take Paul for an example who, after describing the much trouble he had experienced serving in the Gospel, said in 2 Corinthians 4:17, "For our light affliction which is but for a moment worketh for us a far more exceeding and eternal weight of glory." Pastor Massey, in one of his most recent messages, preached concerning afflictions and made reference to the words of the Psalmist David who said, "It is good that I have been afflicted." God is only trying to save us, so in conclusion, we perhaps should say, "Thank God for trouble." You may now ask, so where is God's deliverance in this story? I admit, in anguish and much disappointment, I ask the same question and the answer is "Somewhere in the future." God didn't promise that this would end the way I planned, but rather, He said, "I will lead you to the victory, if you will trust Me." It is at this point when all of the expectations you have conjured up in your own mind have not come to pass and all of your resources are exhausted that you have the opportunity to truly trust God. As Bishop Nugent said only last week, "When you give up on God, you give up on life."

THE BEGINNING